THE FOREST OF LIFE

THE FOREST OF LIFE

Helen Taylor Little

iUniverse, Inc.
New York Lincoln Shanghai

THE FOREST OF LIFE

iUniverse books may be ordered through booksellers or by contacting:

iUniverse
2021 Pine Lake Road, Suite 100
Lincoln, NE 68512
www.iuniverse.com
1-800-Authors (1-800-288-4677)

ISBN-13: 978-0-595-34894-7 (pbk)
ISBN-13: 978-0-595-79612-0 (ebk)
ISBN-10: 0-595-34894-7 (pbk)
ISBN-10: 0-595-79612-5 (ebk)

Printed in the United States of America

This book is dedicated to my Father, Samuel, for his love and acceptance. Thanks for teaching me that all things are possible through God.

CHAPTER 1

▼

I, Alexandra Frances Nottingham, started out fourteen years ago at this prestigious financial consulting company, in the capital city, just after graduation from North Carolina University. I was a young acorn then in the midst of the towering oaks of financial wizards. Not recognizing it at the time, I had planted myself firmly in their garden of ambition and latent greed with deep roots, entwined in their social stratification. Learning from some of the best, I quickly grew in the financial business world, and within a few years felt I too had grown into a tall oak tree of success.

I commuted daily joining the hustle and bustle of the capital city's elite executives, feeling secure and confidant. Canvassing Raleigh's streets as though I somehow personally owned a large portion of them. My success over the years had turned me into a first class number one snooty snob, something I never intended to be. Being the breezy, athletic, tossed hair, and preppy woman about town felt like my birthright.

On this warm May morning I drove into work with the top down on my Porsche 911 Carrera. Speeding through the streets in my sleek oriental red, 315 horsepower machine, I spoke incessantly on my phone. This morning's conversation was to seal an overseas deal I already had frying hot in the pan. Involved totally in my own little world; I was oblivious to the misfortunes of the homeless that had grown in large numbers on our city's streets. Sure I saw them, but only as a blur. My rose colored glasses made them invisible to me as I traversed the tarred black tops.

Entering my plush office with its floor to ceiling windows, which gave me a coveted cross town view of the city's concrete forest of buildings, and which was decorated with the latest in high tech furnishings; I quickly got to work to see what the Wall Street bullies were up to today.

Gyrations and sweeping changes were occurring in the commodity trading industry, and I had to offer my clients a better way to value the market. In this business you had to stay ahead of what drove the market and use that knowledge to your own advantage. I couldn't drop my guard for a moment, or some other broker would topple me from my porcelain pedestal, eager to gain my number one spot as the company's top producer and youngest newly appointed senior officer. It just wasn't the men biting at my ankles every minute of every day; the women were like sharks on a relentless eating frenzy too. Maybe even more dauntless in pursuit of me.

I had worked like a hungry bull, developing systematic strategies and putting together my one, three, and five year detailed plans. Studying trends, technologies, forecasts, and patterns. Staying involved in the daily performance of the top performing sectors. Thriving on larger cumulative gains, I lived and breathed domestic and international statistical trading data. I could give you a market snapshot or put you on a strong buy almost at any given time. I had mastered the roller coaster ride of the commodity market as well as the market would allow. But gaining a serious edge comes with the price of a target on your chest for all the other investment sharpshooters to set their aim; hoping to see you go down in a mighty cloud of dust.

I drank from my bottle of cherry flavored Mylanta as though it was a diet coke to conquer the heartburn that filled my upper chest and scorched my throat. Convincing myself you've gotta feel the burn if you're gonna earn. The ups and downs of the market along with the twenty-hour days were making more than my stomach churn, but I relished my propagating accomplishments. Yes siree, my financial house was in perfect order. I had made this my sole quest in life.

My day had been fruitful to say the least. I had made a multi-million dollar deal in the sizzling energy market. How I loved those light sweet crudes. It had taken me months to put that trade together. Waiting patiently and babysitting the ripening of the fruit was a skill I'd acquired early on. My persistence in keeping one eye continuously focused on NYMEX and the IPE, amongst others, led me to secure substantially high profit margins for my clients and secure millions for our company.

With the taste of victory moving like an electrifying current through my body, I decided to knock off early. It was only six o'clock, which for me was early, and I thought I'd go home to celebrate with Abby.

We'd been together for nearly five years. Longest I'd ever been in a relation-ship. I had met Abby one night while out with my best friend, BeBe, at a local nightclub. Legends, a well-known gay nightclub in Raleigh, and top-notch enliv-enment spot for a grand night out with friends. A place to let your party self go, and let the rhythm move you as the music pumped loud and continuous. On that night BeBe had elbowed me as I danced to the music in my seat, while sip-ping my bourbon and diet coke.

"Alex, don't look now but there's a pretty girl checking you out at three o'clock." Immediately I started to turn my head when BeBe grabbed my face. "I said don't look now," while piercing me with her blue-green eyes.

"What? Hey don't do that. You almost made me spill my drink all over myself."

"Okay, you can look now."

Giving BeBe a look of discontent first, before turning to have a look-see. "Her?!," I asked with a look of fascination, pointing discreetly in the direction of a fantastic looking blonde, petite and radiant. She was dressed like a modern day Barbie doll, and the dance floor lights illuminated her shoulder length, golden hair with a star-like quality.

"Yeah man."

"You're sure?" At that moment Abby and I first locked eyes, and it's now nearly five years later. It was as they say, love at first sight. Or as close to love as I'd ever felt. Our fifth anniversary would be this Sunday. I'd decided I wouldn't go to work as usual. My plans were to spend the whole day with her, which was a luxury with my work schedule being so hectic and time consuming. Anyway, I had bought a super special gift to mark the occasion. An Olivia Cruise from Bos-ton, Massachusetts to Montreal, Canada. Entertainers onboard would include k.d. lang, Meg Christian, Marge Gomez, Suede, Vicki Shaw, Zoe Lewis, Lucie Blue Tremblay, and Amy Boyd. Sounded like a romantic and fun-filled trip to me. I was looking forward to seeing her face when she unwrapped her surprise. Seeing her happy would put a smile in my heart.

On the drive home, I breathed in the sweetness of the springtime's aromatic fragrant blossoms on the trees, and the flowers that covered the rolling hills. Pass-ing by the Jordan Lake on Mt. Carmel Church Road, I was almost home. I loved the way Edwards Mountain provided the backdrop for our community. My thoughts were, *Thank God It's Friday!*

I pulled into our subdivision's main gate located in the Governor's Club in Chapel Hill. Waving at Charlie, the security guard, as he hailed me through the massive gate. The plush twenty-seven holes, Jack Nicklaus signature golf course meandered along through the heart of the community and to our circular drive-way. I had purchased this home for us four years ago, and it was the eminence of success and ranking file. Certainly not the largest home, but it made a powerful statement, and that was important to me. We had a little over an acre of property with terrific year-round views from nearly every window. It was a stunning estate home overlooking the tree-lined fairway. Exquisite detail and craftsmanship prevailed throughout the spacious home. It even had two kitchens, which allowed Abby to pursue and grow her catering business.

Her business had now gained in popularity; so much, that she no longer depended on me to meet her payroll expenses. I was proud of her accomplishments. Helping her fulfill her life's dream had been another priority on my achievement list.

Hitting my remote, I pulled into the garage, and went in through the kitchen door. The smell of some delightful desert filled the air, and soft romantic music echoed throughout the house. She must have called the office and found out I was coming home early. She's such a love. I checked the kitchen, family room and living room. Not finding her, I figured she must be upstairs in the bedroom waiting on me. So I poured myself a drink, all the while humming to the music playing, and began the twelve steps up the mahogany staircase to our bedroom. Happy to know she had a special evening in store for me. This was the way I liked to celebrate.

Not wanting to scare her, I gently tapped on the door and said, "Hey babe, I'm home."

As I slowly opened the door and entered, my thoughts of a romantic evening quickly turned to horror.

CHAPTER 2

▼

Quickly the cloud nine of excitement I had felt immediately evaporated and was replaced with agony. Standing there frozen in disbelief and total shock, I was temporarily mute and emotionally short-circuited. Four eyes stared back at me from our king size bed with mortifying looks. Naked bodies scurried under the sheets like flies to dog piles. I caught the whiff of pot in the air. Their glazed eyes were further evidence that they had imbibed the drug. I recognized Abby's bed partner as I started coming back to my senses. She was Susie, her assistant manager for the past year and a half, give or take a month or two. Very butchie looking, in her mid-twenties, and a little on the heavy side with jet-black spikish hair. Certainly not anyone I would have ever dreamed that I would need to worry about.

Suddenly my mouth flew open in contempt, "What the hell is going on here?" I made a move towards the bed. Abby jumped up and got between Susie and the bed.

"It's not what you think Alex."

"Shit woman, my eyes aren't deceiving me. Don't try handing me any crap."

"We were drinking wine while putting the Clermont's order together for tomorrow, and I suppose we over did it," she whined.

"You over did it alright. Get the hell out of my bed Susie, before I snatch you bald all over your bouncy body." I picked up her clothes and threw them at her. She caught them and ran into the bathroom, and I heard the door lock. I had her scared, which was my intention at that particular moment. I yelled, "You'd better be out of there in one minute or I'm coming in and throwing you out, you cheap hussy," all the while looking at Abby with her makeup smeared face, and shaking my head that reeled from her betrayal.

The bathroom door opened with a gentle sway, and timidly Susie tiptoed out with her head lowered while scooting past me. I truly wanted to hall off and punch the pure daylight out of her. But all I did was give her a little shove out the bedroom door. "And don't you ever bother coming back to this house, or I'll put a restraining order on you. You're lucky I don't horse whip you." Violence isn't part of my nature, but I did discover a rage I'd never been introduced to before, and it wasn't a pleasant side of me at all.

I heard the front door close downstairs. Abby had stood by silently wrapped in a sheet from the evil love nest. All I could say was, "Please go take a bath." Still silent she honored my request.

I went downstairs and replayed the entire scene over and over again in my head, while anger built inside my body. I slammed my drink into the fireplace, and the glass shattered and ricocheted in all directions. I was madder than I had ever been before in my life. Betrayal is a nasty vicious monster. How long had this been going on? Were there others? I'm so stupid. I thought she loved me. Why? Why? My head was filled with thoughts, and none of them were good. I sank down onto the chocolate-leathered couch and tears started pouring. I felt a tremendous loss. Her secret love affair had crushed my peace of mind, and I could feel my heart breaking more apart with each breath that I took. I didn't hear Abby come down the stairs or into the room, so the suddenness of her voice startled me.

"Can I fix you a drink Alex? Looks like you've dropped yours."

I didn't find her comment funny. I guess it was her attempt to lighten up things a bit, but I'd have nothing to do with it. I was mad, and I had a right to be mad. I wasn't about to let her make this seem so trivial. "I don't want a drink right now Abby. I just want you to explain to me what I just saw upstairs in our bed. In our bed Abby, for goodness sakes! And don't you dare give me that cock-eyed line about too much to drink, or smoking that shit you bring in this house. It didn't drag you upstairs."

She sat down next to me and tried to grab my hand, which I immediately pulled away. "I don't want you touching me now."

"Will you at least look at me Alex?"

I turned towards her and felt nothing but utter disdain. The coolness of it swept over my face. She could see and perhaps even feel its draftiness.

"It's just you're away all the time. I get so lonely, and this time I gave in to Susie's attentiveness. We drank and smoked some pot. We danced and then, well, one thing led to another. I don't know how we ended upstairs in our bed-room. I feel just awful Alex. You've got to forgive me."

"I think there's more to this story than you're telling me. I'm too mad and too hurt to discuss this any further with you right now. I'm going to stay in the guest suite tonight. I don't think I can ever sleep in what used to be our bed again. You've soiled the peacefulness it had always brought me, with your drunken tryst. We'll talk more about it tomorrow," telling her as I left her sitting on the couch with tears streaming down her face. Tears, which once would have had me doing anything to stop their flow.

Something inside me told me she wasn't being completely honest with me. The feeling consumed my gut instincts. I needed more time to figure out what I wanted to do. No one had ever dumped on me before, and I didn't like it. No siree, not one tiny bit. Imagine her trying to put the blame on me. I'll not stand for that. Sure I'm gone a lot. Making money for us. I buy her nice things. I bought her car, financed the start-up of her business, and that two-carat rock on her hand didn't come out of a Cracker Jack box. She pays nothing to stay in this grand house. Took her to Paris last year. The more I thought, the madder I got.

I called BeBe. "BeBe, can you come over? I really need to talk to you."

"What's up Alex, you sound down in the dumps."

"Just come on over now, please?"

"I'm out the door and on my way. See you in ten minutes, tops."

"Thanks good buddy."

I could always count on BeBe to be there when I needed her. We've been friends for most of our lives. She's a realtor and owns her own company. It's one of the most eminently successful in the college town of Chapel Hill. Having been friends for the past thirty years, we've supported and watched one another make our marks in the surrounding business communities. But work hadn't occupied all our time, especially in our younger years. Doing everything together from rac-ing cars to skydiving, we've always enjoyed each other's company. She's always been like a sister to me. We girl hunted together, double-dated and took up for one another, even if we knew the other was wrong. Two peas in a pod we are. She's the taller one and I'm the brain of the twosome. At least, she allows me to think so, which is another thing I love about her. Heck, she's as smart as a whip. But sometimes she goes on and on about any subject; so much so, that at times it can be kinda tedious, so I shush her when she gets too wound up. We take care of each other. Some people go through their whole life and never have a friend so true and blue. I know I'm lucky to have BeBe. Probably should tell her that sometime.

I went outside and sat on the front porch to wait on her. Right on time, she pulled into the drive. I met her halfway down the sidewalk.

"Okay Alex, tell me what's going on with you. You look just awful girl."

After spending the next several minutes describing the entire incident, with tear drenched eyes, I dropped my head and trembled. Now the tears turned to a pathetic wail. BeBe sat down beside me on the garden bench and gave me a strong and comforting hug.

"Alex, it's going to be alright. I had a feeling Abby was screwing around on you. She doesn't deserve you. I've told you that many times before."

"What made you think she might be messing around?" I brought my weeping under control.

"Remember a couple of months back when you asked me to come by your house and pick up a report you had left on your desk?" I shook my head yes. "Well I figured Abby wasn't home since she didn't answer your calls, so I didn't bother to ring the bell before I came inside the house. I heard laughter coming from the game room, so I peeked in and saw Abby and Susie sitting mighty close on the couch. Too close, if you know what I mean. When I said hello, they both nearly fell in the floor. Abby said they were planning a menu and looking through some new cookbooks; so I took her at her word and minimized what I thought I had seen. But it's bothered me every since, and now I know why. That little blonde shithead."

"So she lied to me. She led me to believe this was just a one-time thing that came about from drinking too much. I wonder how many more lies she's been telling me?"

"We can go over to Susie's house and rouse her into telling us the true story," BeBe said with a devilish grin.

"I'm probably better off not knowing. Anyway, the way I'm feeling right now, I might take a poke or two at her and get myself thrown in jail. I need to face the fact that my relationship with Abby is over and done."

"How are you going to tell her that? You know she'll plead with you and use all her charm to change your mind. Can you overcome her temptations?"

"I have to, BeBe; I just have to."

CHAPTER 3

─────────────── ▼ ───────────────

Tossing and turning all night from restlessness, sleep had only come to me in short intervals. It was almost six thirty. I couldn't stay in bed any longer. My mind was going in several directions at once. Watching the sun coming through the French doors leading to the beautiful rock garden, I wearily shuffled over and went outside into the warmth of the early morning air. Looking up into the sky I had a prayerful and soft-spoken talk with God.

"Lord you know I'm broken-hearted this morning. I'm not going to ask you why this happened. But please Lord; help me through this. Please, I feel like a little child with a deep and sorrowful lost feeling. I need your help to handle this situation right. Don't let Abby seduce me into prolonging the inevitable. I've lost all my trust in her, and I can't handle love without trust. Don't let my anger make me vengeful, but let me be fair to her Father. Please Jesus. Amen."

When I opened my eyes I could feel God's peace and love surrounding me. A tiny sparrow landed in the birdbath, just a foot or so from me. It sipped some water and then seemed to look at me. It gave me a short song, and then fluttered away towards the rising sun. I thought of the words from a church song, something like, His eye is on the sparrow, and I know He watches over me. What great comfort I felt at that moment. Wiping the tears away that washed down my face, I received God's gift which gave me strength and courage. Looking up to the sky I whispered, "Thank you Father."

I got dressed and went to the kitchen to fix some coffee. Abby sat at the breakfast bar reading the morning paper with a cup of coffee in front of her. I walked in without words and poured myself a cup of coffee.

Abby put the newspaper down and said, "Aren't you speaking to me this morning?"

"Not until I've had my first cup of coffee." I headed to the family room and turned on the television to CNN to catch the latest news, which wasn't so good here lately with the Iraq war. Abby came in moments later. Picking up the remote she switched the television off. I just looked at her with indifference as she sat in my lap and tried to hug me. My arms remained stubbornly at my sides. She started kissing my neck and cooing I love you in my ear. I stood up defiantly, slipping out of her arms and leaving her sitting crossways in the chair. She gave me a sad quizzical look.

"Are you ready to talk about what I witnessed last evening?" She straightened herself in the chair seeing the seriousness on my face and hearing the tone of my voice.

"I guess so," she droned.

"Abby, it's not that I don't love you anymore, it's that I don't trust you anymore. And I can't be in a relationship without trust." She tried to interrupt my monologue, but I over talked her attempt. "I don't know how many times you were with Susie, or who else you've played around with, and frankly that's of little consequence to me now. You've betrayed my love, and you've not been honest with me about heaven knows what else. Tomorrow would have been five years for us. Now it's all over. It breaks my heart, but Abby it's over."

She ran to me. "You don't mean that Alex. We were meant to be together. I never loved any one else. I didn't mean to mess things up. Please forgive me. Let me make it up to you."

She sat at my feet hugging my knees. I could feel her tears trickle down my legs. I reached down and helped her up. She tried to kiss me. I leaned back from reach. This was a pitiful sight that was tugging at my broken heart. I still loved her and wanted to comfort her, but I knew that would spell disaster. I held firm to the stance I had taken. If I gave an inch I knew I would give a mile.

Then her sadness quickly turned to madness. Her face became engulfed in bright red. With her hands on her hips she vehemently let go on me. "You think you can just dump me. I'm the one who has had to spend all those lonely evenings alone in this sandcastle in the sky you've created, while you've wined and dined people all over town calling it business. Was I invited? No! You think you are so important with your fancy spancy job and your million-dollar image. I only got leftovers from you Alex. Cold leftovers. You need to accept some of the blame for this too. If you had been with me, none of this would have happened. You can't expect someone to be alone all the time, and not be tempted when someone else gives her undivided attention. I'm a hot-blooded woman Alex. That's what you loved about me. Remember that? I have needs, and I had to have them fed one way or another. God knows you weren't around."

I stood there and took what she gave. Maybe I was partially to blame. She was right; I did love the fact that she was so hot-blooded. I was gone a lot. She did have to spend a lot of time without me at home. I felt myself getting pulled in too deep and beginning to blame myself. I refocused to the fact that she'd slept around on me. That's why we were breaking up. There's other ways to fight loneliness without sleeping around and betraying your partner.

"Okay Abby you're right, but you're dead wrong about the part where you had to get your needs fed else where. All you had to do was tell me. Haven't I always been there whenever you called me? There was nothing I wouldn't have done for you. But now it's ruined, and the pieces can't be put back together."

"They could if you'd let them. Let's try one more time," Abby said with her voice once again sweetened.

I was surprised to hear her say that after what she had said only moments before, but I stood my ground and held firm. "I'm sorry Abby, it's over, and we need to let go so that we both can move on with our lives. I want to be fair to you Abby. I'll help you all I can. I'll call BeBe about helping us find you a new place. One you can continue to operate your catering business from and live comfortably. I'll pay a generous down payment so that it'll be affordable for you."

"I don't want your damn money Alex. I never did. I just wanted you with me. You think everything is about money. Someday you'll realize money doesn't buy love. I hope it won't be too late for you Alex."

"Abby, I did everything the best way I knew how. I am truly sorry it wasn't enough."

Then she gave me a cold scowl of bitterness. "I'm going to go and stay with my sister for a while. I'll come by next week and pick up my things." With that statement she nearly ran from the room and up the stairs.

My how I wanted to run after her. It took all my strength not to follow her up to what was once our bedroom. But then the vision of last night's betrayal once again filled my head and it erased all that desire.

I pulled out my phone and called BeBe. Hearing her familiar hello, I preceded with, "It's done. I broke it off with Abby."

"Are you okay good buddy?"

"Yeah, I guess. It wasn't an easy thing to do. I'm going to miss her so much BeBe." Then the crying commenced again.

"Why don't I come by and pick you up, and we'll do something together today? Like old times."

"But you have to work today, don't you?"

"I just have one showing at ten o'clock this morning, and then I'm as free as a bird. I'll have little Debbie take all my calls. She'll probably surprise me with a sale, if her past history prevails. So you see, I'm good to go."

"I appreciate you BeBe. Hey, let's go to the lake and rent a boat."

"Sailing, excellent suggestion. Sounds great. Grab your cooler, and I'll stop and pick up some Pepsi. You could probably use a six pack of beer."

"That'll work. What time do you think you'll be by for me?"

"Let's shoot for noon. If that changes I'll call you."

"Then it's a date my friend. See you later."

Looking at my watch and noticing it was only a little before nine, I headed back to the kitchen to fix me an egg, bacon and cheese sandwich. I fixed one for Abby too, remembering she always liked my breakfast sandwiches. I ran up the stairs to give it to her while it was still hot. I heard the shower going so I laid the sandwich beside her make-up mirror. I knew she'd be using that before she'd venture from the house. I double-timed it back downstairs to eat my breakfast before it got cold. I grabbed my sandwich and a glass of milk, while tucking the newspaper under my arm and went to my favorite chair in the family room. After reading the paper completely through, the good and the bad, I heard the living room grandfather clock strike eleven as Abby entered the room.

"Thanks for the sandwich. No body makes a better breakfast sandwich than you."

"You look nice Abby." My chest heaved from the ache inside. "Can I help you with your bag?"

"No, no, I can handle it just fine."

Paying no attention to her declining my help I walked over and took the suitcase from her hand. Together we walked out the door in silence to her Lexus SUV parked in the garage. I placed her bag in the backseat, while she climbed inside the driver's seat. I closed her car door for her and stepped back a few steps. The garage door opened while she started her car engine. For several seconds our eyes fastened together, each filled with tears for a love gone wrong, and for what could have been. She backed slowly into the circular drive, stopping briefly to turn and wave the most heart wrenching good-bye I'd ever received. The look on her face imbedded in my heart.

The garage door went down with me still watching in the direction she had left. Had I done the right thing, breaking up with her? Grief permeated me as I walked into the empty house, and realized how Abby must have felt all the times I wasn't home. Knowing that I was now the lone occupant of this big place made me aware of a desolation I'd never felt inside these walls before now. I heard sounds that had always been covered up with music, friends about, or word exchanges with Abby. Now the clocks ticked loudly, the refrigerator icemaker's noises, and the hum of the cooling system clicking on and off seemed to be taunting me. Immediately I filled the whole house with music. Anything to take away the eerie smog that now drearily filtered throughout my home, and made it feel foreign to me. Or was this home anymore? That question beckoned some serious thought from me.

Then the doorbell chimes broke my concentration. I welcomed the intrusion. Gotta be BeBe, I thought to myself as I looked at my watch, which was nearly signaling noon. I opened the front door happy to see a smiling face, and asked her in while I fetched the things we needed for our day of sailing.

In minutes we were out the door, gear loaded, and in her old red 1968 Pontiac GTO convertible heading to the lake. Just like always the pristine condition of her GTO drew head turns, horn blows, and shouts as we sped down the road. She drove every bit as fast as I normally do. But what could one expect when they were sitting on 400 cubic inches of muscle car? Safe drivers for sure, but a little more pedal to the metal than the law allowed. How we've managed to avoid citations will forever be a mystery to me. I just hope our luck remains and it stays that a way.

Our sailboat was ready to launch when we arrived. BeBe had called ahead and asked Lucas to have it prepared for us. On board the day's gentle wind propelled us smoothly and swiftly into the abyss, located about three-fourths of a mile off shore. We seldom spoke while we navigated through the waters, and that remained constant today. The looks we gave each other, accompanied by a few hand signals, were the only communication we needed when we were absorbed in one of our adventures. The water sprayed us, cooling us as we clipped along with the red, white and blue sails whisking above. Finally though we dropped anchor, popped a top, turned on the radio, and settled back in the comfort of the sun's glow.

"Gentle ride out today."

"Perfect Alex. So peaceful."

"Just what I needed. The last two days have been torturous." I drank down a beer not noticing that I was gulping it like water.

But BeBe took notice and said, "Slow down girl, there's plenty more where that came from, and we've got all day."

I shook my can and felt that it was already more than half empty in only two swallows. "I guess I'm trying to drown my sorrows."

"Listen, you did the right thing. It might not feel like it right now. I'm telling you again you deserve better. That crap about you never being there is just that, CRAP! You worked hard to give her the very best of everything. And when you were with her you treated her like a queen. To go and cheat on you, and then tell you it's your fault is really a low blow. I liked Abby, but I don't know if I can forgive her for doing that to you. And shit Alex, in your own bed."

"That's hard for me too. But that's history. My home has been polluted though, and I don't know what I want to do about it."

"What do you mean?"

"Well, sitting there after she left the place didn't feel the same. It didn't feel like home anymore. You know what I'm saying?"

"I think so, like how I felt when Brandy moved out?"

"Probably something like that. It's tough to describe. Sorry, but I don't know if I can stay in that house anymore."

"Do you want to get another house? They have a couple of new ones going up near the back gate, and then there's the Parker place on the market."

"I think there's more to it than that BeBe, but I haven't quite put my finger on it yet. I'll let you know when I figure out things."

The sun's warmth, the classical R&B music on the radio, and the beer's sedation lulled us both into a nap, while we were nestled in the boat's body, like babies in their mother's womb. I woke up first, looked at my watch, and saw we had been sleeping for over two hours. I nudged BeBe. "Hey girlfriend, wake up."

Groggily she sat up with her eyes still at half mask and yawned. "What time is it?"

"It's almost five o'clock. Can you believe we both slept that long?"

"You needed it Alex, after last night. I saw you dozing off so I decided to join you."

"Are you ready to head back Be's?"

"Yeah…Why don't we go over to Landry's for some seafood?"

"We're probably pretty sniffy after being out here on the water and sweating all afternoon."

"They're used to patrons like us. Let's go? They don't care how we smell."

"I could go for some oysters and then some steak and lobster. Let's do it."

So we got to shore, loaded up the car, and headed to the restaurant to fill our tanks with a good meal and some cocktails.

After our meal BeBe talked me into going by a new women's bar in town. It was near the UNC campus, and was supposed to cater to the thirties plus crowd. I didn't want to go home to that big empty house so I agreed. It was early, only around eight in the evening, so I didn't expect much of a crowd. Parking within a block of the bar I helped her put the convertible top up on her GTO, before we ventured inside to check things out. It wasn't as large as Legends over in Raleigh, but it had a good feel about it. There were only about twenty or so people sitting around the bar and at tables beside the small dance floor. And of course the moment we made our entrance all eyes turned to the door to look us over, for either approval or disapproval.

"Let's sit next to the pool table Alex."

"Now how did I know you'd pick that table?"

"Cause you know me and love me, that's why," BeBe said in her little girl voice.

"Yeah, I reckon." So I sat down and she went up to the bar to order us a drink. I placed two quarters on the pool table for BeBe. She loved the game and she's a pro at it, so I knew she would be ready to play.

She returned with my bourbon and diet coke, while sipping on a cherry coke through a plastic red straw. Skewered atop her glass were three maraschino cherries, which she always talked a bartender into giving her. It was her personal trademark. My buddy could tie those cherry stems into knots with her tongue, which always amazed me.

"I'm the designated driver tonight, so you just enjoy yourself, " she said. Then she walked over to the pool table to check out her competition.

The music was good, not too loud, but loud enough to feel the beat through the floor. I'd only taken a few sips of my drink when a good-looking woman approached the table and asked me to dance. I wasn't prepared for anything like that and she caught me completely off guard. She was too pretty for me to refuse, so I stood and walked onto the dance floor with her. She looked to be around thirty-two to thirty-four, my age, with brown hair touching her collar, and sweeping to and fro as we danced. Her eyes were dark brown and had a nice twinkling to them when she smiled, which was continuously as we danced to an old song by Cindy Lauper, 'Girls Just Want To Have Fun.' I thanked her after the dance and proceeded back to my table.

"Who's that?"

"I don't know. She came over and asked me to dance so I danced with her."

"Look at you. Not in the bar five minutes and the babes are after you."

"Hush, no big deal. Anyway she caught me off guard."

"Have fun. You're foot loose and fancy-free."

"Yeah, I guess, but I'm not even interested in anything like that."

"It's only dancing for gosh sakes Alex." With that she went back over to the pool table. She was only trying to cheer me up, and I was being an old sourpuss back to her. I watched her play a couple of games of pool and whip the pants off her contenders. I got a little happier with another drink and started cheering for her.

The barmaid brought a drink over to me from my dance partner from earlier. I turned to lift my glass in thanks to her, and without any hesitation she got up and headed towards my table. *Please don't come over here*, I'm thinking, but it's too late.

"May I sit down?" she inquired.

"Certainly, please have a seat." I said in my most polite way, but not meaning a word of it.

"I'm Annie."

"Hi Annie, I'm Alex. Thanks for the drink and the dance."

"You looked so lonely sitting over here by yourself."

"Oh, I'm not alone. I'm with my best friend BeBe."

"Is she your girlfriend?"

"Yep, but not in that way. Like I said she's my best friend, and we're out enjoying each other's company."

"Am I interrupting you?"

Lord knows I wanted to say yes you are, but my manners wouldn't allow impoliteness. "No, no, it's alright. She's trying to cheer me up tonight"

"Cheer you up?"

I could tell she wanted to know what that was about. "Had a bad breakup this week."

With a genuine look of concern she touched my hand which was resting on the table, and said she was sorry to hear that.

"Thanks," I said and softly pulled my hand away, acting like I was signaling for BeBe to come over and meet her. BeBe caught my motion and came to my rescue. It wasn't that Annie wasn't attractive, but the timing was all-wrong, and frankly I wasn't in the mood for that kind of company. "This is my friend BeBe. We've been best buddies forever. BeBe this is Annie."

They exchanged pleasantries and BeBe said, "It's almost ten o'clock Alex and I need to get home. Are you ready?"

"Oh it sure is. Sorry Annie. I need to go. Hope I'll see you around the next time I'm here. Sure was nice meeting you. Good-night." As we walked out the door I thanked my buddy for the save. "Whew, she was on the prowl and I was her intended victim, I do believe."

"No doubt about that. See how cute you are with your flaxen blonde hair and athletic body? And if that doesn't get them, then those big round cocoa doe eyes will. You have the women chasing after you, and that's not a bad thing to have going for you."

"You don't have any problems with the women yourself my friend."

"You don't hear me complaining, do you?"

"Nope, let's hit the highway. Thanks for getting me out of the house today."

"Well, what do you want to do tomorrow? I know it was supposed to be your anniversary?"

The good thing was that I had completely forgotten for the moment, but now the onset of that day approaching made me sink a few inches in the car seat and lower my head. "I think I'd just like to be alone tomorrow and contemplate my life."

"I don't like the idea of you being alone tomorrow Alex. Let me come over?"

"No, I'll be fine," I promised. "My wounds need licking and that's a private thing. Please understand, okay?"

"Only if you're sure you'll be alright. You know I'll worry."

We pulled into my driveway, and I promised her I'd call her tomorrow morning at nine. She sat there until I opened the front door and went inside, before she pulled out of the driveway to head to her house. Seconds later the phone rang. "Are you sure you don't want me to spend the night?"

"No good buddy, but thanks. I love you. Now drive safely home, and I'll talk to you in the morning."

CHAPTER 4

▼

It had been a fitful night, and I didn't get much sleep for the second night in a row. Once again I couldn't turn my mind off. It flitted from one thing to another. I was glad to see the sun peeking through the trees bringing in a new day, even if it was supposed to be our anniversary. But I quickly put that thought out of my mind, and headed to retrieve the morning paper and make a giant cup of coffee. The headline read, *Seven More U.S. Soldiers Killed In Ambush.* Having several friends over there fighting this war in Iraq, that kind of news always disturbed me. So far they were all fine, and I prayed daily that they stayed that way. I corresponded through letters and e-mails with them a couple of times a month. I don't like war, but as they say freedom doesn't come free. I admired their willingness to take up arms to defend our nation, and to facilitate the spread of democracy in countries ruled by torturous leaders. They were willing to lay down their own lives if it was required of them. That made them heroes in my eyes.

Not wanting to dwell on the uneasiness this provoked, I moved on to the financial section to check out the latest index predictions. They were forecasting that stocks would lift to new heights in several sectors. With the jitters about the expected increase in interest rates, the ongoing war, and inflation looming about us, I predicted a sluggish week. But even with the mixed bag of economic news my business savvy sensed something good on the horizon. So I'd be closely monitoring this over the upcoming months.

The travel section of the paper had a story on The Blue Ridge Mountains. Reading each word my interest was aroused when I discovered that a secluded mountain wilderness existed only hours away. I'd always loved the mountains. When I was in my early twenties, I'd often dreamed of retiring there and becoming a writer. BeBe and I used to make a jaunt in that direction almost every weekend. Asheville, Cherokee, and even into Tennessee to visit Dolly's place at Pigeon Forge. We'd get off the beaten path from time to time and meet some real locals. We had a blast. I don't know why we stopped, unless the pursuit of money distorted our pleasure buttons.

Enthralled by the story I put down the rest of the paper and went into my office located in the rear of the house. Sitting at my desk I started searching on the computer for secluded mountain land in the Blue Ridge Mountains. Impressive properties from several real estate companies grabbed my attention. One in particular caught my eye. The description read: *Thirty-four acres with a charming 1930's farmhouse and two barns grace a gentle hill. Inviting green meadows wind along peaceful streams caressing throughout the natural forestland. Splendid mountain views surround this property. Located in Aliceston, near Bryson City, North Carolina.*

They were asking $389,900 for the property. Can't be I thought. Something must be wrong with it. But I was hooked and wanted to know more. Immediately I got on the phone to BeBe.

"Morning, didn't wake you, did I?"

"No, you sound chipper this morning. What's up?"

"Remember how much we used to love going to the mountains?"

"Yeah."

"Well, I think I want to buy a place there. I found this place on the Internet, and I'd like you to get the specifics for me. Maybe we could take a couple of days off work this week and drive over to personally check it out, if the details look good to you." I gave her the web-site address and she went online to see what had gotten me all excited this morning.

"Let me make a couple of telephone calls Al. I'll get some more information and bring it over to your house."

"Good idea. Come for lunch. I'll throw some burgers on the grill for us and whip up some frozen margaritas."

"Alrightee then, I'll be there before noon."

Hanging up the phone I went to the kitchen to grab some burgers from the freezer to thaw and to make sure I had everything we'd need for lunch. Still excited, I went back to my computer and researched that area for the next two hours. It was almost eleven-thirty when I signed off. With only about thirty minutes before BeBe's arrival, I quickly took a shower; towel dried my short blonde hair, and threw on some jogging pants and a tank top. Zipping to the game room, I mixed a blender full of margaritas and stored them in the freezer underneath the bar.

Always prompt, my buddy came through the front door with mounds of papers. We quickly hugged each other and strolled into the game room and plopped down on the sofa.

"Gees Alex, if this place looks as good in person as it sounds on paper, then man oh man, what a deal!" Now she sounded as excited as I was. I couldn't wait to get my hands on those papers, but she had them systematically arranged to give me the details in her very professional way, and I didn't want to disrupt her presentation.

"Hurry up Be's a Be, I'm bursting at the seams over here. Show me what you've got."

She went over everything with me, and we were both glassy eyed with anticipation of seeing it in person. She called the realtor and asked if we could visit the property on Thursday.

"Okay then Christy, Alex and I will meet you at your office Thursday morning at ten." After she hung up we giggled and hugged like we had already made a deal.

"So you'll have no problem taking off for a few days?"

"No, I'm long overdue for some time off," I told Be's.

"Hey, I can make this a business trip and deduct all the expenses. It really is a business trip. I'll get that price down for you Alex."

"If it's as good as we think, I don't mind paying full sticker."

"We'll see how things turn out when we get there," she said fidgeting around with her calculator.

We drank margaritas, grilled our burgers and chatted non-stop about the property. The day turned out all right. I wasn't all misty and downtrodden as I had envisioned. I'd made it through, not alone as I had planned, but with the company of my best bud. And the call of the mountains that was now filling my head.

At work the next morning before getting underway with the business of the day, I stopped by Mr. Farrington's office, the owner of the company, to get my time off approved. His secretary announced me and then ushered me right in.

"Good morning Ms. Nottingham. What's on your mind this beautiful morning?"

"Good morning sir. I'd like to take a few days off this week. Say Wednesday, Thursday and Friday?"

"For my top producer, it's not a problem. Going somewhere in particular for a short getaway?"

"Yes sir. Going to head over to the mountains for some R&R."

"Have fun and watch out for the bears. Just like you have to do around here."

With a chuckle I added, "Thank you sir, I will."

As I turned to leave he called me back and congratulated me on the high-ticket deal; I had closed last Friday.

"Nottingham, you've got an excellent future with this company. You have what it takes to be a partner. How does Farrington, Weinstein, and Nottingham sound to you?" He stood there and starred at my stunned expression. I was dumbfounded and probably looked it too. "Just think about it Nottingham, and we'll discuss it when you return on Monday."

"Yes sir, I will sir." That was all I could muster up. I left in a fog. A good fog, but nonetheless a fog. Me become a partner? It was a goal of mine, but I figured it was at least three or four years down the road. Slowly I walked the hallway to my plush office engaged with his words. My secretary saw the look of bewilderment on my face.

"Are you alright Ms. Nottingham?"

"I'm fine Charlotte, but thanks for your concern. Just preoccupied I guess. I'll be taking the latter part of the week off, so make a note of that. I'll get Wade to handle my accounts while I'm away. I'll bring him up to date before I leave."

"You had a call from Abby about five minutes ago. Would you like me to call her back and pass her through to you?"

"No thanks, I'll call her back in a few minutes."

I wasn't prepared to speak with Abby. My wound was too fresh and my pride still burnt from betrayal, but decided I might as well put this behind me rather than have it hovering over me all day. Sitting down with a cup of coffee and my bottle of Mylanta, I preceded to dial her number, instead of hitting the speed dial. With each number that I touched I tightened my emotions to prepare for the unknown, and felt the apprehension settling within my heart and the pit of my stomach. I needed to concentrate and be prepared for anything, I thought to myself. Her phone rang four times and I was preparing to leave a message, but on the fifth ring I heard her voice.

"Hi Alex," in the sweet tone I had come to know instantly.

"Good morning Abby. Charlotte said that you had called a short while ago."

"Just wanted to see how you are doing, and ask you if it would be alright for me to come by this evening to pick up some clothes? I didn't take much with me when I left. It was a strange time, and I wasn't thinking too clearly."

"Sure thing. I'll be home by seven this evening. Do you want to come by then?"

"Yeah, that will work fine for me. Can I fix you dinner?"

There's the shocker I had tried to prepare myself for. I knew if I said yes to that I'd be setting myself up for more than just dinner. Abby knew my love buttons and how to undo them. It would be so easy to say yes and have another night of lovemaking with her, but then I'd start the whole thing over. That wouldn't be the right thing for either one of us. I thought fast. "That's a kind gesture, but BeBe and I have made some plans for this evening so I need to head out by eight. I'm sorry to have to rush you."

"Can't you tell her that I'm coming over tonight and postpone whatever the two of you had planned? We really need to talk."

"I know we do Abby, but tonight's not good for me."

Her tone changed. "It's always about you, isn't it Alex? Did you just stop caring about my feelings all together?"

"No, but after what happened, I've chosen to move forward with my life."

"How can you call off five years so easily, that's what I'd like to know?"

"I believe you're the one that did that Abby."

She shot back at me, "It takes two to tango Ms. Bigshot."

"Do you still want to come over this evening or not Abby?" I felt myself getting quite annoyed with her digs at me.

"I'll be there at six-thirty," and boom she slammed the receiver down, reverberating in my eardrum, and rattling my head.

"Damn," I said aloud as I grabbed my ear to rub the impact. She did it; she said six-thirty, knowing all along I had said seven this evening. She got another dig in before she pelted my eardrum with her thunderous end to our conversation. Just more of a reason for me to realize our relationship could not and would not be saved. Drinking two big sips from my Mylanta bottle, I filed the unpleasant ordeal away in the back of my head and got to work.

I worked up until five and called BeBe to tell her what happened earlier with Abby.

"She said WHAT? She's losing it Alex. Be glad it's over between you two. At least she's seeing what a giant mistake she made with you. I'm proud of you for staying so strong. Just keep it up tonight. Maybe I should come over and be there with you?"

"Thanks, but I can handle it. Just say a prayer that we don't get into a shouting match. She's really out to get my goose good. Strange as it may sound, I'm ready for pretty much she might throw at me."

I left the office at five-thirty, and stopped to pick up a burger and fries to eat on the drive home. I wanted to make it home before she got there. After walking in through the kitchen door I ran upstairs to brush my teeth and put on some comfortable clothes. What had once been our bedroom now totally gave me the creeps. I didn't like to be in there any longer than I needed too. Maybe I should move all my clothes into the guest suite.

I heard the front doorbell. Six-fifteen, it's too early for Abby I thought. Taking the steps down by twos and leaping over the last four steps with ease, I unlocked the door to find not only Abby, but also her sister and two brothers. The looks on their faces said it all. Sour and gloomy faces exhibiting a body language that reeked with hostility. Totally unprepared for this curve ball, I was thrown back a few steps.

Abby picked up on my cautious behavior and a cunning smile crossed her lips as she watched me squirm. Not saying a word, Abby led them beyond me. Her two brothers, ages thirty and twenty-eight, both bumped my shoulder hard and intentionally as they followed her up the steps. The two guys I had found jobs for only a couple of months ago, and who had said I was one of the best people that they had ever met. The same two guys I had purchased a couple of used cars for, while they were down on their luck, and took groceries over to feed their families. Now suddenly I was their enemy. I didn't know what their sister had told them, but I'd bet my Porsche it wasn't the truth.

The tension I was feeling with them in the house was scaring me. I heard them all laughing upstairs. Probably aimed at my reaction to seeing them all at the door. I looked around not knowing what to do. This wasn't a situation I thought I should be alone with. I could sense my body shaking from the fright of the unknown. Why would she want to frighten me like this? This wasn't the person I had loved. But here lately I didn't know her, and was almost wishing I'd never known her.

Then her older brother, Joey, came down the stairs and walked directly over to me as I gazed out the family room window towards the mountain in the distance. "Sis says to ask you where's the ring you gave her?"

"Doesn't she have it on? She did when she left here the other night."

"She said she left it on the bathroom counter. Now where is it?" His look was fierce.

"Joey, honest she had it on the other night when I walked her out to her car."

"Are you calling my sis a liar?" Without warning he punched me in the face. I fell against the sofa from the force of his blow, striking the coffee table on the way down. Blood immediately flowed as I lay stunned on the floor, too bewildered to speak. I heard Abby scream and felt my body go limp as I slid into darkness.

CHAPTER 5

▼

I woke up in the hospital nearly twenty-four hours later. As I came around the first face I saw was BeBe's as she sat at the side of my bed holding my hand. I couldn't recall what had happened or even where I was. "Where are we?" I nearly scared my poor friend to death with my unexpected question, after so many hours of stilled silence.

"Dear God Alex, you're back." She ran to the door and yelled for the nurse. Instantly the nurse hurried into the room and to my bedside.

"My, you've had us worried." She checked my pulse and blood pressure. "Looks like you're out of the woods now. Eyes are clear, heart sounds good, but I need to go and call your doctor." With that she proceeded out of the room.

I turned back to BeBe. "What's happening? Why am I here, and why's my head hurting so bad?"

"You don't remember anything?"

"Remember what? What on God's green earth are you talking about? I need to get out of here." With that, I tried to lift myself from the bed.

"Stop that Alex. Lie back down. You're in no shape to go anywhere. Hell girl, you've been in a coma for the last twenty four hours."

"In a coma? Did I have a car accident?"

"No, you were attacked," BeBe said, giving me a curious glare.

"Attacked, by who?" Then it all started coming back to me. "Ooh, I remember now. Abby's brother Joey. He hit me. That despicable piece of horse manure. How bad is my face? The sucker hit me in the face."

"Well, let's put it this way. If I didn't know that was you lying there in that bed, I'd never recognize you. You've got a couple of raccoon eyes, a busted nose that looks twice it's size, two stitches in your upper lip, and five stitches in the back of your head. Not to mention the eight stitches in your arm from hitting the coffee table."

"My hair, did they cut my hair off in the back?"

"Still your vain old self. Couldn't knock that out of you. They only shaved a little. Don't worry you'll be your beautiful self again in no time."

Doctor Aycock, my doctor since childhood, entered the room. "There's my girl. Let me have a look see here. Hmm, good job on those stitches. Doesn't look like it will leave much of a scar, if any at all. You're right nurse Mindy, her vitals look and sound good. I think she's going to pull through this just fine."

"When can I go home Doc?"

"Patience Alex. You took an extreme blow to the back of your head when you hit the floor, accompanied by that hit to your face young lady, so you'll need to stay here again tonight. We'll wait until tomorrow before we talk about releasing you. Mindy, please get Alex another drip and chase all those people waiting to see her outta here in thirty minutes. What you need now is rest and plenty of it. I'll order up something to help you rest."

"Can my friend stay until I fall asleep?"

"Sure Alex."

After he left I questioned BeBe, "Who's outside waiting to see me?"

"The story of the attack on you made this morning's paper. They started pouring in after that. Your Dad just left to go and get something to eat a few minutes before you woke up. Abby's sitting out there. She followed the ambulance to the hospital and has been here ever since. She called me right after she called the ambulance. I called the police and rushed over as fast as my car would go. She really thought you were dead. She was crying hysterically.

Of course your sister, Bonnie, is sitting out there ready to rip Abby's head off at any given moment. Some of your co-workers and several of our friends are out in the waiting room too. I asked your nurse to have Abby move over to the far side of the room, because right now no one out there can stand the sight of her, and I'm on the tip-top of that list."

"I don't want to see her. She did this to me. She had them scare the hell out of me intentionally. That sorry brother of hers. Where's he?"

"He's locked up tight Alex, don't worry. And it will be my pleasure to get Abby out of here. I don't think she meant for things to go so far, but you're right she's responsible for you being here. Too bad we can't have her locked up. You could have been killed. That was no kind of a game to be playing with you. She's got some terribly loose screws."

"You're right Be's, and I don't think they can be tightened without some medical screwdrivers. Please go tell her I'm going to make it, and I'd like for her to leave. Would you?"

"Your wish is my command," she said saluting me as she stood at attention.

"Get outta here crazy woman," and I motioned her away.

The next day Doc Aycock let BeBe take me home around noon with strict orders for me to get plenty of rest. It was Wednesday and I was off work as I had arranged on Monday. My friend took me to her house. She had gone over to my house earlier that morning and packed some clothes for me for the next several days. While she was there she had Sears come out and shampoo the large Scottish tartan plaid rug underneath the coffee table, in the family room, to remove all the blood, my blood. She knew if I saw all that blood I'd freak out. And of course she was right.

When we pulled up to her home little Debbie was there to help get me in the house like I was some helpless person. "Hey now you guys, I can do this by myself. Get your hands off me."

"Alex, stop being such a brat. The doctor said you'd be shaky on your feet today and would need steadying. Let us help you."

"Okay, okay, you win." Like two orderlies they escorted me into the house and sat me in BeBe's own prize chair, that she always dared others to even try to sit in. "My oh my, aren't I special?"

"I just want you to be comfy and relaxed. Doctor's orders."

Debbie began bringing in flowers, two vases at a time, and placing them about me on the surrounding tables. Altogether she brought in fourteen vases. "Wow, are all these for me?"

"There's more in your bedroom. Thought you might like them spread around a bit. Here's the cards, and I've labeled the flowers so you'll know who they are from."

"Gees Bees, I see why you keep her around now. She's a jewel."

With that Debbie headed back to BeBe's office to take care of business for the next few days.

"When do we leave for Bryson City? I can't wait to see the place."

"You've got to be kidding. You've got to rest. I called and cancelled our appointment with Christy."

"Well, you'd better get right back on the phone and set it up again. I'm going even if I have to go alone."

"Calm down. Don't be getting yourself in a dither. I should have known you'd act this way. I'll call Christy back and make the appointment for around one o'clock tomorrow, if you'll promise to get a good night's rest tonight."

A huge smile came across my face. "I promise mommy."

"I don't suppose you'll ever change, will you Alex?"

"Do you want me too?"

Nope, but I just figured your vanity would interfere with you wanting anyone to see you looking so, you know, unlike yourself?"

"Crap, I'd forgot all about that. Do you think you can get her to give you the key and directions tomorrow and let us go over alone? You're right, I don't want anyone seeing me and thinking I'm some wrestler that went toe to toe and lost."

"I'd just tell them you won and that they should see the other guy. Don't worry I'll get things worked out."

The doorbell rang. "Must be the delivery man. I ordered some Chinese for us. I want you to eat and then I'm putting you to bed. No lip either Ms. Pris."

I did as I'd been instructed, thankful to be in my friend's home and tender care. Sleep did come easily as I drifted off with mountain visions lulling me.

My buddy brought me in a tray of French toast, bacon, coffee, and orange juice about nine the next morning. I had slept for nearly fifteen hours. She said she was beginning to worry that I'd slipped back into another coma, but that my snoring proved otherwise. I really felt good and rested, but I still looked like crap-ola. Thank goodness I wouldn't be seeing anyone I knew for a few days. I tried to cover my multi-colored face with as much make-up as I could, without looking like a pie face. I put on a baseball cap and sunglasses to conceal the rest. BeBe just laughed at me.

It was a beautiful day for a drive. We took her yellow baby Hummer to climb the mountains and do some four wheeling over the property. "If I move up here maybe I'll need to trade my car in for one of these. Yuh think?"

"Oh yeah, you'd love it."

We pulled up in front of the real estate office and BeBe went inside to get things squared away for us. She was back in a few minutes grinning from ear to ear.

"So what's that about?"

"What?"

"That cat-eating grin on your face, that's what."

"Me to know and you to find out."

"Don't do me that way good buddy."

"It's a surprise. You'll find out later when we get there. Just indulge me for once, will ya?"

"You know I can't stand not knowing what's going on."

"You'll just have to hold your horses this time Alex. It's only five miles from here to Aliceston."

"Did she tell you how big Aliceston is? I've never heard of it before, have you?"

She nodded her head no. "Christy said the town only has ninety-eight residents. It's very small."

"No shit Sherlock. Ninety-eight people? That's the smallest town I've ever heard of."

"Well,we're about to see, cause there it is ahead."

I'll be darned. A sign along the road said, *Welcome to Aliceston, Home of the Best Chicken and Dumplings in the good old USA.* We looked at one another and laughed. Just past the sign was a little café named, The Apple Dumpling Café. Then a tiny gas station that doubled as a Post Office, and across the road was a Lil General Store.

"That's the town? That's it?" I said crinkling my bruised face.

"Afraid so, cause Christy said at the end of town at the Lil General Store go two-tenths of a mile, take the dirt road to the left, and follow it to the property." She slowed the car down and turned left onto the red clay road. "Almost there now." We zigzagged bouncing our way up the road until we came to a chained gate blocking further entrance.

"Oh no, can we get through?"

"Yep, I've got the key. Hang tight while I get the gate open."

Then we were on our way again. Once we rounded a couple more sloped curves and a cluster of thick evergreen trees, the view was magnificent. Just as it had been pictured, no tens times better. She stopped the Hummer so we could just drink in the panoramic view in its entirety. My swollen eyes opened wide to take it all in.

"Gosh Be's, it's beautiful, isn't it?"

The look on her face said she agreed with me, as she quietly drove us closer. She pulled under a huge Willow tree and parked in front of the old farmhouse.

"Wait, let me come around and help you."

"For Christ sakes Be's, let me be. I'm doing fine and dainty. Thank you ma'am." I hopped out with no problem and stood awed as I looked out across the fields. "This is all so surreal. You know, I feel like I've been here before. Hard to explain this tranquility that has surrounded me. I've got to see more," shaking my head in wonder.

We went up the five steps to the front porch of the unpretentious country home. From the porch you could see for miles to all the surrounding mountains. Everything was green, with wildflowers swaying white, pink, and purple in the valley. Trees everywhere and some seemingly reaching to the heavens. Sweet honeysuckle odorized the air, mixed with other pleasant scents unbeknown to me. Four high-back rocking chairs, and an old weathered swing that moved gently with the soft breeze of the day, occupied the porch. As BeBe unlocked the door I asked her, "Do you feel it?"

"Feel what Al?"

"The peacefulness that this place exudes."

Giving me a strange look and holding the door for me to step inside she said, "Those drugs the doctor gave you must still have you feeling pretty good."

"It's not that, oh just forget it. You know sentimental me. Anyway look how homey this is." Decorated in what appeared to be Victorian style with old antiques, even an old-fashioned player piano, which made me jump after I bumped it, and it began to play *Camptown Lady*. We both giggled and began to sign along, "Oh The Doo-Dah Day." We continued humming as we looked around while the piano played on. It looked as though the family just up and moved without taking a single thing with them.

"Someone must come out and clean cause it smells fresh, and there's no dust or cob webs. Actually, it looks like someone still lives here, doesn't it Be's?"

"Christy said that it hasn't been lived in for over four years, but it's only been on the market for a few weeks."

"Wonder why there's been no takers?"

"That is strange, it's a wonderful place. I'll ask Christy about that later. Let's go out to the barns."

"Right behind you. I'm going to leave the door open and close the screen since we'll be back in a few minutes."

Both barns were painted in chipping and flaking red paint, but still their character reflected a nostalgic part of the past. I envisioned them freshly painted and brought back to their original glory. Inside the barn were things I had no idea of what they were, or what possible purpose they could have. But they intrigued me.

"What's this? Looks like someone sleeps out here in the barn."

"That's the surprise Al. His name is Running Horse. He's lived on this land since he was a young man. He's in his sixties now, and he still watches after the place. Christy said he'd like to stay on if the new owner would agree. She said he's harmless."

"How much would I need to pay him?"

"Christy just said room and board."

"Oh no, I'd have to pay him. Room and board wouldn't be enough. He'd need spending money for clothes, goodies and other what have yous."

"Are you saying you want to buy this place?"

"I simply adore this place Be's. I feel like it's home already. I guess the population is going up to ninety-nine, cause Alexander Frances Nottingham is ready to sign the dotted line, and I see no reason to dicker around with the price."

"It's going to need a lot of work you know. You haven't met Running Horse yet either."

"This is the place for me. I can feel it in my bones. Get those papers ready."

"Alright Alex, you know what you want. Let me call Christy and tell her you want to buy it lock, stock, and barrel."

CHAPTER 6

▼

While she made the call, I went back up to the house about a football field's length away. The path was aged and well marked from the thousands of other feet that had made their marks over the years, to and fro. This place was over seventy years old, and had the grace and character of a southern steel magnolia. It was obvious that much love had abounded on this splendid land, from the variety of trees and flowers that grew in testament. Only with much care and love could they have thrived and grown so beautiful.

I tried to imagine what the family that had built this home must have been like. It would have been a period of time between the great wars. Did they migrant from afar or were they newly wed, just starting out from around here? Were they from a notable family? Did they raise sizable families here, lots of little ones running about chasing butterflies or playing hide-and-seek? The questions in my mind only increased the desire I had to hopefully call this my home.

As I stepped up on the porch and re-entered the house my thoughts settled down, and I began to take in the enchantment of the time-honored home. Its furnishings were unobtrusive by today's standards. Certainly not the loftiest refinement that I had become accustomed to, and had surrounded myself with over the past several years. But none of that had ever brought me true happiness. None of that had the personality that could ever endure the seasons of seven decades with the harmony that these walls preserved. None of that brought the peace that I felt as I walked through each room, immersed in each new find.

The master bedroom was large with a stone fireplace occupying one corner of the yellow with blue toile wallpapered walls. Quaint white woodened shutters framed the two windows facing the valley below, surrounded on all sides by the grandeur of the Great Smokey Mountains. The attached bathroom was ample size, with an old claw-footed bathtub and a white porcelain pedestal sink. Not reproductions for modern day decorating, but honest to goodness well cared for antiques. The commode's tank hung on the upper wall behind it, with a pull chain. That was something different than I had ever seen, but I thought it a magnificent reflection of the past.

As I merrily skipped down the stairway humming once again, "Oh The Doo-Dah Day," BeBe came in through the front door.

"Well the papers are drawn up. Just need your John Hancock. Christy is on her way out here now."

"I don't want her to see me looking like this"

"It's okay; I told her about what happened when I went in to pick up the keys. I gave her a copy of the news article. She felt so sorry for you. She said that she has read several of your articles in the financial section of the Raleigh Times. She's a big fan of yours Alex."

"We'll see. I don't want anyone feeling sorry for me. Is my make-up still hiding most of the bruises alright?"

"Yeah, yeah, yeah, you vain child. The swelling has gone down a lot today, and you look like Alex again, so stop fretting."

"Let's look at the kitchen." Together we walked in. "Will you look at this?" I said, pleased with the find. Another stone fireplace was on the wall next to the back door. The walls were exquisitely wood paneled in knotty pine, and the flooring was covered in quarry tiles, aged and exuding a timeless quality. "Gracious, this is just totally awesome. I can't believe my luck."

We went out to sit on the front porch in the swing to await Christy's arrival. We sat motionless for a few minutes as we both looked out over the vastness of the farmland. Bird-songs filled the blue-skied summer's air with pleasant melodies, that only they could create. The massive willow tree that shaded almost the entire front yard fanned us with gentle mountain breezes.

Abruptly BeBe spoke, making me jump in response, as the brief silence was broken. "Sorry, guess we both got kinda lost there for awhile. I think I hear a car coming up the road."

Sure enough a red jeep blowing dust came into sight, slowing as it came nearer the house. Parking behind our car under the huge willow tree, the engine shut down, and Christy emerged and came to the front porch to join us. "Howdy, gorgeous day isn't it ladies?"

I pulled over a rocking chair as we stood to welcome Christy and get the formalities out of the way. BeBe went to her car to get us each a Pepsi from her cooler before we got too buried in the details of the purchase.

"Christy, please forgive my looks. That Mack truck hit me pretty darn hard."

"So I heard. I'm so sorry you had to go through that calamity Alexandra."

"Please call me Alex. Oh no big deal anymore. I just want to put the whole thing behind me and move on to better pastures. And this here is the pastures I'd be talking about. It already feels like home."

"Okay, BeBe said that you'd like to offer $380,000 for the property. I think that's a reasonable place to start."

I threw BeBe a look of astonishment since she hadn't conferred with me before bidding lower than we had previously discussed. "What do you think my chances are of buying the farm for that Christy?"

"Well, it's only been on the market for a little over two weeks, but the locals have known it would be sold for a long time now, so all we can do is submit the offer and see what the owner thinks."

"Excuse us Christy; BeBe and I need to talk alone for a second." I motioned for BeBe to follow me inside and shut the front door behind us. "What are you doing? I don't want to chance losing this place."

"Just trying to save you a few bucks. You'll need it trying to fix this place up. You know how persnickety you are about having everything just so-so!"

"Thanks, but no thanks, if it could possibly mean me not being able to make this purchase. I appreciate your good intentions, but let's not gamble since we have this bird in our hands right now. Okay good buddy?"

"I get your drift. You're the boss on this one. I'll tell Christy that you're wanting this deal closed right away; so you're willing to go the full asking price to guarantee a speedy delivery."

"Thanks for understanding."

I went to the bathroom while she spoke with Christy about upping the offer. When I came back out Christy looked at me and said, "Looks like you've got yourself a country mountain farm. Let me step out and call the owner to get a verbal approval before we proceed."

She walked down towards the barns following that old age worn path. We could see her smiling in the distance, with her free arm twirling like a windmill as she talked. Minutes later she approached the porch. "When would you like to close Alex?"

Now I beamed like a floodlight with excitement, squinting through my swollen eyes. "Next week? Is that possible?"

"So happens the owner will be in town next week to speak with Running Horse about what his plans will be."

"I thought he wanted to stay here?"

"Oh my, yes, he does, but that would be totally up to you."

"I couldn't make him leave his home. Anyway, look how well he's kept this place up. Heck, together we could probably make it look like it's brand new again."

"Would you like to meet him first?"

"I'd love to meet him, but my mind's made up, he stays."

My buddy added, "Trust me Christy, if Alex says that her mind is made up, then the matter is settled, and there'd be no changing her mind without a team of wild horses. You'd have an easier time painting that dirt road out there blue."

Turning back to me Christy asked," When would you care to meet him?"

"Gracious, I'd hate for him to see me looking like this. How about next Saturday? Let's say about four o'clock? You'll come with me, won't you BeBe?"

"I'll sure try."

Christy said that she would set the meeting up here on the farm. We all shook hands while bidding ado. She pulled away leaving her trail of dust in the distance.

"Can you believe it? I'm going to be a country girl. No more seven-day workweeks for me. No more traffic jams. No more back stabbing friendly faces."

"Wait a minute Alex, what are you saying?"

"I'm saying I'm quitting the company."

With a look of shock and disbelief Be's protested, "But you said you've been offered partnership. What about that? You need to think about this."

"I have been thinking about it. Only habit ties me to that job. That money pit has enslaved me long enough. I have no one to hold me there. And let's face it, not everyone can up and go to follow their dreams. It's a life changing opportunity. Partnership I can refuse, but the chance to make my dreams come true is a gift from God. I told God, that if I could buy this property, I'd take a leap on faith; take off my rose colored glasses that have blinded me for too long, and study the art of living for a change. My social lines have been too narrow. I want to live where there is no pecking order of who to be friends with because of whom they are or what they have"

"Gosh, you do sound as though you've given this some thought. This is a side of you I've never seen before. I like it, but it scares me at the same time."

"Think of it, just me and nature. The chance to write my thoughts in this beautiful and peaceful valley, surrounded by ancient mountains and forest. No deadlines or oscillating markets to decipher. I'll be able to finally take the target off my chest and discover what real peace of mind is."

"Can you afford to do that? Will you be alright financially?"

"I've made some keen investments in the financial arena. You know that. My portfolio is well beyond the goals I had set for myself, and with the sell of the house, well I should be able to support myself just fine for many years. I'll just repurpose myself, and adjust my lifestyle."

"What will I do without you? We've been friends for so long."

"Don't even go there girlfriend. We'll always be the best of friends. Nothing will ever change that. We might only see each other every other week or so, but heck before all this mess with Abby, that was about the only time we saw each other anyway. Right?"

"Yeah, I suppose, but you were only minutes away, not hours," her face looking forlorn.

"Listen, I'll give you a key and you can fix a bedroom upstairs just for yourself. I'll not let anyone else stay in there. It will be all yours. Okay? Put your coca-cola stuff all around. Do what you want. You're my family; you know that."

She gave me a broad emotional smile in accordance, and tiny flicks of gold dust sparkled in her green eyes. We hugged and sealed that promise of eternal friendship and sisterly love on the front porch of my soon-to-be new home.

CHAPTER 7

BeBe had dropped me off late last night around one in the morning. We had checked out some sights around Asheville, inconspicuously due to my gruesome appearance, before heading home. We found the nightlife jamming around that town. On the drive back to Chapel Hill we chatted like busy beavers, about the mountain life I would soon be embarking. Funny how two city-slickers like us could get so excited about the country life. We'd packed a lot into our thirty-four years and grown in awareness. We were cut from the same cloth, and that cloth was turning from French silk to country gingham. And we weren't afraid to admit it. Time has a way of changing you, if you're willing.

I got up around noon on Sunday grabbing my usual giant cup of coffee, but instead of the Sunday paper, I grabbed the papers on the farm. Sitting down in my chair I reread every page. I could feel my facial muscles more relaxed than I'd noticed in years, and I felt the smile that just naturally spread across my face this morning. I was at peace with my decision, even amongst the last week's incidents. I realized that the bad that I went through only helped lead me to the good I was now experiencing. It had been a rainbow in disguise.

The phone rang breaking my daydream state of mind. "Hello."

"Morning girlfriend. How'd you sleep?"

"Like a baby. How about you?"

"Same oh here. You know I've been thinking. Now that you done gone and got yourself a farm, whatcha gonna call it?"

"Well, you know I haven't even given that a thought. You got any ideas?"

"Got to be your call Al. Anyway give it some thought. Wanna go to a matinee movie around two? Three movies start at the Plaza then, so we can pick one out when we get there."

"Sounds good Be's. Want me to come and get you?"

"I'm driving. You still need another day to rest. Sides it's closer to your house than mine."

"When will you be by?"

"Pick you up in an hour."

"Okie dokie, see you then." I still had to apply make-up to hide the bruising, but not as much today, thank goodness. BeBe's question about what to call the farm engrossed my brain cells as I dressed. All kinds of names ran through my mind, but none that stuck more than a second or two. Then it came to me. Eureka, that's it. Heck, with a last name like Nottingham, how could it not have just jumped right out of me? NOTTINGHAM FOREST, that's perfect. Nottingham Forest, I couldn't wait to tell BeBe. She'd get a kick out of that.

After the movie we picked up some to go food and drove back to my place to eat, and get a little more rest before our workweek would start over again.

"What are you going to tell your boss tomorrow?"

"Well, I've been rehearsing it over and over again in my mind. Something like that time in the hospital made me really give some serious thought to what I really want from life. You know something along those lines. I'm still working on it."

"What do you think he's going to say? Do you think he'll try to change your mind?"

"I'm not for sure, but tomorrow will tell. Oh yeah, guess what?"

"Good or bad?"

"Good for heaven's sakes. It's something you told me to think about."

"You came up with a name for the farm?"

"Precisely. How does Nottingham Forest sound to you?"

"Excellent, I love it. Has a ring to it."

"It does, doesn't it? I want to have a sign made up to put across the entrance onto the property. Think you can get your sign man to give me a good deal? I'll need your help to design it too."

"He'll give you a good deal. I'll see to that."

After BeBe left I practiced what I would tell Mr. Farrington tomorrow, about my reasons for deciding to resign at this time. Particularly after the mention of a partnership he'd out of the blue spoken of last week. Two weeks ago, the thought of leaving the company I had put so much of myself into had never crossed my mind. But the incidents that had occurred since then made me contemplate another side of myself, which I had been postponing for the last fourteen years. My voracious desire for money, prestige, and power never before allowed me the thought of walking away. Not in my wildest dreams. My frivolous vanities had prevented that type of thinking only days before. But the peace and tranquility that I had experienced at the farm seduced me into another realm of ambition. I wanted to become my own apprentice in life, drop the daily Deja Moo, and find the key to my spirit.

Thomas Buchanan Read wrote, *All in their lifetime carve their own soul's statue.*

Up to this point I didn't like the way my statue looked, so I needed to start over and bring my true soul's picture out of the rock. I was going on a search to find myself. Nottingham Forest would be the perfect place to start my journey.

As I strolled past Charlotte on the way into my office I was all smiles and humming that Oh The Doo-Dah Day song, which had been stuck in my head since I heard it play out at the farm house. I stopped briefly and said a cheerful, Good Morning Charlotte."

"Good morning. How are you feeling?"

"A few battle scars to clear yet, but otherwise I'm on top of the world. Thanks for asking. I really like that dress you have on this morning. Makes your eyes glow like sapphires. That's a terrific color on you Charlotte."

"Thank you Ms. Nottingham. We've missed you this past week. It seemed too quiet with you not around."

"That was probably a welcome reprieve for you."

"No ma'am, I like the way you hustle about getting things done. I'd like to be just like you."

"That's nice Charlotte, but I wouldn't advise it. Do I have any appointments this morning?"

She gave me a questioning look. "Mr. Farrington wants you to have lunch with him at noon over at The Cardinal Club. Should I call his secretary and confirm?"

"Yes, please do. And by the way Charlotte, thank you for being so efficient and keeping everything organized while I was gone. You've done an outstanding job."

She blushed in gratitude and sheepishly accepted my compliments. Her considerate conduct made me realize just how ungrateful I had been. I should have been praising her more all along for the work she's willingly jumped to do for me, over the past year she's been onboard with the company. I'd be sure to make every effort to bestow more words of kindness in her direction, up until my last day. I had been too preoccupied with my own concerns before to go out of my way to extend the like to anyone, other than my compensating clients. Sure I was nice to her, but not like I should have been. Now with the rose colored glasses removed, I could see that.

I called my florist and asked him to send her some flowers to the office today. "Roses, coral, two dozen of them please. Just sign the card, thanks for all your hard work. Always, Alex Nottingham. Thanks Frank" This should show her my appreciation, and diminish some of the guilt I was feeling for having taken her for granted these past months.

Sitting at my desk, I answered e-mails, opened stacks of correspondence, and returned calls. Time quickly passed. Charlotte popped her head into my office at eleven-thirty.

"Time for you to head for The Cardinal Club, Ms. Nottingham."

"Good gracious, where has the time gone this morning? Thanks Charlotte."

Once I entered the club's dining room I saw Mr. Farrington waving me over. Mr. Weinstein was also sitting at the table, and they both stood as Mr. Farrington pulled out my chair for me. This had to be a celebratory luncheon of sorts, probably my partnership invitation. I swallowed hard, feeling a bit nervous and slightly overwhelmed at the task at hand. I knew they were thinking I'd be elated and eager to accept their prestigious offer. This was indeed something that used to be my huge goal in life. Funny how your priorities change through episodes you encounter.

"It's so good to see you Alexandra. We're so sorry about that dreadful experience you went through. We both came by your hospital room, but needless to say, you wouldn't recall that. Did you receive our flowers?"

"Yes sirs, and they were stunning. You really shouldn't have, but thank you both so much."

"I see you still have a couple of stitches."

"They come out today, matter of fact. I'm almost back to normal. I was pretty lucky. Good thing I'm a tough old girl."

"Tough maybe, but old girl, no way. You're a striking and remarkable young Lady."

"Thank you Mr. Weinstein."

"Please call me Howard. Roger and I have been closely monitoring your performance over the past years. When you first came to us I told Roger, now there's a shining star. You've always been at the top of the game and worked like a powerhouse. You've made the best we can tally up, around one hundred and sixty million dollars for our company, and thirty million of that has been this year alone."

Roger Farrington piped in, "Success like that should be rewarded Alexandra. I spoke briefly with you in my office about partnership in the company. Now Howard and I would like to make that a formal declaration. We'd pay you five percent of our net profits each year to start. That would be on top of a five-hundred and fifty thousand dollar salary. You're worth every penny of it too. We'd be proud to add Nottingham to our company stationery, if you'd accept our offer."

Then silence stilled the air as I prepared to speak. Quietly I cleared my throat in readiness. But before I got the first word out, the club's director, Gerald, brought over an excellent bottle of French Chardonnay, 1998 Le Montrachet, which I knew to cost about three-hundred dollars or more a bottle.

"Allow me to be the first to congratulate you Ms. Nottingham. On behalf of The Cardinal Club, please have the first toast on us," he said in his haughty British accent.

Then he poured four glasses and arms rose in salute. By now we had the attention of the full restaurant. I had no other choice but to let the toast be finalized. My face felt the blood come to the surface, and I'm sure I glowed with its luminescence. After Gerald left our table, the attention once again was focused on me as Roger and Howard sat in anticipation.

"Gracious gentlemen what a generous offer. I'm honored that you would even consider me for a partner. It's been a dream of mine for some time." Their smiling faces only added to the anxiety I was feeling, as I tried to put into words a declination speech. Halfway through my remarks their smiles were replaced with more somber looks. Looks of understanding that also presented astonishment, that I would be so bold to turn down such a lucrative position and step out to follow my dreams. As I concluded, "I've learned so much from the both of you. You gave a young girl straight out of college the chance to fulfill one dream and prepared me for the next. For that I shall forever be grateful."

"I admire you Alexandra and I'm sure I can speak for Howard too. It's our loss, but I expect we'll be hearing more from you someday through your literary works. I only wish we could share you a while longer, but I see the fire in your soul, and know you'll pursue this quest just as vigorously as you've worked for us." He leaned over and spoke with Howard privately for several moments. "I'm sorry, didn't mean to be rude. Howard and I want to give you a parting gift. You've given us so much of yourself over the years." He pulled out his checkbook. He quickly wrote and tore off the check and slid it discreetly over to me.

I was blown away. Five-hundred thousand dollars. *That can't be right* I was thinking. Carefully I counted the zeros in my head again. But that's what it said. I looked back and forth between the two, shaking my head in total disbelief. "I don't know what to say."

"All you have to say is that if you ever decide to get back into this business, you'll come back to us. And if you don't, well you'll send us free autographed copies of all your books."

I beamed, "That you can count on," and we sealed our deal with fond handshakes.

We ate our meal and talked in great depth about my new venture. They seemed almost envious and lit up with excitement for me, as I described the mountain farm. I promised to invite them both out to the country once I got the place in order.

After I left The Cardinal Club I drove over to the doctor's office and had my stitches removed. The facial and head scars were barely visible and would heal probably un-noticeable in time. However, the scar on my arm wasn't quite so diminishing and would leave tell-tell signs, as a reminder of a love gone miserably wrong.

I swung by BeBe's office before I headed home and told her about my luncheon, proudly displaying my check with youthful candor.

"You lucky son of a gun. You go and quit them, and they give you a check for five-hundred thousand dollars. How do you do it? I just want to know, how do you do it?

For the life of me Al, I'll never figure that out."

"God loves me my friend. That's all I can say about that. He wants me to fulfill my dream. Now you believe me don't you?"

"Yeah. God, I want to fulfill my dream too."

"I think you are right here, aren't you Be's?"

"You're right Alex, I am. But there's another part to my dream."

"I know, woman of your dreams. Not to worry, hang on, and it'll happen."

I went by the bank and deposited my check. My long time Customer Service Officer friend, Judy, gave me an exaggerated "Oohh, musta been a king size deal this time," smiling at me broadly from behind her desk.

"You'd better believe it."

The news spread fast through the company that I had submitted my resigna-
tion and would be leaving in thirty days. Wade and Charlotte were in my office
waiting on me the following morning.

Wade piped up first, "Say it isn't true! You're really not leaving us are you?"

"Oh, so you've already heard."

"Then it is true. Why Alex?"

"Then Charlotte, "Yes, why Ms Nottingham? Was it that dreadful incident at
your home?"

"That was the straw that broke the camel's back I suppose, but it goes far
beyond that. I've dreamed of being a novelist since Lord knows when. I used to
make up church hymns in my head, before I even knew how to write the words.
It has always been my dream, but my love of competition in the corporate world,
chasing materialistic conformity, and financial power sidetracked me. It took a
physical blow to wake me up out of the trance I had become so absorbed in, to
get it through this thick noggin of mind that that's not really who or what I'm all
about. I came out of that coma at the hospital realizing that I had other mountains to climb and rivers to fish. I want the things that no money can buy, and I
can't find that here. I need to explore the caves of my imagination and run to
meet life on it's own terms, with me at the helm. I want to feel the wind in my
face as I walk this earth, not just as I speed down the highway in my car. I've
sashayed around my dreams too long. Time for me to refocus and dance my way
to the real meaning of my life."

A hush and amazed looks permeated for several hung seconds.

"WOW, you are really something else Ms. Nottingham. I don't think I would
have the guts to do that. You turned down a partnership here to go for your
dreams."

"Yeah," Wade said, "I wouldn't have the balls to pass up an offer like that.
You're either a crazy woman or a miracle in motion."

"I like that Wade, a miracle in motion. I must remember that phrase. But
you're right, God is working through me in some pretty awesome ways at this
junction in my life, and I'm gonna follow where He leads."

The rest of the week went zooming by, filled with conversations from nearly
everyone I ran into in the office, about why, what, and where. I was trying to tie
up loose ends with clients and redirect my accounts. I made sure to take good
care of my protégé, Wade, by sharing my mental investment intelligence play-

book, and cluing him in on how to spot bull-market powerhouses on the horizon.

On Friday I walked him through a large account I had been working on quite profitably over the last six years. The timing was perfect. He was awestruck by the mechanics of momentum fund investing, as he watched as I made eye-popping transactions that reaped seven figure gains.

I would work hard for Frank and Howard until the end. Leaving a strong profit record and an example for others to follow in my wake, would be a proper parting gift. Satisfied with the outcome, I left work that evening feeling worth my stuff.

My buddy had some people coming in from out of town unexpectantly for the weekend to look at some commercial properties, so I had to drive over to Aliceston alone. I got there about one o'clock on Saturday and decided to stop in at the Apple Dumpling Café for lunch, since I'd not eaten all day.

A quaint little café painted green with yellow trim on the outside like a John Deere tractor. Inside the gray-planked walls were decorated with memorabilia of all sorts, like old tin signs, black and white pictures, and dated cooking utensils. The tables and booths had yellow and green-checkered tablecloths, with artificial sunflowers in green dollar store vases centered on top. There was only seating room for about forty people, but with a population of ninety-eight, I guessed that certainly was adequate. Every since I'd read that sign proclaiming "The Home of the Best Chicken and Dumplings in the Good Old USA," my mouth had been watering to give them the old taste test.

I didn't even bother looking at the menu before my waitress came over wearing an apron matching the tablecloths, and handed me a cold fogged mason jar of fresh lemonade. An aged hospitable woman, tall in statue, burly in size, and she had a smile that would melt the butter on your biscuits instantly. Her silver hair framed her round golden face, and was tied back in an old fashioned bun. Her black eyes danced in my direction and made the corners of my mouth spread upward involuntarily. That contagious smile was illuminating. Like some magical power she possessed. I felt a strange connection of familiarity.

"Com'a fur piece today, hat'ya young'em? Bet yew tarred and hungree. What's ya be a'wontin?"

I stared at her while trying to figure out what she had said to me, repeating her sounds in my head, until I deciphered what I thought she had said. "I'm hungry enough to eat the buttons off of my shirt, and those chicken and dumplings sound mighty good. I'll take a large bowl of those, please ma'am," I said right proudly.

There were only about ten people scattered around inside the country café, and they all clapped in unity. I looked about to see what they were clapping at, but they were all looking at me with smirks spread across their faces. Puzzled I looked up at my waitress and saw her clapping too.

"Oh, honey we're just joking around with you. We like to put on a bit with new people. They kind of expect us to be talking that a way around these parts. But since you're going to be joining us, we'll go easy on you."

"Gee thanks, I think. How did you know I'm moving here?"

"Don't nothing much get past us locals. You know small town and all. We know you're here to meet Running Horse."

Now this was going to take some getting used to for me. I had always considered myself a very private person and now, well now, it appeared that I wouldn't be keeping too many secrets anymore.

"Would you like some sweet milk to wash those dumplings down with Alexandra? You don't mind me calling you Alexandra, do you?"

"No ma'am, that's fine. What may I call you?"

"Oh sweetie, call me Mama Willa. Everyone in these parts does." She graced me with another one of those larger than life smiles and strolled back into the kitchen.

A strange looking gentleman, dressed in faded bib overalls, walked across the room and stood over me. "Got any kin in these hills?" He asked me as he rocked back and forth beside me, pinning his eyes to mine, awaiting my reply.

"No sir, none that I'm aware of."

Without another word directed to me, he grumbled to himself and sauntered out the front door.

"Don't mind Uncle Opie, he'll warm up to you." With that she placed a monstrous platter of chicken and dumplings in front of me, along with a plate of fried green tomatoes to the side. "On the house today neighbor."

"Gosh, thanks. Everything smells delicious, but I don't think I can eat all this."

"What yer can't eat I'll wrap up for you to take to your new home. Just enjoy your meal Alexandra." She left me alone and went over to speak with some other patrons, who were playing cards and drinking not just tea, but sweet tea I'd soon learn to say.

I ate about three-fourths of what was without a doubt everything they had claimed to be, The Best Chicken and Dumplings in the Good Old USA. They passed my taste test with flying colors. Mama Willa tried her best to get me to eat some of her fresh cooked apple dumplings and ice cream, but sensing my fullness she kept to her promise and fixed me a to-go bag. I left a five-dollar tip on the table and waved good-bye as I exited. Everyone in the café, all men except for Mama Willa, cheerfully sent me on my way with a friendly, "See ya real soon," while their hands waved in the air.

As I walked to my little sports car, I could feel eyes at my back. I turned around and sure enough everyone had followed me out to watch me drive away. Smiling to myself, I peeled out onto the road and threw up my hand quickly to wave, before shifting into second gear. I had just met over a tenth of the town's residents, and I liked them all, even Uncle Opie.

I slowed down to make my turn onto the dirt road, which led to my property, or soon to be my property. Anxious to meet Running Horse, my mind conjured up fascinating images of the Indians of years past. Then tossing the silly images aside as utterly ridiculous, I laughed at myself for being so trite.

My Carrera took the hills with ease, while mud from the early morning rain splashed inside the car and threw sprinkles of clay on my face, without me even noticing. I was so caught up about seeing the farm again and meeting Running Horse, that I wasn't mindful to much else. The gate to the entrance was open so I slowly drove on through, and rounded the cluster of evergreens; to the spot I had first laid eyes on the farm. Sitting ahead, like a reminiscent picture of time gone by, was the place I would soon call home. I should have someone paint this view for me to hang over the fireplace in the kitchen, I thought to myself.

Sitting there for several minutes captivated by the fan-tabulous spreading sight, a lone deer skipped down the road ahead of me leading to the house. "Outstanding," I whooped and proceeded to follow in total delight. Feeling like a little kid I drove under the willow tree and parked as the deer continued to run through the meadow. I couldn't take my eyes off of it, and watched until it disappeared into the greenness of the woods.

It was only about two o'clock, so I'd have a couple of hours to myself before any others arrived. I walked up on the front porch and stood and stared out across the land, taking in a little at a time as my eyes panoramically scanned Nottingham Forest. I saw five horses out in the field by the big barn. Two gorgeous Pintos, one palomino, a frisky black stallion stomping in the dirt, and the reddest chestnut I'd ever seen. "Now I wonder whose horses they are?" I said aloud. "Just beautiful."

Then from behind me came a voice. "Yes they are, aren't they Ms. Nottingham?"

Nearly falling down the steps, I was caught by two strong arms just in time.

"I didn't mean to sneak up on you, but then we Indians are known for that. Are you alright?"

Turning around I looked into the bronze and smoothly aged skin of Running Horse. He had a high brow, chiseled cheekbones, and hair as black as his eyes. Strong eyes that reflected knowledge more than age, and penetrated me with a genuine kindness. His square jaw jutted out proudly as he let me go and stepped back. He was handsome, built like a man twenty years less his age of sixty-two, and dressed in jeans and a crisp chambray, working shirt.

Just like Mama Willa, his smile beckoned a return. Smiling back, I apologized for my reaction and thanked him for catching me.

"You have to be Running Horse."

"Yes, Ms.Nottingham."

Extending my hand, "Please call me Alex, all my friends do. I hope we can be friends Running Horse."

"It would be my honor Alex." His handshake was warm and firm.

I don't know what it was, but I had that same feeling of familiarity that I had felt when I met Mama Willa. It was perplexing me, but I had too much to do to give it much thought right then.

He walked me about the property for the next two hours telling me stories that enthralled me. I sensed an uncommon wisdom from him. His manner of speaking was clear and expressive, not at all as I had expected, and he was the most sententious man I'd ever come across. He said things like, "What befalls the birds of the air and the animals of the land will in the future befall on us. That is why we must balance the land's energies." Pretty heavy, but right on, I thought as we continued.

After only spending two hours with him the familiarity I had felt was now feeling almost paternal. It was effortless talking with him. It wasn't like two strangers meeting for the first time, although I didn't know what to make of it.

"We have company Alex."

"Who is that Running Horse?"

"Mr. Terrace Blake, current owner of the property. He's driven in from Atlanta for the closing today."

"What's he like?"

"A bit stuffy, all business, hides his heart, but deep inside a kindred spirit. He just hasn't realized it yet. Some never do."

"Before we go to meet him I'd like to tell you something. It's important to me that you know this will always be your home for as long as you want Running

Horse. And I know you are used to getting room and board for helping out around here, but I insist that I pay you a hundred and fifty dollars a week also. I know it's not much, but it's all I can handle right now, until we see what the future brings."

"I need very little Alex. I make money in various other ways. To be able to stay here on this land is all I ask. Thank you for your kindness, but please keep your money."

"It's all or nothing Running Horse, take it or leave it," giving him a tenacious look, with my head cocked to the side.

"Seems you speak powerful language young lady. How can one deny a mind so set in rock? I will accept your offer."

Christy's red jeep was headed for the house, and we could see she carried a passenger with her. So together we made our way back to the house.

Christy's passenger had been Gladys, the mortgage-closing officer. It took only twenty minutes to get things finalized, as I had sent the money to her office earlier in the week to expedite the process. Mr. Blake was a man of few words, even when I asked him questions he responded with only a short sentence or two. Seems he had inherited the property several years ago, and had planned to use the farm as a vacation home for his family. Things however didn't work out, so he decided to sell. I read between the lines for myself with my active imagination. His manner made me sense a divorce must have occurred, and halted his plans to stay out here on vacation. Evidently I was benefiting from the pain of another. Odd how that works sometimes. I thanked him for the information I was able to extract from him about the property, and didn't pursue with further questions.

Anyway I had the expert on the land with Running Horse on site. He probably knew more about this land than anyone. In his colorful way he could answer my questions with interesting stories of its history.

After Mr. Blake pulled away in his black clay dusted Mercedes, followed by Christy's jeep, Running Horse invited me to have supper with him. I agreed and he said he'd bring it over at seven. That gave me a couple of hours to relax, take a bath, and change clothes. What a day this had been. A mountain farm to call home, a new friend, and a complete new start brightened my horizons.

My thoughts were like visions skipping around in my head. Feelings of euphoria ignited me and twirled my brain. Catching myself in the mirror, the spectacle stopped me cold. My face and hair were covered with mud freckles, like a child who'd been playing out in the rain splashing in mud holes. I looked preposterous. I had to laugh at myself. No one had said a word. I guess no one wanted to do anything that might put a splinter in the closing. But I'd have to ask Running

Horse why he hadn't questioned me about my unusual appearance. My oh my, what must they have thought of me? No wonder Mr. Blake hardly said a word. He probably thought I was some wild demented woman that he needed to flee from as quickly as possible. Wait until I tell BeBe this story. She's going to roll with laughter. I made a beastly face at myself in the mirror, and then headed to wash off the plastered mud and make myself more presentable.

Promptly at seven supper, not dinner like I was used to calling it was served. Fry bread, boiled crawdads, barbequed fish, wild onions, roasted corn on the cob, and for dessert grape dumplings. It was all new to me except for the corn on the cob. It smelled divine. "How'd you cook all this?"

"Over the fire-pit where I do most of my cooking."

"Amazing," I said shaking my head. The only problem I had was with those crawdads, ugly little things, but when Running Horse showed me the trick on how to retrieve the sparse but succulent meat, I was hooked. Eating until I was about to burst, then pushing my chair from the table in defeat of finishing my dessert, I looked into my new friend's wise eyes. "Simply delicious meal. I can't imagine you cooking it all outside. You must teach me, if you wouldn't mind."

He took my compliments with the charm of a true gentleman. "Running Horse, I need to ask you a question. Earlier today unknown to me at the time, I had mud all over my face and in my hair. Yet no one said a word about the way that I looked. I'm just curious why you didn't say anything."

With an uneasy look he carefully tried to tell me. "I don't get to big cities very often and that's my choice. I know women's fashions and trends change rapidly in these times, and I didn't know if you had purposefully applied that mud or not. So I just assumed you had and held my tongue." The seriousness of his expression was priceless.

I started laughing uncontrollably and he joined in. We laughed until tears flowed from both our eyes. His laughter only further spurred my own.

"That's too much," I said when I caught my breathe. Then the laughter started again.

Once composed, "Please don't let me ever walk around wearing mud on my face again. Give me your word?"

"You have it Alex, now that I know it's not a fashion statement," his eyes flashed impishly.

The evening had been wonderful. We talked for hours, which seemed to pass like minutes. Around mid-night he marched out to the big barn where he made his home, and I readied myself for bed. Courteously he had put fresh sheets on the bed prior to my arrival that day. I'd be changing some of the furniture later on, but for now I was contended to climb into that plump feather bed with zest, knowing I'd sleep like a baby from my busy and engaging day.

The next day as I gingerly awakened and glanced at my watch, I could hardly believe my eyes. Ten o'clock on a beautiful Sunday morning. I couldn't recall sleeping in that late in like forever. Feeling rested and invigorated, I quickly threw on some shorts and a shirt with my hiking boots, and bounded down the stairs. I grabbed a diet Pepsi from the frig and headed outside to explore.

Seeing the horses in the field I proceeded in that direction. As I neared those magnificent animals the black stallion neighed a warning of my arrival, and together the five of them trotted further away, so I held back and spoke to them. "It's alright, I won't hurt you. Just want to make friends with you." Slowly I walked towards them again and stopped about thirty feet shy of them. They didn't move but cautiously watched me.

Something inside told me to sit on the ground. I don't know that much about horses, and where the idea to sit on the ground came from is beyond me. So I sat there and drank my diet Pepsi, completely caught up in the mountain air and everything around me.

The morning was glorious. Looking out across the meadow, blanketed with pink and white mountain laurel, and still finding it hard to believe that this was all mine, I didn't see or hear as one of the pintos snuck up behind me. With her nose she nudged me in the shoulder from behind. "Hey," turning and seeing her, "Well, hello big girl. Come here girl." The other horses stood back and watched. I stood up and stuck my hand out to her. She took two steps, smelled my hand, and let me rub the side of her face. "See I told you I wouldn't hurt you." Then the black stallion neighed again, and my newfound friend retreated back to the others. Now I knew who the boss was of the bunch. I'd have to work to win his trust, but at least it was a start. Next time I'd bring some apples with me. I brushed off the back of my pants, and headed for one of the paths leading into the woods. The horses followed me until I left the clearing.

Amongst the pine thickets were poplars, sweet gums, dogwoods, and some oaks mixed in with the evergreens. Chipmunks barked at me from overhead, while chickadees and brown thrashers filled the morning with song. Like a comforting salve to my stressed and stretched nerves, the forest wrapped its arms around me. My own piece of heaven surrounded me, with Cherokee roses winding up the trees and snowy trillium by the thousands, spreading their fragrant perfume. My very soul was being re-charged as I drank in the ancient beauty of this land.

Sunlight filtered through the tree's branches and fell gently on my beckoning path. The sound of babbling water made me walk a little faster to investigate. Off the path down in a hollow was a pristine streamed lined with weeping willows and river birches. Rhododendron tunnels grew sideways out of the earth. Its awesome majesty charmed my senses.

Scooping a handful of the cooled waters tumbling over a large rock, I brought it to my lips and found that it tasted as good as the bottled water costing a dollar at the Seven-Eleven. I leaned against a willow tree and watched the skinks and salamanders play on the rocks. Soothing songs of mourning doves echoed through the woods. So this is what stopping to smell the flowers is all about. Before now that had never held any meaning to me. Now I was enveloped in flora and fauna. My eyes couldn't get enough of it.

Everywhere I looked I discovered more of God's incredible workmanship. A family of bunnies played on the other side of the creek. I sat motionless so as not to scare them away. Feeling so totally relaxed I catnapped under the willows soothing branches, that gently fanned me. The soil beneath cushioned me as my sleep deepened.

Then I snapped to when I felt something wet on my cheek. Looking squarely into two big hazel eyes that scared the begebees out of me, I nearly knocked myself out trying to get up and away. Tripping I fell in the creek and laid there looking at my intruder. I wasn't sure what it was at first. Skinny, mangy, and barking at me like an out of tune bugle was a floppy-eared dog of some sort. Fearing he might be mad and bite me, I stayed low and tried to calm him. "Whoa boy, you came up to me remember? I'm going to get up now. Take it easy on me, alright?"

He stopped barking and stepped into the creek with me, looking up at me with his remarkable eyes. "Hey boy, see it's okay." He licked my hand and I petted his matted hair. "Who do you belong to? They sure haven't been taking care of you, now have they? Are you lost? You look hungry. I've got some chicken and dumplings back at the house. If you come with me I'll feed them to you. Come on boy," I said as I slapped my knees.

Like a trooper he followed me back through the woods and across the meadow to the house. "You stay out here on the porch boy. I'll be right back." He was lying right where I'd left him, and jumped up when I came out the door. "Here you go boy. The best chicken and dumplings in the good old USA." He gobbled those up and looked at me for more. "Sorry fella, that's all I've got." I sat down in a rocking chair and the fella came over and laid his head in my lap, tugging at my soft heart with his sad colorful eyes.

"Whew boy, you stink. What say I give you a bath? You won't bite me, now will ya?" I got the hose off the back of the house; along with a bar of Irish Spring soap I had brought with me and proceeded to give that boy a bath. He didn't have the mange like I had thought at first. He was just all matted up and plastered with dirt, prickly burrs, and briars.

After I finished he looked like a different dog. I didn't know what kind of dog. Looked like a hunting dog. His hair was black with a red brindle trim. "Well, you sure were a good boy. I hate to leave you fella, but I've got to get back to the city this afternoon. I'll put you a water bucket down. I don't have any more food for you. Wait a minute." Going over to the car I found a bag of chips and some graham crackers with peanut butter. "Here lets see if you like these." He ate them as fast as I could hand them to him. "Gosh boy, you were starving weren't you?"

I went into the house and got my purse and car keys. I walked back down to the barn to see if Running Horse was about so that I could tell him good-bye. My forest find was trailing my every move. Not finding Running Horse, I stuck a note on the door telling him I'd be back next Friday. As I opened my car door the fella was on my heels. "I've got to go boy. You better be heading home. Stay boy." As I drove away he chased along behind me all the way to the gate. "No boy, go back, go home boy." I hated to do it, but I stomped my feet at him after I closed the gate behind me, and he took several steps backward. Gazing in my rear view mirror I could see him still sitting there starring at my departure. His floppy ears surrounded his sad and distinct hazel eyes.

CHAPTER 8

▼

Getting all my business transactions and loose ends organized, and assigned to top performing associates, that I held in high-esteem, kept me scrambling the next week. By Thursday I had pretty much finished the process of transferring accounts. Working eighteen-hour days, skipping meals, and spending nights on the couch in my office put me ahead of schedule in my departure preparations. Being somewhat of a perfectionist, I knew my files would support and describe my previous and future approaches in minute detail. Wanting this to be a smooth transition, I'd leave no stone unturned or door unopened for my replacements. That evening at eight I ran into Mr. Farrington, I mean Roger, on my way out of the building.

"Alexandra, gracious young lady you've been putting in some long hours. I should have expected that from you. Your stats, reports, profiles, accounts, and recommendations have been placed on my desk at a continuous pace all week. Looks like you're nearing completion."

"Yes sir, I just finished the finale. Should be on your desk by tomorrow morning."

"Very well handled. You've always done the work of three people. Would you care to join me for dinner?"

"Thanks Roger, but I'm showing my house at nine tonight, so I need to get there pretty quickly. You know light some candles, turn on some classical music, stick some cookies in the oven, and pray they like it enough to buy it."

"You're moving along rapidly with this adventure of yours. Good luck with the house. See you in the morning."

I could feel my momentum jading, so as I entered the house I grabbed a Snicker's bar to give me a sugar rush, and propelled forward to ready the house for showing. Running through the house like a woman on a mission; I finished my task just as the doorbell rang. Catching my breath with a deep sigh, I straightened my wearisome body.

"Hello, please come in and make yourself at home. BeBe knows her way around, so I'll be in the family room if you should need me." Hearing some aaahs in the back of the house as they toured my home, I took those as a good sign. With that peace of mind I was finally able to kick my shoes off, and lean back to relax on the sofa. It was after ten-thirty when they left. BeBe called me about ten minutes later.

"Start packing Al. They loved the house. It has everything on their list and then some."

"Are you writing a contract?" I asked her.

"They want to sleep on it. They'll get back to me in the morning. But I'm telling you girl, I know that look, and we've got a buyer here."

"What kind of price do you think they'll come back with?"

"They'll probably start at about ten thousand less than you are asking, but we can negotiate and cinch the deal by compromising to split the difference. That would give you a hefty profit."

"Hey good buddy that sounds too good to be for real. Great job."

"I'll call you as soon as I hear from them tomorrow."

"Alright then, I'm going to get some sleep. I'm sure you need to do the same. Good-night, and thanks for getting some qualified buyers out here so fast."

By ten o'clock the next morning we had closed the deal exactly the way BeBe had predicted. Damn she's good. So needless to say I was back on cloud nine again, with that obstacle removed from my life. They wanted to finalize as soon as possible. The wheels were spinning some kind of fast, and I liked it that way. Never had been one to drag my feet once I'd settled in on something.

At quarter of noon, Charlotte let me know that I was needed in the conference room for an impromptu meeting.

"Did they say what it was about Charlotte?"

"No ma'am, just they needed you."

"Well, I'm off to check it out."

When I opened the conference room door people ignited in applause and revelry, balloons covered the ceiling and walls, a huge cake, shaped like a red barn, adorned the conference table, along with a big spread of catered food, and a brightly wrapped king-size present suspended above the table. Champagne bottles popped from every corner of the spacious room, maxed out with well-wishers, all yelling their congratulations at once. I had stepped into a surprise party meant just for me.

I'd never been given a surprise party by anyone, and the act touched me deeply, impelling tears of gratitude from my eyes. Both Mr. Farrington and Mr. Weinstein said a few affectionate and generous words. Then a good-natured roast by my colleagues pelted away at me, with grand humor and sidesplitting laughter. It was the best time I'd ever had inside these office walls. Gone was the rivalry that had kept distance between us.

Wade brought everyone's attention to the gift drifting above, while he escorted me to the center of the table. Reaching upward he unveiled the gift. It momentarily took me off-guard and more tears, earnest tears, eluded in appreciation for their meaningful presentation. A sign about two feet by six feet, which resembled an old log, was engraved with the words, NOTTINGHAM FOREST, in deep green letters. Underneath those words in much smaller letters read, Proprietor A. F. Nottingham. A cluster of detailed carved evergreen trees framed the words. Its design was almost exactly as I had envisioned for myself. It was truly a prize gift.

Humbly thanking everyone together, and then as individually as I could, the festivities drew to an end. Mr. Farrington concluded the celebration with an added surprise when he announced to everyone, that henceforth, I would only be available by phone or e-mail.

"Ms. Nottingham has worked endlessly, and it's time for her to start following her dreams. Go with God's speed Alexandra."

They all toasted me as I walked out of the double doors. I never turned back. I just went to my office one last time, looked around fleetingly, gathered my briefcase, and then shut that door. Once closed, I placed my hand gently on the thick wooden door and said a silent thank you.

As I was driving away I looked up to see Wade watching me from his window on high. I gave him thumbs up, and left that familiar place with a heavy heart, not from regret, but from respect. Without that place I wouldn't be in any position to be making this move. It was a part of me. It was where I grew up, so to speak. I'd only be taking the best memories with me as I went looking for my true self. The person I wanted to be and knew lived somewhere tucked neatly inside of me.

It was still mid-afternoon so I drove over the Hummer dealership in Cary, which was owned and operated by a friend and former client of mine. I'm one of those car buyers that every sales associate disdains. I only want to deal with the top person, and in my case my friend, Richard. He owned the dealership and spent a lot of time in an office he kept there; to oversee his diversified business deals. Driving around the lot for only less than a minute, I saw something I wasn't expecting. It was a sport utility truck.

"Must be new," I whispered to myself. Parking, I got out to inspect with keen interest. The body's color hit me just right, metallic pewter, with jet-black leather interior. The exterior had a chrome package, which accentuated the coloring. For me accessories are necessities, and best I could note it had everything I could quite possibly need. There was even a mountain bike included. Before I could get back into my car to head up to the showroom to see if Richard was available, a young lady greeted me rattling off Hummer savvy like she'd majored in the technology. Thanking her for the information, I told her I was there to see Richard.

"Which Richard ma'am?"

"The owner please Teresa," reading her nametag.

"If you'll drive over to the showroom I'll tell him you're here. Whom shall I tell him is visiting?"

"Oh yes, Alex Nottingham, and thank you."

I spend about hour and a half with Richard, and he took me for a test drive. He had a special area for me to test the responsiveness of the H2's maneuverability. He'd also sold me my Porsche, almost a year ago. Telling him of my plans and my need of a more rugged vehicle, he jotted some figures down, called the new car prep manager, and out the door I went with the keys to my new 2005 Hummer SUT. Along with those keys was a check for the difference in price, which were more bucks in my pocket than I had anticipated. Car dealers get a bad wrap sometimes, but my friend Richard always treated me fair and square. I had always recommended his dealership to all my clients, which I'm sure was a primary reason he would cut me a mini-deal. Yep, the old saying one hand feeds another is alive and well. Thank goodness!

I liked sitting up high for a change, after riding low for the last several years in whatever sports car I was into at the time. This was a luxury, but a practical luxury. I was making some small steps in the right direction, but I couldn't change my complete lifestyle in only a couple of weeks. My exorbitant materialistic wants would end here I swore to myself, as I headed to the house to pick up some food and clothes. I packed enough for a couple of weeks to last until the movers delivered all my belongings, which BeBe had promised to orchestrate for me.

Before getting into Aliceston, I decided to stop in Asheville, and fill up a couple of the coolers I had brought with me with more food and ice. I picked up lotsa fruits, sodas, milk, canned goods, and snack foods. And just in case that old dog came back around, I bought some Kibbles'n Bits and dog shampoo. After leaving the grocery store I pulled across the street to get some gas. I only had a half tank left and wanted to top it off. Thirty-two dollars later I got back on course.

The sun was getting low now, and the sky was streaked in orange and pink clouds forecasting a clear day tomorrow. By the time I got into Aliceston, what there was to the main drag was closed and deserted. It wasn't even nine o'clock yet as I looked at my watch. Gracious, these folks go to bed with the chickens.

The gate to the drive leading to the house was unlocked and open for me. I'm sure Running Horse had seen to that. My truck took the road brilliantly. My open Pepsi cup never once splashed about, as I took the hilly twists and turns. I could see the front porch light on as I rounded the evergreens. Never seeing the farm from this spot at night, I drove slowly. A light glowed over each barn, another out behind the house, and one from the front porch. An utterly charming sight for my frazzled city eyes. That crazy warm tranquil rush came over me again, and gave me a second wind as I parked beneath the willow.

A giddy delight took over my emotions. "Home, home on the range, where the deer and the antelope play. Where seldom is heard a discouraging word, and the skies are not cloudy all day," I sang like a frog with a bad cold, as I unpacked the truck.

Once finished with the unpacking I opened a bottle of wine to celebrate, and settle back while toasting myself. I sat down and stretched out on the couch and began reading a new novel, I had picked up at the grocery store. Tired from the past week's hectic schedule, today's festivities, the purchase of a new car, and the drive to my new home, I drifted off to sleep in no time.

Awakened by something strange moving loudly around outside, I turned off the coffee table lamp, and walked somewhat fearfully over to one of the front windows. I realized at that moment I had left my 38 revolver out in the truck. At first as I looked out, all I could see were the shadows cast by the nearly full moon. Then I saw Running Horse standing outside the barn's light, looking towards the house. That made me feel a little better, knowing I wasn't alone, but I was still worried because he had heard it too. He began walking up the path to the house. His presence gave me the courage to open the door and step out on the porch. He waved me back inside no sooner than I got both feet out the door. Without any delay, I quickly scooted back inside and watched from the windows.

I darted back and forth. Then I heard a loud scream, like a woman in agony. "What the crap was that?" I whispered. A long silence prevailed…and then a knock on the door. From the window I saw Running Horse standing there with a bloody knife in his hand. "Gees Louise, what in the world?" Gradually I opened the door, my eyes as big as saucers looking at the knife, as he asked if I was all right. "Running Horse what happened out there?"

"Mountain lion prowling around, looking for food. It killed a deer in the clover on the side of the house. That's what made most of the racket before I killed it. Can't have it coming this close to your house hunting for food."

Alarmed, I responded, "A mountain lion! I was just out there about an hour ago. Would it have attacked me? It didn't hurt you did it?"

"No, I'm fine. You don't need to worry Alex. I hated to kill it, but he left me no choice. I'll go and take care of things. Go on back to bed."

"Don't you want me to help you?"

"This is my job, anyway I need to check to make sure he was traveling alone. Please go back to bed, and try not to worry. I'll tell you about everything tomorrow."

"I know thanks sounds so trivial, after what you just did for me, but that's all I can think of to say right now. Gosh, I'm sure glad you were here. Good-night Running Horse."

CHAPTER 9

▼

Running Horse and I caught up in the field along with the horses the next morning. He'd been for an early morning ride, and was busy brushing down the friendly pinto that I'd met the week before. Clutching a bag of apples, I handed her the first one. "Good morning. Didn't know these were riding horses. That's a terrific saddle hanging on the fence."

"Morning Alex. Yep, made that myself several years ago."

"Gees, you can do it all. I don't believe I've ever met anyone so outdoorsy and talented."

His bold eyes blazed me an appreciative smile.

Stroking the pinto's muzzle, while feeding her the yellow skinned apple, I asked, "What's her name?"

"Misty Morning."

"That's lovely, Misty Morning," calling out to her as she nuzzled the side of my face.

"She likes you. She's the shy one, doesn't usually cotton up to strangers. I think she's made a connection with your soul Alex."

"Now what does that mean?"

"She feels your goodness and wants to get to know you."

"Thanks. Don't know if I understand that any better, but I'll leave it alone for now. About last night, I didn't know there were mountain lions around these parts. I thought they were extinct."

"Many say so, but I've heard their cries over the years. First one I've seen on this side of the mountain since I was a young buck."

"What did you do with him?"

"I called the Fish and Wildlife Services last night on their hotline. An officer came by at first light to pick up the carcass. They're protected in these parts, but after I explained the encounter, he agreed that no good comes from a cat encroaching so near home dwellers."

"Betcha he would have attacked me if he'd been out there a little earlier. Was he alone?"

"They're solitary by nature. I only found one set of tracks. He could have been one of two that escaped from a couple's ranch about thirty miles from here, a few months back."

"You mean there could be another one lurking this mountain? That gives me the willies."

"Don't worry, I'll keep my eyes open for any signs." Looking at Misty Morning with her head nested on my shoulder he said "Looks like animals are drawn to you."

"Would you mind if I rode her sometime? Would she let me?"

"Do you ride?"

"Well, only a couple of times, but I'd really like to learn more about it."

"What do you say Misty, would you take Ms. Alex for a ride?"

"Wheeee," Misty neighed.

"Well there's your answer. She said you bet."

We heard barking coming from the front porch. Turning we both saw that skinny black brindle dog lopping towards us.

"You do have your way with animals. He's been coming around every day to that water bucket you put out back. You must have made friends with him last weekend when you were here."

"Yeah, I met him out in the woods on a hike. He scared the begee's outta me at first. Hey boy, come on." He leapt up on me like I was his long lost pal, and nearly knocked me over. "I bet you're hungry, aren't you fella? I'm going up to the house and feed him. Let's go up to the café for lunch. My treat, okay Running Horse? Say noon?"

"You must have tried Mama Willa's chicken and dumplings. Sure, I'll meet you up at the house at noon."

I strolled up to the house with my new companion in cadence with my every step. "You've gone and gotten dirty again so you'll just have to wait out here on the porch." Returning with an old beat up wash pan full of Kibbles'n Bits he barely gave me time to sit it down, before he started gulping it in ladles. "Slow down boy. I'm not going to take it away from you. When you finish I'm going to give you another bath."

I couldn't get over how frisky he was with me. He was starved for more than food. "Well fella, you want a home?" He perked his ears and turned his soulful eyes to mine like he understood me. "Guess we need to come up with a name for you. Let's see, you came out of the woods. This is Nottingham Forest. How about Robin Hood? Do you like Robin Hood?" He began a dance of circling around me and barking in his bugle tones. "Then Robin Hood it will be. Come on Robin Hood, let's get your bath over with, and I'll show you around inside the house."

At noon when I went outside two horses were saddled and stood passive beneath the willow's shade. Running Horse was mounted on the black stallion, while Misty Morning awaited me.

"Ready for that ride Alex?"

"Wow, this is great," I said as I climbed onto Misty Morning's back. Off we went with Robin Hood at our side.

"Got yourself a dog I see. Looks like he's a plott hound. What do you plan on calling him?"

"He likes the name Robin Hood, don't you boy? Plott hound, never heard of that kind of dog."

"Just so happens to be the North Carolina state dog."

"Goodness, really?"

"Came from Germany originally. Great hunters. He'll fill out into a muscular dog. Known for their strength, loyalty, and courage. He'd fight a mountain lion for you Alex, if he thought you were in danger of it."

"For real? Would you do that for me Robin Hood? What do you think of his terrific hazel eyes, Running Horse?"

"They are a sign of his pure heart and bold spirit."

We rode quietly as I tried to comprehend the depth of words that he spoke, while I gazed proudly at Robin Hood with this newfound insight. Misty Morning gave me a leisurely ride and played teasingly with Robin's tale, when he got too close.

Running Horse pointed out the natural herbs that grew along side the road, some of which I had thought were only wildflowers or weeds. He'd stop every so often and have me listen to the sounds of the forest, with ears I'd never used so insightfully. He brought me in tune to the melody that surrounded us. His painted words made me think of what Thoreau wrote, *He hears a different drummer.*

"Rain coming tomorrow," he said.

"How do you know that?"

"See the leaves on the trees? See how we can see their undersides? That means rain's approaching."

I took note of how the leaves showed their detailed venation, and pondered the remarkable observations this veritable wise man was sharing with me. "How do you know so much?" I inquired of him.

"It's the teachings of many generations, carried down by our Mothers and Fathers. Like the trees that are nourished by their own fallen leaves and branches, our ancient ones have nourished us. Our roots have reached deeply into the soils of life, and have made us strong through the wisdom granted us from our Creator. What I have learned has been threaded throughout the beginning of time."

I shook my head, not in disbelief, but in affirmation to his words as I understood them. Drinking in his eloquence as we continued, until we saw the café up ahead of us. "Sure smells good from here."

My wise friend nodded in agreement. "Let's tie our horses up in the back Alex."

As we were about to enter, I leaned down and told Robin Hood to be a good boy and stay out here on the porch. He walked obediently to the side of the door and sat down. "I'll bring you something when I come back boy."

Mama Willa greeted us like kinfolk as we closed the green wooden door behind us.

"Git on in here. Gotta table waiting on ya." She hugged Running Horse and then me. "Well Missy, how do you like my son here? He's a good man. Told me about that mountain lion prowlin about last night."

"Did you say your son? Running Horse you never told me that."

"Didn't see the need to. Figured it would all come out in its own time."

"Yep, that's just the way he is Alexandra. What can I get for ya today? Got some fresh hot chicken I just fried up in the back. Of course, I've got more chicken and dumplings freshly stewed too."

"Mama Willa makes mouth watering fried chicken Alex. You ought to try it."

I knew'd you'd be havin that Thomas. And let's see, you'll have smothered fried taters and corn on the cob, with a side of chicken and dumplings to go along with it."

"You got it Mama."

"You called him Thomas."

"That be the name we gave him honey-child. Running Horse, well, I'll let him tell you that story. Now what would you be a wanting?"

"I'll have the same Mama Willa. Thank you."

"Sweet tea with that for the both of you?"

Before we could answer her she was off to greet the next bell ringer coming in through the front door. I could see Robin Hood still waiting patiently as I'd left him, through the picture window next to our table. "Look at him, he's so smart, isn't he? Wonder what happened to his owner?"

"Probably abandoned him from the city. Dogs like him need plenty of space and someone that will dote on them. You so happen to fit all his needs."

"He's really growing on me. You say he waited around for me to return all last week?"

"Yep, he's a dog that knows who he really belongs with. Shows good qualities and alertness to his nature."

The small café was getting packed. It seemed like every one of the local patrons wanted to speak with Running Horse about the mountain lion, which ventured up to the house last night. Mama Willa shoed them all away when she brought out the steaming chicken piled high on our platters. "Git away now, and let my son and his boss eat in peace. Go on now git, plenty time for talking after they's done. Y'all enjoy now, and don't forget about dessert. Let me know when you're ready."

"Better let that chicken cool down a bit before you go on the attack. It'll scorch your mouth something awful if you don't. That's why I get the chicken and dumplings on the side to tide me over till it's safe to eat," he said, while I eyeballed him with all the questions building up in my mind.

"When are you going to tell me?"

"Tell you what Alex?"

"You know what Thomas."

"Oh yeah. Okay then, Thomas is the name my Papa and Mama gave me. Thomas Jonathan Sykes."

"Nice name."

"Thanks." He took a big swig of tea before beginning. "The story goes something like this. When I was a barefoot little buck of five, Mama Willa took my sis and me to a picnic over to her oldest brother's house. His farm adjoined our property down in the valley. Family and friends came to this annual celebration, and had done so for the last fifty plus years. Papa would be joining us later in the day, after he helped Flossie birth her calf. These get togethers were like a family reunion, a time to catch up with each other, share stories, learn traditions, eat of God's bounty, and make music and dance. It was at these gatherings that I learned to play the flute and drums. I'll tell you more about that some other day. My sister was nine at the time and a very adventuresome soul. Mama had told her to stay away from the horses. But sis had a passion for horses, and whenever she took a notion to gallop away on one not even the sting of a hickory switch could stop her. I was playing with some boys down by the corral. That's when I saw sis climb up the fence and stride atop old Dynamite. Now as the name predicts he was a rip-roaring terror, that only my Uncle Freeman could control and ride."

"What was your sister's name?"

"We called her Little Joy, for a sundry of reasons. But she was anything but a joy that day, I tell you. She mounted that old horse and no sooner than she'd grabbed his cherry mane, he took off like a bat outta you know where. None of the adults could see what was going on. The others kids started yelling and screaming. Dynamite was bucking and galloping madly. I took off running through the meadow as fast as my little feet would carry me, leaping over rocks and streams like a white-tailed deer. I caught up with that mad horse, and grabbed his bushy mane with all the force I could gather. My feet left the ground, but I mulishly kicked him in his front quarters, while continuing to pull violently on his mane. My sister's eyes pleaded my help. Bringing my mouth to his ear, I bite down so powerfully hard that old horse came to an abrupt stop, while we hung on for dear life. He stood there in a stupor, while my sis and I dropped to the ground. Then several of our uncles surrounded us on their horses, while Uncle Freeman ran to hug and comfort us. Then looking at me he said, "From this day forth Thomas, you will be known as Running Horse. You have the swiftness and courage of a mighty stallion. This life-defining event has proclaimed your name of honor."

"At the campfire that night they had a ceremony. Uncle Freeman lifted me up and said, "You flew like the wind today to your purpose in life. Like a horse you have physical and spiritual powers. You took your sister's burden upon yourself. You followed your sacred path. Spirit God has chosen you to be Running Horse. It is a name that must be spoken with respect and caution." He called my earned name to the east, the south, the west, and the north. Then again to the sky and to the earth."

My wise friend looked out through the window up to the clouds and said, "The rest of the pow-wow was filled with our prayers carried on smoke to the heavens, followed by chanting and dancing to the drumbeats." Then turning back to meet my eyes he concluded, "That's about it in a nutshell Alex. Oh, except for one more thing. Old Dynamite settled down after that. I think it was the bite on the ear that did it." He said, giving me a wink and a loud animated chomp of his teeth.

Laughing at his comical conclusion I added, "That's an amazing story. That would make an excellent children's book. I'd like to write your story one day, if you'd allow me Running Horse. That's why I wanted to move to this mountain. Well, at least one of the main reasons."

"You would honor me greatly to do this thing. You were sent here to help me with my quest too Alex. Now let's attack this platter of food Mama Willa brought us," and with that said, he picked up a plump golden-fried chicken breast and plowed his pearly whites into it.

Perplexed by his statement about me helping him with his quest, I followed his lead and began my chicken feast.

In harmony we hummed, "Ummmm!"

CHAPTER 10

▼

When we got to the top of the drive to the house, I saw BeBe's yellow hummer parked next to my new SUT. "Come on Running Horse it's my best friend BeBe. I want her to meet you. Let's gallop in and impress her. She'll get a kick out of that."

Well, he leaned over and swatted Misty Morning's rump, and off we flew in full gallop, with me hanging on for dear life. I'd never galloped on a horse before, and my backside wasn't cooperating with the saddle the way it should have. We jerked to a halt at the foot of the front porch with both horses snorting in the dust.

"Hells bells, would you look at you? You look like a real cowgirl Al. Thought I'd drive over and surprise you."

"Hey good buddy. Like you to meet Running Horse." They shook hands. "He's teaching me all kinds of stuff," I said, easing down from the saddle and rubbing my bottom, which quite frankly smarted.

"Nice meeting you BeBe. I need to get these horses taken care of, so if you ladies will excuse me I'll be seeing to them."

"He seems real nice Al. Where did y'all ride off to?"

"We rode over to the Apple Dumpling Café for lunch. His Mama owns the place. Mama Willa is her name, and she's a real pistol. You'd love her cooking. It's all country style and served up fresh," I said licking my lips.

"Will it be open tomorrow?"

"Nope, closed on the Lord's day. But next time you come we'll go over and eat, okay? Hey, they've got a pig-picking coming up in two weeks. Why don't you come back over then?"

"What in the world is a pig-picking? You're going all country on me, aren't you?"

"Sure am honey-child, and excuse me, but I think I hear a twang in your voice too," I said laughingly. "Must be the air. It's when they roast a pig outside for hours over a wood fire until it gets so tender it falls off the bone. You just go up and pick it apart and cover it with Mama Willa's famous BBQ sauce, or so I'm told. See I'm learning this way of life around here, and I love it...Oh Be's! Running Horse killed a mountain lion right over there, just last night."

"Come on now Al, don't be trying to fooger-boo me," BeBe said giving me that side-ways grin of hers with questioning eyes.

"No shit Sherlock. I'm telling you the truth. And he killed it with a hunting knife. It was screaming like a woman right outside my window. I tell you Be's when I saw him standing on my front porch with a bloody knife in his hand afterwards, I was scared to death. It was like something out of a Stephen King movie, I'm telling you. And then when I found out what he had done, I was nearly speechless. I had just been out there an hour before. It could have attacked me."

"You really weren't kidding, were you? That's incredible. Gosh, you'd better be careful around here. I didn't know you had mountain lions."

"Me neither. Whatcha think of my new truck?" I asked changing the subject.

"I was looking it over before you galloped in. You know I love it. I'd heard these new SUTs were coming out, but yours is the first I've seen up close. Honey of a truck."

"Wonder where Robin Hood got to? Robin Hood, here boy." Bounding towards us at ninety miles an hour, ears flopping and tongue dangling, he heeded my call with gusto. He stopped within inches of me, looking up at my buddy and sniffing her leg; as I squatted down to pet him. "Here fella meet BeBe. She's part of the family."

"Where'd you get that?" Be's said, with her nose all squished up and eyes crinkled in demur.

"He's not a that, he's my dog, Robin Hood. Found him in the woods when I went exploring."

"Sorry Al, but he looks like an old hound dog to me."

"You're somewhat right. He's a plott hound, and just so happens to be the North Carolina state dog, so show some respect. Running Horse said plott hounds are courageous and loyal."

"What about those eyes Al. Weird aren't they?"

"Remembering what Running Horse had said, I repeated it to her, "Those wonderful eyes are a sign of his pure heart and bold spirit. He's unique, aren't you boy?"

I helped BeBe bring in her clothes along with the things she had brought to decorate her room upstairs. She'd also brought the sign with her that the office had given me at my farewell party. I knew she had given them the idea for my gift. Wade had probably called her for help in picking out something perfect for me, and as always she came through with a winner. After we unloaded everything we grabbed an ice-cold longneck Bud, and sat out on the porch to shoot the breeze, while Robin Hood napped at my feet.

"Joey copped a plea for assault Friday to avoid trail. Did Tim get a hold of you?"

"No, I was probably at the car dealership. I had my cell phone turned off for a while. What happened?"

"Well, the judge sentenced him to two years."

"Whew, two years huh, I bet he didn't like that."

"Serves him right though, don't you think? I mean he could have killed you for heaven sakes."

"I guess so. Well, I'm glad the whole mess is over with. You know I don't mean to sound hard-hearted, but I don't think I ever really loved Abby. Don't get me wrong, I truly cared, but loving completely and deeply, I don't think so. Maybe I don't even know what that is. Am I making any sense to you?"

"I'm following you. There were always some questions in my mind about you two."

"What do you mean?"

"She needed you, but you were so independent. I didn't see you needing her. Don't get me wrong, you were good to her, but you were somewhat removed or distant at times."

"Are you looking for a nice way to say I'm egotistical?"

"Now that's your word, not mine."

"Yeah, I hear a but in there somewhere. Spit it out my friend."

"Alex, you were so preoccupied at times is what I'm trying to say. I don't think the two of you were meant to be."

"Well, that's now perfectly obvious in hindsight. Enough of that subject. I'm enjoying this country life. We need to build you a cabin on the property. Who knows you might get lucky and bring a friend one day."

"I like that idea."

"Come on let's go look for a spot to build it."

"I'm right behind you Al."

As we walked through the meadow abounded with the pastel hues of wild-flowers, the grazing horses joined our promenade to escort us to the edge of the clearing, as they had done on my last hike. Warrior, the black stallion, neighed an adieu as we ventured on a beckoning path into the woods. Robin Hood ran ahead to blaze our trail. That darn silly dog lifted his leg and tried to mark his scent on every other tree out there. We laughed at his repeated attempts.

I began showing off what I'd learned from Running Horse on our horse ride to the café, earlier that day. Pointing out and naming the herbs, flowers and trees as we went deeper into the belly of the forest. "Now I know you know this is a cedar tree, but let me tell you the story of the cedar tree. Seeing I had her full attention, I proceeded in detail just as I'd been told. She listened as I had with interest.

"So there you have it, the spirits of the Cherokee ancestors live in the cedar trees. Tradition has it that the wood of these trees holds powerful protective spirits. Running Horse carries a piece of cedar wood in his medicine bag that he wears around his neck. He said that the front and back doors to my house are made of cedar wood, to keep evil spirits away."

"Maybe that's what protected you from that mountain lion last night," BeBe threw in.

"Could be. All this lore captivates me. There's so much to learn. Looks like a clearing over to the east; let's head that way. Come on Robin Hood, this way fella." Within another ten minutes we reached a beautiful dandelion valley, with the color of the sun drenching its floors. Off in the distance deer were grazing unaware of our approach, that was until Robin Hood spotted them. Like a check-ered flag had been lowered at the races, he took off bellowing across the field in pursuit. We watched as the deer fled, high-stepping it into the woods' covering. Feeling proud of his self for chasing them away, my furry friend eyed me for approval.

"You see that house over there?" I said to Be's, while pointing down the hol-low past some mountain pines."

"Yeah, let's go and check it out."

"This valley is as far as my property goes in this direction, but hey, they must be my neighbors. Guess we should go and introduce ourselves."

When we got closer we saw that what we thought was a house was only an old weathered barn. Inside it smelled like tobacco. Be's said, "From the smell of it, I'd say this is an old tobacco barn."

"Clever deduction, however do you do it?" I said mocking her. As we exited out the other side we saw an elaborate three-story log cabin up the hill. "Think we should go up?"

"We've come this far, no sense in turning back now. I don't think they'll shoot at us or anything, do you Al?"

"I've only moved to the country; I haven't gone back in time. For Christ sakes Be's, this isn't Deliverance."

"Quit giving me a hard time, will you Al?" Her face sullen from my unwarranted criticism.

"Okay, sorry for being such a shrew."

As we got closer the front door opened, and out stepped Mama Willa with a bright red bandana covering her head, like something out of 'Gone With The Wind.'

"Hey Alexandra. I wondered how long before you'd make it over the hill to visit me. Who's your friend?"

"Be's, it's Mama Willa I was telling you about. Owns the café. Running Horse's mom. Mama Willa I didn't know you were my neighbor. This is my best bud, BeBe, from Chapel Hill, where I used to live."

"Well hi there BeBe from Chapel Hill. Welcome to the mountain. Come on up here and let me git a good look at you." We ambled up the porch steps while Mama Willa checked BeBe out. "Umm, you look like a mighty friendly young lady. Now both of you sit here on the porch, while I git yous some sweet tea. You must be thirsty from your walk over here." She petted Robin Hood's head on her way into her house.

When she stepped inside BeBe said, "Now that's country."

Returning with a tray carrying three sweet teas and a bowl of water for Robin Hood, she sat down with us on her front porch that spread the length of her house. It was a huge log cabin, at least twice the size of my home.

"I thought I heard some commotion going on down in the valley. Must have been your little fella there chasing after something."

"Yes ma'am, he saw some deer."

"Plenty deer around here. All kinds of critters scurrying about this mountain. Drink up girls. You know my granddaughter's inside with Thomas. Let me go and git her and bring her out to meet y'all. She just got here about an hour ago. She's sitting at the dining room table with her Paw."

When she left I elbowed my buddy, "Isn't she a real hoot, Be's? Best darn cook I'm telling you. Can't wait for you to taste those chicken and dumplings."

"Who's Thomas?"

"Oh that's Running Horse's real name."

"Did you know he had a daughter?"

"Heck no, this is a surprise to me. I think he likes to surprise me."

The screen door opened, and my eyes lit up like high beams on a dark night. Walking out behind Mama Willa, and standing about five foot six, with hair the color of a raven's, was the most mysterious eyed woman my eyes had ever beheld. My eyes were drawn to hers like a magnet. Those same eyes of Running Horse and Mama Willa, only more intoxicating to my whole being. The fluid of them seemed to immediately immerse like an arrow to the core of my heart. The strangeness of it caught me off guard in its depth. She was speaking to me, but I couldn't hear because I was still lost in those eyes. Then seeing her hand out-stretched in front of me, I was able to compose myself.

My ears re-opened and I shook her offered hand, and sat back down still cloudy from the experience. Every since I had arrived, the power of the eyes of my new found friends around me, including Robin Hood's, seemed to penetrate to levels I'd never explored or even known lay within me. It was almost like a mystical happening. Some things are just too hard to explain. BeBe elbowed me and gave me an inquisitive stare. She leaned over and whispered in my ear.

"What's wrong with you Alex?"

I just looked at her and shook my head awkwardly, shrugging my shoulders as I tried desperately to refocus and act normal. Taking a big swallow of tea I noticed everyone was watching me. Even my dog sat at my feet giving me a fragile whimper. Clearing my throat I tried to speak, but the words came out muffled. So I repeated myself. "Please excuse me. My tea went down the wrong way." I had invented the excuse as a cover-up for my unusual behavior. "I'm sorry but I didn't catch your name," I asked her, while looking back into her magnetic eyes and restraining from their pull on me.

"I'm sorry, sometimes I speak so fast that people don't understand me. Bad habit of my mind that I'm trying to break. Most everyone around these parts calls me Willow."

"She's named partially after me, I be proud to declare," Mama Willa chimed in.

"Oh, but it's a lovely name. Isn't it BeBe? Don't think I've ever heard of someone with that name before. Does it have a special meaning? I mean like your Fathers?"

Her voice was as sweet and soft as a gentle rain when she spoke. "My full name is Willow Rose Sykes. Willow is from my Grandma Willa. Her real name is Willow, like mine. It means freedom tree. Rose was my Mother's first name."

Now Willow had a natural captivating radiance about her, which intensified her crystalline beauty. With skin like bronze velvet, wonderful round coffee eyes, full deep pink lips, and long straight ebony hair, her symmetrical body made a dynamic presence. I felt drawn to her like a bee to honey.

I think Running Horse sensed something. He had a strange smile on his face as he sat there staring at me. He nodded his head at me when he caught my attention. "My daughter is a professional like you Alex, but she's decided to come back to these mountains. She's moving back in two weeks. That's why we're having the pig picking. It's a welcome home party for Willow. She's been in Greensboro for the last ten years, lawyering at a big company. I've been mighty proud of her, but I've wanted her back home since the day she left this mountain."

"A lawyer, that's great. Which firm do you work for?" My voice still wasn't up to its normal tone.

"Oh, you've probably never heard of it. Smithfield, Connors and Sykes."

"You don't mean as in Gordon Smithfield, do you?"

"Yes, do you know him?"

"He's been a client of mine, or was a client of mine for five years. But that was in Raleigh."

"We have a satellite office in Raleigh. Well, isn't it a small world after all?" Willow added.

"I'll say it is. And you're a partner in that firm. Gosh, you must be one tough cookie in the courtroom."

"I've been known to rattle some cages and raise the roof a few times."

"Wow, I'm impressed. How about that BeBe?"

BeBe joined in on the conversation. "Didn't I read a while back where you represented Fred McMillan, in that multi-million dollar extortion case? With all the evidence the state had against him, I don't know how you managed to get him found not guilty."

"Simple, he was framed. I knew that from the moment I took his case. Our detectives did a superb job gathering the proof we needed to get him freed."

I commented on the thought that had just entered my mind. "Willow the freedom tree. Now I understand why your name is so fitting."

She studied my eyes endearingly, and I felt my temperature soar. My stomach did a flip-flop like I was on an exciting ride at Disney. The warmness my heart received at that instant was like a flame of fire. An exotic ardor that made my body quiver inside.

"How sweet of you to make that comparison Alex. I'd never looked at it from that angle. Clever deduction. I think I remember Gordon talking about an Alex a few times at the office. Are you his financial wizard, as he's so often called you?"

"Well, I was, but I resigned recently to move here. I want to try my hand at writing. This place seemed like the ideal setting, so here I am."

Mama Willa stood up, straightened her long gingham dress, and cooled my fervor by proclaiming," And we're darn proud to have you here with us Alexandra, aren't we Thomas?"

"Yes ma'am, she's quite the lady." Then looking over at his daughter he said, "I'm sure you two are going to be good friends. Hey Alex, why don't you and BeBe join us for supper this evening? It'll give you and Willow more time to get acquainted. We're going to fry up some trout I caught this morning."

I gave BeBe a questioning look, and she nodded an affirmative. "Sure we'd love too, if you're sure it'd be no trouble. Can we bring something?"

"Just your charming selves," said Willow.

"What time should we come back over?"

Mama Willa said, "We'll be ready to eat about six."

Glancing at my watch, I noticed it was pushing four o'clock. "Well Be's, we'd best be heading back if we're going to get cleaned up for dinner, I mean supper."

Once we had gotten to the dandelion valley on our hike back home, BeBe started laughing. "What in the world are you laughing at?" I asked her.

"You Al, you were the funniest I've ever seen you in all the years since we've known each other."

"Just what do you mean by that?"

"You were almost drooling back there. You should have seen yourself."

"Gosh Be's, was it that noticeable?"

"Heck yeah, man. The two of you were like there was no one else around, the way you looked at each other. Everybody noticed it."

"Oh, golly gees Be's. What must Running Horse and his Mom think of me? I don't know what was happening, but whatever it was, I couldn't help myself. I got totally lost in her."

"No kidding. I think it was mutual from what I could see my friend. Her face was glowing just like yours. It was like a mini-movie we were watching. Mama Willa and Running Horse just smiled at each other like they approved. It was so strange to be watching."

"Isn't she something though? I mean she's gorgeous, isn't she?"

"She is a beautiful woman Al. There's no denying that."

"I saw what looked like an engagement ring on her finger. She's probably happily engaged to some rich attorney in Greensboro. You know all the good ones out there are straight." We both chuckled at that.

"The way she was looking at you Al didn't have the qualities I'd call straight. Y'all two were off in your own little world for a few minutes there. I could tell the moment you laid eyes on her, you were a goner."

"How's that."

"Well, you get this corny little grin on your face, and your eyes start bugging out."

"Say it isn't so Be's, that's awful. I looked absolutely stupid, didn't I? She must think I'm off my rocker."

"I think she liked it Al. She couldn't take her eyes off of you."

A bright smile filled my face, as I pondered her words over and over in my mind. So Willow had shown an interest in me too.

We walked along without further comment for the next several minutes, soaking in the beauty of the forest surrounding us. Butterflies waltzed merrily together on the path in front of us. This enchanted land so drenched in history with ancient traditions inspired meditation. Even the soil beneath our feet seemed alive with its earthy essence. The harmonious parade of nature songs played in our ears, and crept silently into our very souls, while we were unaware. We were both basking in the splendor.

"Hey over there. I didn't see that on the way over, did you?"

"What Al? Where?"

Off the path, to the left about fifty yards, was a stream coursing gently over some large round-shouldered rocks, with a verdant growth of fiddleheads growing on its mossy banks. A grove of Frazier fir stretched high in the background. Huge holly bushes nestled in front of them, standing tall as trees. As we neared we found the remains of a crumbled old chimney lying on the ground, and signs of burnt ruins from a long ago house. The stones of the off-grade foundation were still very much in tact. Azalea bushes flowered all about giving more evidence of past dwellers on this piece of land.

"See Be's, someone used to live here. This would be a perfect place to build your cabin. Look at the view."

"Great view. Wonder what happened to the house that used to be here?" BeBe queried.

"It was probably ancient. All this stuff looks older than dirt to me. I'll ask Running Horse this evening. He'll know."

BeBe walked around kicking at the dirt, and squatted down every once in a while to investigate. I saw her holding something in her hand and studying it with interest.

"Find something?" I asked her.

"Look at this. What do you make of it?"

I reached for it. "Let me hold it. Hmm, maybe an old piece of jewelry. It's rusted together. Must have belonged to the lady of the house. It's shaped like a locket of some sort. Let's take it home and try to clean it up."

CHAPTER 11

▼

We climbed into my Hummer shortly before six that evening and drove over to the Sykes' household for supper. We had decided against walking back through the woods, since it would be dark by the time we returned, and after last night's ordeal with the mountain lion I wasn't about to take any chances. Besides, I'd probably get us lost in those woods, since I wasn't all that familiar with them. Not wanting to go for supper empty-handed, I grabbed the two bottles of wine I'd brought from the back seat, and we strolled towards the log cabin porch. Fresh fried fish aromas saturated the evening air and brought comforting expectations to our inhaling nostrils.

The sun still blazed in the western sky, peeking between two mountains and covering the valley below, granting us shadows of shade and hisses of nimble breezes. A brassy glow framed the Sykes' cabin in a whimsical welcoming fashion. A pleasant feeling enveloped me as I climbed the porch steps.

"Are you going to be okay Al? You look flustered again."

"Oh, I guess I'm justa little nervous. You know Willow and all. I'll be okay." Before I could knock on the door Willow appeared and invited us in.

"Welcome back. Perfect timing. Dad almost has the fish done, and I'm just finishing up some hush puppies in the kitchen. Follow me on back." She had on one of the gingham aprons from the Apple Dumpling Café over her clothes, and she looked right at home in the kitchen. There was nothing pretentious about her. Sophisticated but down to earth too. I really liked that. She was comfortable in her own skin, which was something that I was just beginning to learn for myself.

I gave her the bottles of wine and as she took them she placed her hands over mine, while thanking me with direct eye contact. Sensual shivers stirred through me, but this time I maintained my composure, and looked deeply back into her eyes with confidence and admiration. We both were now on the same page. I turned and looked at BeBe with my ear-to-ear smile. She gave me a quick wink of encouragement.

"Please have a seat at the table. I need to run and check on Mama Willa. She's been working too hard here lately. She got winded right after you left earlier. I convinced her to go and lie down for a while. I'll be right back."

"Is there anything we can do to help you?" I asked her.

"No, just make yourselves at home."

As she left the room, Be's punched me softly in the arm and said, "You go girl. See I told you she was flirting with you."

"Gosh, I hope so. She has my stomach turning summersaults. I hope Mama Willa is alright." The back screened door opened, and Running Horse came in with a large pan of golden fried trout still steaming. "Running Horse, Willow said that Mama Willa wasn't feeling well. Is she going to be okay?"

He placed the hot pan onto a folded dishtowel on the large family dining table. "She's been having these episodes for the last few months. I keep trying to get her to slow down and cut back on the hours at the café, but she'll have nothing to do with what I say. Mama's her own person. Stubborn as an old hen and twice as proud."

"Can we do something?"

"She'd never let you. But thanks for offering. I never could talk any sense into her. Willow has a way with her though. Got her to go and lie down a while. Here comes the Indian Queen now."

"Thomas you know better than that Indian Queen stuff."

"Yes Ma'am, come on up to the table."

"I's coming, ain't no cripple. Don't be embarrassing me in front of our company." Then she turned to us with her eyes softened. "How are you girls this fine evening?"

Together we both answered. "Fine."

I continued, "Sorry you're not feeling well Mama Willa."

"Oh girl, I'm doing just fine. Had a little case of the short winds earlier, but that's all gone now. My baby girl here took good care of me. She's got the touch like her Paw," she said patting Willow's hand and beaming with pride at her granddaughter. "Thomas bless this food before it gets cold, and let's eat."

Our scrumptious meal was accompanied by tons of laughter. Mama Willa was a natural born comedian. The way she could put a country twist on almost everything reminded me of Granny, from those old *Beverly Hillbilly's* reruns on television. Willow and Running Horse laughed every bit as hard as BeBe and I did. This family energized me. I felt refreshed.

"That was one heck of a great meal Mama Willa," I said leaning back in retreat.

"Thomas and baby girl fixed it all. I taught them well, don't you think?"

"Without a doubt. My compliments to the cooks."

Mama Willa chased us all from the kitchen, and refused to let any of us help with cleaning the table or washing the dishes."Shoo now, get outta here or I'll git my broom to yas."

We all high stepped it out of there in obedience. Running Horse and BeBe took off together down through the valley, leaving Willow and myself alone on the front porch. We settled into the porch swing, side by side, with a glass of wine in our hands.

"I'd like to make a toast to the cook, if I may."

"You may," she added.

"To a cook I'd be pleased to have in my kitchen any ole time. Thank you for nourishing my body with good food, and my heart with good laughter." She gave me an exuberant smile, and we clanged our glasses high in the air. For several moments our eyes were fixated attentively on one another's, while we sipped our wine.

"Alex, I don't know what's going on here, but from the moment I met you, I've been strongly attracted to you. I knew in my soul that I should come home. I wasn't sure why exactly, but I believe now it has something to do with you being here. There's more to it than that, but you fit in there somewhere, I'm positive."

She completely caught me off guard with her bold statement. She didn't mix words, just came right out and said it. I'd just met her that afternoon. Now I was a straight shooter, but her impulsiveness was in your face, literally, as we were only a foot apart cheek to cheek. I found myself stuttering. "Ex…excuse my voice, I'm a little nervous Willow. You see it was the same for me today when I first laid eyes on you. My insides started trembling, and I know I probably sounded and looked like a darn jackass, but the sight of you struck a chord deep in my heart. I'm better at writing words than I am at speaking them, but I'm going to try, if I can get this frog out of my throat. I have no idea where this is going. All I know is that I want to get to know you and spend some time with you, if you'll allow me that opportunity."

"Then let's toast again," she said, while she continued to examine deep into my eyes, as she proposed the toast. "This time let's toast to the future, and our path along the way."

I was happy that Mama Willa joined us on the porch, so that I could calm down my heart and the feelings rushing through me. I needed to digest our spur of the moment conversation.

"You girls have a lot in common, now don't cha?" I was thrown to left field by her statement, but Willow rescued me with her returned comment.

"Yes we do Grams. Both of us have been out into the big city world to slay a few dragons, and now we've come home for a more peaceful existence. We're ready to listen to our true selves now and heed to the call of Mother Earth."

"Well, it's about darn time, I'd say. But there's something else your old Granny is noticing. I guess you'll discuss that with me whenever you're ready." She stared hard but warmly at the both of us.

We squirmed in the porch swing. I felt Willow's eyes on me, but I was too uncomfortable at that moment to return her look, because Mama Willa still had me in her questioning glare. I drank my wine to keep from talking.

Then thank goodness the subject was changed and we moved on to talking about the pig-picking party that was coming up in a couple of weeks. Mama Willa had nearly completed making all the arrangements. Uncle Opie would provide her with three freshly slaughtered young pigs the night before the party. She and Running Horse would tend the roasting throughout the night. Friends and family had been invited, which included everyone on Aliceston Mountain. Willow's homecoming was a big deal around here. It was to be the biggest celebration on Aliceston Mountain in recent years. I turned to Willow. "They really love you around here. That must make you feel so special. I envy you."

"I am blessed to be a part of Grams' tribe. It is her that should be honored, not me. She is so wise with the wisdom of our ancestors. All that I am, I owe to her and my Father. They have so unselfishly given me the greatest opportunities."

"Now baby girl, your Paw and me saw the light in you. And you poured that light on us, through your love. We've received our honors over the years. Now you must step forward to accept your inner calling. We're mighty proud of our little Willow Rose."

Willow got up and went over and wrapped her arms around Mama Willa. Tears streamed down both their faces, while they clung to one another. I dabbed at my misty eyes with my shirtsleeve. Their love and devotion was remarkable.

Minutes later, we saw Be's and Running Horse coming up towards the house carrying an old log, about five feet long and a foot in diameter. I yelled out, "What's that for?"

"Running Horse wants to make you something from this Al," was Be's reply. It's a secret and I can't tell you what it's going to be, so don't go trying to pry it out of me."

They each grunted when they laid the log on the porch. Robin Hood immediately went to sniff it out, and finding that he couldn't eat it, he returned back to lie beside my feet and finish his nap. He was stuffed from a ham bone that had been loaded with meat, that Mama Willa had fed him. He had cleaned that bone as clean as a whistle, and his belly bulged in appreciation. I bent over and scratched his sleepy head.

"Dad said that your dog picked you to be his special person, out of all the people in these hills. That says a lot about you, doesn't it Grams?"

"Matter of fact it does. Says you're a good person with a caring heart and a soul to match. He sensed that in you Alexandra. You display a genuineness that drew him to you. He wants to be your side-kick through life."

"Pardon me for asking this, but how do you know all these things? Do you see it or just feel it?"

"A person's story is written in their eyes Alexandra, if you will look closely and take the time to read."

I threw that statement around in my head. So that's why Mama Willa, Running Horse, and now Willow gazed so earnestly into my eyes. They were reading my story. Could it be that simple? "Can everyone do that Mama Willa?"

"If they truly desire to do this thing and practice its principles, it's as easy as reading a book. But unlike a book that is read from the outside in, reading a person is from the inside out."

They could see that I was baffled by my confused expression. BeBe sat silently listening off to the side in an old pine rocking chair, that squeaked as she rocked. Running Horse had his head bowed and eyes closed, as though he were asleep.

Willow patted my leg. "Grams, I think we've given Alex something to think about for awhile. She looks a little perplexed, and as if she's wondering if she's stepped into The Twilight Zone."

"Oh no, I'm fascinated by your ways. I'm devouring every word. Trust me, I have nothing but the greatest respect for all of your beliefs. I guess I'm just a little scared by what you might read in me."

"Your story reads like a tree in the great forest. Like why you chose to call your farm Nottingham Forest. You are a part of that forest. Like a fir tree, blessed to be green year round, and add beauty to these hills. You're a mysterious individual Alexandra. You have extraordinary tastes and great dignity. You love beauty. Sometimes you're moody and for sure you can be stubborn. But you can be relied upon. Your word is your bond. You possess many talents. You're driven by self-motivated ambition."

I was held speechless by Grams' words as she continued.

"These are all good qualities, if used correctly. The bible says that, the trees of our Creator are full of sap. He has blessed you with much sap my dear."

"Well, I'm totally dumbfounded Mama Willa. Don't reckon I can hide very much from you, now can I?"

"No child. I see what you have yet to see."

"I don't understand."

"You will in good time. Be patient." She turned to her granddaughter and said, "You too baby girl."

There she went again. Had she figured out that Willow and I were attracted to each other? If so, she seemed to be all right with it.

A watermelon slice of yellow moon floated above, amongst the millions of twinkling stars enameling the night sky. The golden dots on the mountains in the distance were the home fires burning of our surrounding neighbors. How peaceful it all was. I filled my lungs with the fine misty pristine air. I had been pumped with a new vitality tonight. The howl of a coyote broke the momentary silence that had existed.

BeBe shot up straight in the air out of her chair before the howl ended and whooped, "Sheets, what's that?"

Running Horse answered with a chuckle. "That's old Greystone. He's right on cue tonight, as usual. He's letting us know that he's secured the woods for the night."

Robin Hood answered with a bugle howl of his own. "That's a good boy," I said while petting his proud and courageous stance. "I guess old Greystone is telling us it's time to be on our way Be's. We had a wonderful evening. The food and the company were great. Thank you all so much for having us. I learned some things this evening."

"Hope we didn't scare you off Alex." Willow stood and said.

"No way. I had a most unusual and interesting time. Can't wait for more of the same, if we didn't wear out our welcome tonight. What time will you be driving back to Greensboro tomorrow Willow?"

"I won't leave until around three tomorrow afternoon."

"Good, would you come over and join Be's and me for breakfast in the morning?"

"I'd love to Alex."

"Great, see you about nine o'clock then?"

"I'll be there."

BeBe and I said our good-byes to the others, and Willow walked with me to the truck. With my truck between the cabin and us, she took both my hands and squeezed them tenderly. "I'll see you in the morning Alex. Sleep tight tonight." Before she released my hands, I gently kissed the top of her right hand. She stroked my cheek lovingly and gave me a soft wave.

As I got into the car my buddy remarked, "I saw that. There's definitely a potent chemistry going on with you two. And strangely enough, I think you have her family's blessings."

"Really?"

"It's too-too strange Al, but I saw it with my own eyes. What a great family, huh?"

"She told me while you were out walking with Running Horse that she's attracted to me, and you saw her hold my hands just then. There's electricity flashing through my veins with her every word. I'm mesmerized. I feel intoxicated when she touches me. Her eyes reach into my heart and spark a desire. I've only known her for less than a day and she's affecting me this way."

"Look out the love bug is attacking. Sounds like you're getting bit pretty good to me."

"Heck, I'd spoon feed myself to her if she asked. Wish she didn't have to leave tomorrow. Thank God she's coming back in ten days."

"Do you want me to leave before she gets to the house in the morning, so that you can be alone with her?"

"Gosh no Be's, I won't see you for two more weeks either. I need you to help me stay balanced. You know I don't want you to go, silly woman."

"Alright then, if you're sure."

The next morning I got up before daylight. I didn't wake Be's, since we had stayed up talking until two in the morning. I had only slept about three hours when my eyes opened, and my mind moved into high thinking gear. I knew from experience that when that happens I might as well just get up and get cracking. I tidied up the house and got the fixings for my omelet's ready to go. After cutting up some tomatoes, peppers, onions, cheese and frying some bacon, I placed it all into the refrigerator.

As the sun began to rise, I took a cup of hot tea to the porch to watch the day begin. Thoughts of Willow flooded through my mind. Memories of her touch seared my being. "Come on boy, let's go and pick Lady Willow some flowers for the breakfast table." He bounded behind me; tail wagging like he understood my every word. Frankly, I wasn't so sure that he didn't. He led me right over to some wild miniature roses that grew up the wall on the side of the house. Gathering a hand full, I spotted some daisies along the fence rails. Strange mixture, but oddly enough they looked good together. I rinsed them off under the faucet in the back of the house, and took them inside to find a suitable vase for the table. Unable to locate one, I settled for a large pilsner glass. I wrapped the glass in a pink napkin and arranged the flowers the best I knew how, which surprisingly turned out pretty good-looking. Pleased with myself, I poured another cup of tea.

Returning back to the front porch, I found Be's still slant-eyed, only half awake, but sitting there with a kid's grin on her drowsy face.

"What's the stupid grin for? And why are you up? I wasn't going to get you up until eight. It's only seven."

"I got up to go to the bathroom and saw you out the window picking flowers. I bet they're not for me, are they?"

"Well yes, they're for you and Willow."

"Pooh, you know you can't fool me. Since when have you ever picked flowers for me, or anybody else for that fact? You're gone girl. Totally gone, and I'm glad that I was here to see it happen."

"This is all happening so fast. I'm afraid we're moving too fast. Don't you?"

"Remember what Mama Willa said last night?"

"What part?"

"You know the part about where she sees what you have yet to see?"

"Yeah, what of it?"

"I think she can see into your heart in a way. That woman's intuition is incredible. She's got the two of you all figured out Al. It's only too fast if you think it is. Read Willow's eyes Al, like Mama Willa said. What do you see when you look into them?"

"It's more of a feeling Be's. Sounds a little stupid I suppose, but it's like we're dancing to a beautiful slow song underneath a full moon's glow, showering silver rays down on us. Like we're the only ones for miles around. It's totally absorbing in the most unexplainable way. Sounds corny, huh?"

"Did you hear yourself? You said dancing to a very slow song. Not a fast song Al, a slow song. You're not moving too fast. Sounds like things are moving at the speed they are intended to me."

"Thanks. See, I need you to help me see things in prospective. You're right; everything is on its own course. Can I get you a cup of tea? I need to run upstairs and get cleaned up before she gets here. I got hot and sweaty picking those flowers earlier."

"Run on and take care of business. I'll get my own tea."

I sang in the shower to an oldies song on my Bose CD player, which I had turned up loud enough to shake the rafters. Robin Hood napped, oblivious to my squawking, on the bathroom rug. Happiness pierced through every atom of my body. "R-E-S-P-E-C-T, find out what it means to me," I bellowed from my hot vaporizing shower. I remembered my Mom singing that one, as she danced enthusiastically around the kitchen, when I was a little girl. So long ago, I thought. I took my time getting ready. Put on a little make-up, spritzed and blow-dried my hair, sprayed on some perfume, and put on some white shorts with a navy polo shirt. "What do you think fella? Is this okay?" He licked my hand in reply. "Thanks boy."

Together we strode down the steps like we had music in our feet. I turned on the radio to keep the melodious liveliness going. I had brought my satellite radio in from the car, so I easily found my favorite jazz station. Spyro Gyra was playing. I picked up Robin Hood's front paws and began to dance him around the living room while singing. BeBe caught us as she came down the stairs.

"So you're teaching him to dance. Can I cut in?"

"He's a good sport. Puts up with my antics. Willow should be here anytime now. Is my hair okay in the back? Not sticking out is it? Does the place look alright?"

"Perfect as usual. She already likes you. Stop worrying. Ooh, I see a car up at the top of the hill. That must be her."

Approaching the house was a little silver Mercedes sport's convertible. A black ponytail blowing in the wind revealed my expected guest. A sudden rush of excitement swept over me as she parked under the huge willow tree, along with our cars. Now that willow tree took on a new meaning to me. Like her its branches, covered with feathery leaves like hair, blew gently in the wind too. Like her, it was beautiful and stately.

BeBe and I stepped out onto the porch to welcome her. "Welcome to Nottingham Forest. Beautiful day, isn't it?"

She said good-morning to Be's, and then angled in my direction, handing me a warm pan of cinnamon rolls. They were partially covered with a red and white-checkered cloth, and their sugary-spice aromas curtained her arrival. She had gotten up early to bake them to go along with our breakfast. Her thoughtfulness only added to all the other wonderful qualities she possessed.

"Lovely morning indeed Alex. I couldn't sleep last night, so I got up and baked these. Hope you'll like them."

"Al didn't sleep too well last night either. Got up before the sun." BeBe exposed me.

"Really," she said as I stepped aside to let her go into the house first.

After breakfast we all did the dishes. I washed, Willow dried and Be's put them away. Willow suggested we all go for a horse ride, up to the waterfall, on their property.

"A waterfall nearby, that sounds super. What do you say Be's?"

"Oh Al, I can't. I've got to get back to the office this afternoon to get the paperwork ready for tomorrow. Little Debbie is out of town this week, so I have to do all the research and market analysis' myself. Sorry, but this should be a big commercial deal for me. You and Willow go on, and I'll get on the road when you leave."

"Are you sure good buddy? I don't want to go off and leave you."

"Please go you two. I'll be fine."

I excused myself and took Be's out on the porch. "You don't need to do this. I don't want you to leave."

"Seriously Al, I had planned to leave early anyway. I really do have to get things ready for tomorrow. It's the large Gori Corporation account. Could mean a bundle."

"Okay then. Since you're talking money, I understand where you're coming from. Good luck with it. You're coming back for the party, right?"

"That's the plan. Now get back in there with Willow, and y'all go horseback riding."

Stepping back inside I told Willow, "Looks like it's just you and me, if that's alright."

"Oh BeBe, I'm sorry you can't go. Another time then?"

"Gladly, now you kids get going. Looks like it's beginning to cloud up out there."

"Your Dad did tell me that it was going to rain today. Something about the underside of the tree's leaves."

CHAPTER 12

▼

The trees provided a soft green light to the morning, and the sun's gold pierced through their canopy as we traipsed down an old logging road. I rode Misty Morning, while she sat the saddle on her palomino named, Peanut Butter. She had named the horse when her Father gave it to her on her twelfth birthday.

Willow showed me magnificent sights along the way. Like her Father, she knew the flora at every turn. She'd have me pause to hear the animals sharing our arrival with others of the forest. She could name each sound. I marveled at her woodsy knowledge. Riding just to the side of her, a foot or so back, I could take in her natural beauty without her seeing my intent watching of her every move.

Only about thirty minutes into our ride and before we had made it to the waterfall, thunder rumbled and bounced in the hills.

"Storm moving in fast Alex. We'd better high tail it back to the house, or it will be on top of us."

"You can tell all that just from some distant thunder?"

"It's a summer flash. Let's get." With that she slapped Peanut Butter and took off, galloping back through the woods towards Nottingham. Not to be out done, I kicked in my heels, and Misty Morning chased after them. The clouds thickened rapidly. I hung on by the seat of my pants, and managed to stay on board precariously all the way back home.

Running Horse met us at the barn and sent us up to the house, while he took care of the horses for us. We ran as Robin Hood barked excessively at our mad scramble. Before we made it to the front porch, Texas size raindrops drenched us to the bone.

"Now I see why it's called a summer flash. That just came out of nowhere it seemed. Let's get into the house and dry off."

Willow took one look at me and began laughing. "Look at us. Two drown rats, dripping all over your living room floor."

Her clinging t-shirt revealed her shapely breast and the effects the cold rain created beneath. She saw me staring, and a smile spread across her face as she said, "Guess we'd better dry off."

"Oh yes, let me get some towels." I ran upstairs and grabbed two large soft bath towels, and came down and wrapped one around her shoulders. "Here keep this on you, and I'll go and get some dry clothes for you to put on."

"You don't need to do that. The towel will be fine."

"And have your Grams think I didn't take care of you. No way." I flew back up the stairs, and returned instantly with some shorts and a pink jersey tank top for her to put on. Then she shocked me by removing her clothes right in front of me. Trying not to ogle at the sight of her curvaceous velvety body, I stuttered. "I—I'm going to run upstairs and change too."

Up in my bedroom, the lasting vision of her naked body in my mind turned on a tidal wave of desire. She had to know what the sight of her would do to me. I'm sure that was her intention. Times like these, I wish I wasn't so morally straight laced. My upbringing had abated my sexual impulsiveness. But my thoughts now were to shed that prehistoric skin, and give in to the sensual signals she was throwing my way. Signals, that if I was reading them correctly, promised exploration and gratification. I felt the heat sweep over me as I exited down the steps, and back into her presence. "How about a glass of wine to help warm us back up?" Not that I needed to be warmed any further. My blood was already at a simmering boil.

"That would be nice Alex. Can I help you?" The pink tank top showed the excitement in her breast. Straining gemstones puckered through the thin jersey cloth. She brushed up against me from the back in an arousing way, as I removed a Chardonnay from the refrigerator. I could feel the heat of her desire with that touch. The immense heat that was flooding back and forth between us was hollowing my breath. I turned and looked into her eyes. I swear I saw fire. It burned into me.

Setting the wine bottle down, I placed my arms around her and brought her body tightly to me. Dizziness came over me from the heat and passion encircling us. Our lips found one another's with a thirsty torrid kiss. Deep, probing, and emotionally longing for more. An immense rush of sexual excitement heightened through our first kiss. I took her hand and we climbed the stairs to my bedroom.

Willingly and eagerly we flowed together, and onto the downy bed, while returning to the power charging through our burning kisses. Our bodies were swelter-
ing from the steamful ardor that overtook us. Her body atop mine pressed and
aroused the fibers of my soul. I buried my head into the valley of her breast as she
heaved them to me. I kissed and suckled each breast tenderly with an enormous
hunger, while she made yearning tones of desire. The passion was so intense that
it was hard to be gentle lovers.

For two hours we mapped each other's bodies with almost wild pleasures. Just
a mere look into each other's eyes rekindled those desires. Like ancient lovers, we
fulfilled and gratified until we lay exhausted, wrapped around each other as sleep
overtook us.

Two hours later I awoke in her embrace and stared into her golden sleeping
face. The loveliness of it etched into my heart. This wonderful beautiful woman
had captivated me and loved me in only a couple of days. Funny though, everything about her felt so comfortable and long knowing to me. It didn't feel as
though we'd only recently met. Our naked bodies fit together like they were
made for one another's. My heart was feeling such happiness. As uncanny as it
may sound, I think I fell head over heels in love with Willow Rose Sykes, at that
moment.

Robin Hood started barking loudly and ran down the stairs. Willow's eyes
sprang open. She looked at me with such sweetness that I felt my heart begin rac-
ing again. But Robin Hood's continued barking required my attention. "Excuse
me. Let me see what's up with him." I grabbed my terry cloth robe from the
rocking chair next to my bed, and made my way downstairs to check things out.
I could see Running Horse through the parted curtains on the front door.

"Oh shit," popped out of my mouth before I realized it. Thinking to myself,
I'd better answer the door because he knows we're in here. But what will he
think? I have his daughter upstairs in my bed. I ran back up the steps. "It's your
Dad at the door."

She had put back on her clothes."Well, let me go and see what he wants.
Don't look so upset. Coming with me?"

"Let me throw on my clothes, and I'll be right behind you."

Seconds later I was with her as she was talking with her Dad in the living
room. My face still flushed with afterglow. "Hi Running Horse," I said as I has-
tened to the kitchen. Seeing the bottle of wine I had earlier sat opened on the
cabinet, I poured a glass and gulped it down in my nervousness. Willow walked
into the kitchen. Her face shined with laughter.

"You should have seen your face Alex, when you told me my Dad was at the door. You looked scared to death. Poor baby. We're big girls, dear one."

"I know Willow. But for Christ sakes, I've never been caught with my pants down, so to speak. You don't think he knew do you?"

"If he did he looked pleased. Stop worrying. He really likes you. Pour me a glass of wine, and I'll tell you a story."

I poured us each a glass of wine and we sat at the kitchen table, while she told me the Cherokee story of 'two-spirits'. Her story collared my full attention with exceptional interest, and I sat glued to her words.

"You see Alex, homophobia is not an indigenous trait to our culture. Since ancient times it has been treated with a positive attitude amongst our people. 'Two-spirits' are seen as genders other than man or woman. They are maleness and femaleness interlaced in one body. We are all connected in this circle of life, and sexuality is inseparable from the other aspects of life. We are what nature has made us, and we are not afraid of the differences between us. To be a 'two-spirit' is to be considered an emissary from our creator, God. We're regarded as possessing special intellectual, artistic and spiritual qualities. My family has allowed my nature to manifest itself, and they have never questioned my sexuality, one way or another. They love and respect me for who I am."

"Gracious, what a great way of thinking. I've never heard of 'two-spirits'. There's so much about your traditions that I can identify with. Then you're saying that if they knew about us, they'd be alright with everything?"

"Now you're probably not going to believe this, but I swear to you it's the gospel truth. Last Christmas when I came home for a visit, Grams sat me down one night and told me that I needed to start planning on moving back home. She said that in the summer my true love would return to these mountains, and if I didn't return, I would forever miss love's opportunity."

"Are you talking about me Willow?"

"Yes Alex. I knew the moment I saw you. I'm sure Grams knew too. That's what she meant when she said; she saw what we were yet to see. She's always right. She's the wisest woman I've ever known."

"Did you just tell me in an off-hand kind of way, that you love me? Because if you did, I know I'm the luckiest person in the world!" My eyes implored her.

"I love you Alex Nottingham. It's a love like I've never felt. So strong, so deep, and so completely consuming my heart, that I'm afraid you're only a dream."

My arms went out to her, and I held on to her like a life preserver while whispering, "I love you, I love you, gosh how very much I love you." Our kisses of wine quickly ignited our desires once again. The magnitude of passion took on a life of its own, and love climaxed relentlessly through the afternoon. It was the closest to heaven I had ever been. I knew God had brought us together.

It was getting dark outside and our stomachs were growling. "I never want to let you go Willow. Let's stay here forever."

"I wish we could. I feel like I belong with you. No, I know I belong with you. But I have to go back to work for two more weeks. Then no one can separate us again."

CHAPTER 13

▼

Saying our good-byes last night had been difficult for the both of us. It had taken us over an hour to get from the front porch to her car, parked only about forty steps beyond. Gazing into the eyes of one another for several minutes at a time without speaking, revealed the physical force of unspoken words. This incredible chemistry flowed between us with dazzling effects. I had heard of drowning in love, but thought it to be unmitigated bullshit. But Willow had thankfully found the chink in my protective armor and tenderly ensnared my heart.

After she had called me the final time last night to let me know that she had gotten back home in Greensboro safe and sound; I took the pink tank top she had worn that day to bed with me. Her lingering fragrant scent helped me drift off into a peaceful sleep. The next morning I awakened refreshed and on top of the world. "Good morning boy. Listen to those birds singing. What a gorgeous day out, huh boy?" Robin Hood's tail thumped the floor rapidly, and his hazel eyes sparkled with the thrill of the new day. "Betcha hungry. Let's go make breakfast. I'm famished. How about another omelet this morning for me, and some Kibbles'n Bits for my fella?"

Once breakfast was devoured my shadow, Robin Hood, followed me out to the barn where we met Running Horse. At first I felt a little apprehensive about the day before, but then I remembered Willow's story about the 'two-spirits', and a calmness came over me. "Morning Running Horse. You were right about that rain yesterday. Sure was a drencher. Anyway, I was wondering if you'd help me put up my Nottingham Forest sign today? You know up there where the gate is?"

"Already put that up for you yesterday after the rain ended. Came up to the house to tell you, but my timing wasn't too swift. Willow told me y'all were busy."

Goodness, if the color of a cherry red blush burned a body, I would have been a heaping pile of ashes. I was only used to this manner of frankness in my business life, but never my personal life, which I usually kept to myself. But not with this family. They spoke pretty much what was on their minds, which I liked, but it would require some getting used too. Noticing him watching me wriggling around for words, I managed to say, "That's great, let's go take a look see."

Robin Hood led the way gleefully chasing bees and June bugs here and yonder, but always staying close by me.

"Your dog keeps pretty good tabs on you Alex. Are you getting used to him?"

"He's wormed his way into my heart. As with most things around here, it seems like we've been together much longer than we have. Strange how that is, don't you think?"

"The Great Creator works in mysterious ways. Just part of your life's plan. It's good that you listen with your heart. Many people consider that foolish, and in turn miss many of His blessings."

"Funny you would bring up that subject. Seems like every since I decided to move out to these mountains, I've been receiving more than my fair share of blessings. Mind you, I'm thankful, but I get a little uneasy when things are going so well. You know, like when's the other shoe going to drop, or my good fortune run out?"

"Don't dwell on that Alex. Haven't you had many disappointments throughout your life? Didn't you ever ask yourself when are things going to turn around for me?"

"Well, yeah."

"Your whole journey has been leading you here. You fought it for many years. God could not shower you with all the good He had for you, until you listened with your heart and followed where He would lead you. So now keep your arms and heart open to receive His gifts."

I held out my arms as wide as I could stretch them and said, "Here I am God, right where you've wanted me. I'll take all the blessings you have to give me."

My humorous display amused Running Horse.

Looking up at the well-crafted sign my business associates have given me at my going away party, I marveled. "That looks fantastic. It fits perfectly. You did an outstanding job getting it up there straight and even. Thanks. I know it couldn't have been easy by yourself." I stepped around looking at it from all angles. My furry fella took every step I did, and looked up at the sign as if giving his approval along with mine. "You like it too, don't you boy?"

"Good Alex, pleased to do that for you. You don't ask me to do very much around here, so I have to go looking to see what needs to be done. I hope you won't ever hesitate asking me to fix or do anything for you."

"Well, I have been thinking about painting the old barns. How do you feel about red with green trim?"

"Sounds like a good plan. When do you want to get started?"

"Are you always this agreeable? You know, you're a good man Running Horse. I truly do admire you."

My cell phone rang, and I held my hand up to him and said, "Excuse me," and answered the call. It was Willow. I stepped several feet away. "Hi my Indian Princess. Gosh, I'm missing you more with each minute that passes." We only spoke briefly. She was between court appearances and in a rush, so we bustled through our conversation. "Thanks for calling. Call me again later? You know I do too." I turned back to Running Horse. The full force of his gently seamed face and penetrative eyes studied me, like I was standing directly in the spotlight on a stage.

"So she's your Indian Princess?"

I was taken back by his comment, since I hadn't meant for him to overhear me. He came over and hugged me, lifting me almost a foot from the ground. My dog jumped on him in protest. As he put me down, I reprimanded Robin Hood. "It's okay boy. He's not hurting me." Flabbergasted, I just gawked back at him standing in front of me giving me his noble Indian smile.

"We've been waiting for this. I knew the day I first shook your hand. Mama Willa called me from the café that day when you stopped in for chicken and dumplings. Our girl's soul flame has finally arrived, she told me."

"I don't understand how y'all know all these things. For the life of me, I can't grasp any of this. It's like I'm in another place and time."

"You've just come home my new daughter. And I might add, you were as slow as molasses about it too. Like Willow, I guess you had valuable life lessons to learn in preparation. We're just so happy you're here, and our Willow is coming home. We don't expect you to understand all our ways Alex. We have had generations to learn these ways of our people."

"Maybe this explains why I felt such a vein of recognition when I first met all of you. It was weird. Well maybe weird's not a good word for it, but well you know, uncanny? No that's not it either."

"I understand you. We awoke something in your spirit that was reaching out to connect."

"Well yeah, that's sorta it, I guess. Whatever it is I'm glad that y'all are happy about it, because really Running Horse, I love your daughter. I know it's fast and all that, but I can't help it. She's touched a part of me that no one else has ever managed to reach."

"There's that connection I just told you about. It has been my quest to help lead my daughter to her destiny. Remember I told you that you were sent here to help me with my quest?"

"Sure, but I didn't have a clue as to what you were talking about. So you really knew all along?"

"Mama told me when Willow was only a day old that she was a 'two-spirit', like my Aunt Ruth had been. My aunt died the day before Willow was born. Willow shares her gentle enlightened spirit."

"How did Mama Willa know back then that Willow was a 'two-spirit'?" I wasn't doubtful of his story, but my heightened curiosity needed more detail, and I listened closely as he continued.

"The story has been told among our ancestors even before Mama was born, and it has been passed through to all of us by our tribesmen. To possess the female and male gender in one body is a gift from our Creator. With this gift come heavy burdens of responsibility. We never mentioned this to Willow, until she was in her final year at college. It was inherent that she came to realize this on her own. She came home that summer all upset and confused. Mama had a long talk with her, and it was during their conversation that baby girl revealed her attraction to women. Mama told her the story of the 'two-spirits' and of her Aunt's esteem among our tribe. It is a great honor for my family to have another 'two-spirit'. You are both strong and powerful women, the same yet different. You both have been picked to fulfill the design of your birth." The reverence in his face indicated the sincerity of his words.

"It would be nice if everyone saw things the same way as the Cherokee. So many of us have tortured ourselves over our identities, and lived in secret to hide from ridicule and rejection. I came here to find my true meaning in life. Wow, if I'd known all this awaited me, I'd have gotten the molasses out of my breeches a lot sooner." We both laughed and walked arm in arm, absorbed in mutual expression back to the barn.

When I left him I felt better about myself, and proceeded up to the house. Along the way I called and left a message for Willow to call me the first chance that she got. "I've got some great news for you, my Princess Willow Rose. Call me when you get a moment. Love you."

That evening after finishing dinner I sat down at the kitchen table with my laptop. My head was filled with mental notes needing to be saved, while they were still fresh in my mind. Things I'd been shown, stories I'd been told, new phrases I'd heard, wisdom that had been shared, and new feelings that had been stirred. The soup pot of my brain was boiling and brimming, and I lost track of time as my fingers tapped out steadily, page after page. The effusion of words came forth with a life all their own. These mountain forests had unfurled my senses, and allowed me to gain clarity of mind in my Appalachian hamlet. My mind and spirit were becoming a team as I adjusted to the rhythms of life around me.

I pushed through the invasion of fatigue that sought me. Knowing that ink lasts longer than memory, I continued as my fingers kept pace with my prolific thoughts. It was nearly mid-night when the phone rang, and put an end to the body bracelet of magnificent meditation that had encompassed me, for the past six hours.

My Willow Rose sounded all worn out from a full day of putting together her closing arguments, in preparation for the finale of her firm's noted trial. Tonight she was going to sleep on her office couch, so that she could get an early start tomorrow. Another thing we had in common. I shared with her how I had often done that at my previous office, to get a jump-start on things. Then putting the business aside, we spoke about my talk with her Dad earlier in the day. She was happy that everything was out in the open for me. Her voice was the nightcap that I needed to settle my thoughts, and get to bed myself. She had a soothing effect on me. Carrying her loving words to bed with me, and holding on once again to the pink tank top, sleep came contently.

The next morning when I let Robin Hood out to do his business, I spotted a note taped to the front door. It was from Running Horse. He'd gone into Bryson City, to Clampitt's Hardware store, to pick up the paint for the barns and some grain for the horses. It said that he'd be back around ten, and ready to get those barns taken care of. Bless his heart, he thinks we'll get those barns painted today, and I'm thinking no-way man. It looked like an easy two-week job to me. But I liked his attitude. I stood with my hands on my hips, looking out across the pasture at the task at hand. I couldn't wait to get them done. They were going to look tremendous against the plush green hills. Glancing at my watch, I yawned and headed back inside to have my morning coffee. "Let's go boy."

My satellite TV wasn't installed yet, so I twisted and turned the portable TV antenna every which a way, until I got the one channel I could pick up out here. It was a snowy picture with vague shadows. I listened as I sat at the kitchen table eating my sausage and jelly biscuits; while my fury fella lapped up the sausage gravy I had made and poured over his breakfast. More bad news from Iraq. Another ambush and eight Americans had been killed. I hadn't heard from my friends stationed overseas in the last month. Tonight I would try to get through to them.

Hearing rumblings coming from outside, I went to the door to see what in the world was causing all the racket. Over the hill and down the drive came a caravan of trucks and cars kicking up dust. Arms waved back and forth at me from their rolled down windows. "What the heck?" I said out loud, as Robin Hood took off in the direction of the barns barking, in his now familiar horn tones. Shaking my head, I preceded after him to welcome all the guest that was still coming over the hill.

"Morning neighbor," came repeatedly time after time, from faces I'd seen and others I'd never met. Smiling, warm and generous faces stepping out from the caravan like long lost relatives. They were dressed some in overalls, some in jeans and t-shirts, some in cut-offs, and others in flowery dresses. There was Mama Willa toting a picnic basket in each hand.

"Hear there's a barn painting going on here today Missy." Then other ladies carrying baskets made their way over to me, while Mama Willa introduced us. Must have been fifty or more people marching about as though they were on a mission. Robin Hood stood by my side as I surveyed the group. I had just told Running Horse yesterday about wanting to paint the barns. How could he have put this together so fast? I scratched my head in disbelief at the generosity of my neighbors. Their animated and loving spirits were a joyous sight. Never had I witnessed this type of sharing. I watched as ladders went up, old sawhorses were turned into tables, paint was poured, and all able bodies hit the barns with brushes in hand. I felt honored and fought to keep my emotions at bay.

"Don't be just a standing there Alexandra. There's work to be done." Grams said, handing me a paintbrush and promptly leading me to the barn.

"Yes ma'am." I obeyed with a zest of delight amidst my neighbors and Mama Willa. One of the ladies from Bear Creek Valley Baptist Church started singing hymns, and we all joined in while the sun climbed overhead, defying the mountain breezes. Hymns switched over to 'Suwannee River', and other old tunes I hadn't heard since elementary school, or some never at all.

It was only a matter of hours and both barns looked sparkling new. Stepping back to admire the fresh dressing of paint, my eyes were drawn to the top of the main barn. Anchored atop was a weather vane carved from wood. A detailed carving of an eagle in flight perched above the directional arrow, and turned into the wind. Looking over at Running Horse, I couldn't keep my feelings of gratitude at bay any longer. With fluid filled eyes of appreciation, I thanked him with a heart felt hug.

"Did you carve that from that log you and BeBe brought home that day? It's totally extraordinary. You're an artist." Then I tried to go around and personally thank each of my newfound friends with a shake of hands or a hug.

Mama Willa, accompanied by most of the other ladies, was busy getting all the food laid out for everyone. Now I'm not a social butterfly as I've been accused of before, but I felt such a comradeship with the people of Aliceston. So much so, that talk and laughter came tumbling from my mouth without any effort at all. They embraced me as though I had lived on Aliceston Mountain for all my life. Even Uncle Opie's brow lifted, as he returned my hug and teasingly offered me a chew of his tobacco. His tobacco stained shirtsleeves gave evidence to his daily habit. But his kind gesture, along with his nearly toothless smile of acceptance, endeared him to me.

CHAPTER 14

▼

It was after six before everyone went home. Robin Hood was still busy burying all the bones he hadn't managed to gobble down earlier in the day. He frolicked from one place in the yard to another, searching for the perfect spots to hide his treasures. Now back in the city I would have had a fit if a dog started digging one hole in my perfectly manicured yard, much less about ten of them. Instead now, the sight of my fury fella scrambling about kicking dirt into the air entertained and tickled me.

Plopping myself down in a rocking chair on the front porch with a satisfied stomach expanded from the picnic in the meadow, my eyes grew heavy from a day that had been packed with pleasant surprises. The overhead whirls of the porch fans batted the evening heat, and I drifted off into a nap. Couldn't have been asleep too long before Robin Hood took notice that he didn't have my attention any longer. He doesn't cut me much slack. There he stood to the side of me, with his front paws raised up on one arm of my rocker. His head lobbing forward and his wet and dirt covered tongue licking me squarely on my mouth and nose. "Hey, hey, whoa boy." Wiping my face and stretching, I laughed at him. "Can't a woman get a nap around here? Oh well, let's go in and call our Willow Rose."

I spent the next week writing ten to twelve hours a day. Amazingly, the words poured onto the computer screen almost faster than I could keep up with them. Sometimes even I didn't know where they came from so abundantly. They were exploding from me as though they had been arrested for too long. Coming out in battalions of exhilaration transfusing from me. This was a dream coming true. I looked forward to each day of writing, eager to see what would evoke in front of me. Time passed quickly when I wrote, which thankfully eased my separation from my Willow Rose. Only a few more days and she'd be home with me.

On Tuesday I drove in to Bryson City to pick up some groceries, and a few other things I needed around the house. It was good to get out for a while. When I got back home and put things a way, Robin Hood and I took a walk through the meadows and played Frisbee. I hadn't spent much playtime with him the past week, so we tried to make up for the lost time. He'd leap into the air about three feet and catch the Frisbee. He seldom missed. Usually he freely gave me the Frisbee back, but ever so often he wanted me to chase him for it. The boy is a big clown. Don't believe I could stand to be without him now. He keeps me company, and he keeps me smiling.

"Okay boy you've worn me out. We both need a drink of water. Come on and let's go back to the house."As we entered into the house my cell phone was ringing somewhere. I had forgot where I left it, and shuffled around frantically until I spotted it in the fruit bowl on the kitchen table. I made a mad dash to grab it before it went to voice mail. "Hello."

"Hey Al. What cha up to?"

"Just getting ready to send out a few e-mails. You know, to Roger, Fran, Kim and Tyrone. I've been so busy with the move and all that I haven't had time to let them know what's going on around here. How about with you?"

"You haven't heard, have you?"

"Heard what Be's?" I didn't like the sound in her voice.

"Are you sitting down?"

"No."

"Please sit down then."

"Okay I'm sitting. What's going on?"

"I wish I didn't have to be the one to tell you…Fran's helicopter was shot down last Saturday Al." Then she hesitated briefly before releasing the following stunning words. "Everyone on board was killed."

Silence, silence, silence…

"Al, are you still there?"

I had slumped almost parallel to the floor in my chair. My head felt like it weighed a hundred pounds. Not Frannie. We three had been friends since the fifth grade, after her family moved around the block from us. We were the three musketeeretts. We did almost everything together before she joined the service. BeBe and I had been there when she received her flight wings. We threw her a going a way party before she left for Iraq. Beautiful, little petite Frannie couldn't be a casualty of this malign war. "No, no, no," burst from me.

"Al, I'm going to get in my car and come over there. I can be there in about three hours, if I push it."

"I'm sorry. No. I'm all right. But thanks good buddy. I need to come there. When's the funeral? How's her family?"

"There's a service on Thursday evening. Afterwards there's a party in her honor down at Legend's. Alex, there's no body to bury. No remains were recovered, due to the intense explosion. Her Mom told me that the military officers said they never had time to know what hit them, and that their deaths had been immediate."

"Whew! I suppose that's something to be thankful for. It's too hard for me to believe. I should have written her weeks ago. Shit, I've been so preoccupied with my own matters. I'm so self centered at times."

"Now stop doing that to yourself. She knew how much you and I both loved her. She'll be watching out for us now. You know she will."

"Yeah, she was the angel of the three of us. That's for sure. Can I come and stay with you for a few days?"

"You know you don't even have to ask that question. Come on."

"Thanks. I'll leave here tomorrow afternoon. Need to take care of a few things around here before I head out."

"Well, you've got the key to the house, so just go on in until I get there. I have a closing at four, and I'll be home after that."

Feeling emotionally drained, I wanted some time to myself. "I'll call you later. I need some time to sort this out right now."

"Okay Al."

"Thanks for understanding Be's. Bye-bye."

Grabbing a Pepsi from the frig, I called Robin Hood and slammed the door behind us. Walking in a daze, oblivious to all but Frannie's face in my mind's eye, until we reached my spot in the woods where I had found my fury fella. I hurled my drink bottle madly, and fell to the ground like a rock. The floodgates of my heart burst forth. I buried my head in my arms crossing over my knees, and tears dripped from my chin and onto the already moist ground beneath me. Robin Hood had his head lying on my feet with his large sad eyes turned upward, watching me respectfully, as I mourned the lost of a brave and courageous person, and dearly beloved friend.

Remembering what Frannie had told me that morning before she boarded the plane to Iraq put a smile on my soggy face. She had said, "Our country needs me

Alex. It's what I've been trained to do. You know I've always wanted to do this. Don't worry; I'll be in good hands. And any way, if I get to heaven before you do, I'll help your Mom look after you. Lord knows, you could use the extra help. Stay out of trouble, you hear me," she had said while holding my jaw firmly between her slender fingers, and looking up into my face with her resplendent green eyes. Her golden smile added a twinkle to her eyes as she winked at me, before turning to hug her family good-bye. She had looked so happy that she sparkled that day. That's how I'll always remember Lt. Commander Frances Allen....

As I walked from the woods and across the pasture, the horses seemed to sense my sorrow, and joined Robin Hood in a quiet procession behind me. When I opened the gate to head back up to the house, I'd be willing to take an oath that those horses bowed in reverence before I left them. Feeling it as gift from God, I returned the gesture. Then looking to the sky I whispered, "Frannie did you ask God to do that for me?"

When I walked back into the house I wanted so badly to call Willow, but knew I shouldn't interrupt her. I'd just wait for her to call me when she had the opportunity. While washing my hands at the sink, my attention was drawn to the bauble that BeBe had found at the sight of the burnt down cabin in the woods. I'd had it soaking in a bowl of Pepsi Cola since the day she'd found it.

Drying my hands I continued staring into the bowl. Curiosity overcame me, so I drained the bowl and laid the item on some paper towels. Taking an old toothbrush from underneath the sink, I began softly rubbing away the loosened rust. The Pepsi had performed its cleansing task remarkably well. It looked like an old locket, just as I'd thought the first time I saw it. The shape resembled a baby shoe. I couldn't get it opened. Bending down, I searched under the sink for the metal polish I had bought for my car's wheels. Finding the bottle I applied it to the locket's surface for a few minutes, and then began to buff it with a chamois. Gold filtered through. Now I could see that it was a tiny baby shoe. Also, there was a dainty enamel red rose engraved on the top of the miniature shoe. It still needed more polishing, but at least I had figured out what it was.

Then a knock came at my door. Looking through the curtains I could see Running Horse standing outside discerningly. I answered the door in the best spirit I could muster up."Hi, and what do I owe the honor?" Stepping aside, I invited him in.

"I just came to see if you are alright. There's a trail of tears leading up to the house. Can I do something to help you Alex? Mama Willa is on her way over here too."

Then my tears began again. He let me cry on his shoulder and hugged me in comfort, until Mama Willa plunged through the door seconds later.

"Come here child." Her arms rocked me in their pillow of softness. I dropped the locket from my hand without realizing its release. It bounced on the knotty pine flooring into the corner, just behind the doorway. "Come sit down honey child." She kept me in her arms as we sat together on the couch. "Tell me all about your loss sweet girl."

Without me ever saying one word, they had felt my pain and came to my side. I'll never figure out how they know all this stuff about me. It's like magic on Aliceston Mountain. Do the trees and animals really talk to my new Cherokee family? Can that really be true?

For the next hour we talked about Frannie. I told them childhood memories. I told them how much I loved my friend, and I told them how very proud of her I was. It did me good to talk about Frannie with them. They cried with me.

Running Horse addressed us. "War doesn't recognize its victims. It destroys many lives with each body it consumes. Tonight Alex, I will send a tribute to Frannie through the clouds. I'll send your love in music to the heavens."

I didn't understand what he meant, but I nodded and thanked him.

"Thomas, go out to my car and bring in that pitcher of lemonade I brought over please." She lifted my face in her gentle aged hands and said, "You're my girl too now Alexandra. Have you told Willow about your sorrow?"

"No ma'am. I didn't want to bother her. She's way too busy with her final presentation."

She gave me an astonished look. "Too busy. I should say not. She'd cook my goose if I didn't let her know you're hurting. She loves you child. Don't cha know that?"

Drying my eyes with my shirttail, I answered. "Yes ma'am."

"Then give me your phone. We're gonna call her right this minute."

I brought her my phone. I must admit I felt just like a little girl doing what I was told. But her mothering was appreciated and well received.

"Let me speak with my grand-daughter, Willow Sykes. Yes I'll hold, but tell her to hurry up. It's an emergency." Seconds later she had Willow on the line. "I'm fine sugar-pie. Alexandra got some sad news today. One of her best friends got killed in that God-awful war, and she's hurting something fierce. She didn't want to call and bother you, but I told her you'd cook my goose if I didn't let you know. We're right here with her. Okay, here she is." She put the phone to my ear and went into the kitchen with her son to give me some privacy.

"Hi Willow Rose."

Her tender words were like a balmy ointment, which further consoled my heavy heart. She said she'd drive home tonight to be with me, and leave early tomorrow morning for court. I protested until she finally agreed not to make the drive. I don't know how I got so lucky to fall into this wonderful and loving family, but I'd not let a day go by without thanking God for His marvelous blessings.

Mama Willa brought the lemonade in the living room once she knew I had finished talking with Willow. We all sat down. "Thomas said that you dropped this earlier."

Looking I could see the locket in her hand.

"Yes ma'am, BeBe found that at that old burned down cabin we stumbled upon, when we walked back over from your place the other week. Looks like a locket, doesn't it?"

"It is child. It's the locket Thomas gave to his wife, Rose, right before our little Willow was born. It's been missing for over thirty years. It's a sign Alexandra."

"It was your wife's, Running Horse?" He nodded as he took the locket from his Mother and held it to his chest, as though it was a cherished item, which I could see it was.

"It's my Rose's sign giving her approval of you Alex. That was our cabin out there. She's letting us all know that she sees what is going on. She died in that fire. I've gone to that spot at least once a week for all these past years. I turned over every rock and limb, and even dug in the dirt hunting for this locket. And now here it is. She left it there for you to find and give back to me."

"But BeBe found it, not me."

"But who cleaned it up and got it back to me? You did Alex. Don't you see how effective her plan was? BeBe played an important role, but you brought it back to me."

Gracious, this was totally overwhelming. Now dead people were giving me their sanction. Really strange, but in a wondrous way. "I couldn't get it opened Running Horse. Can you?"

"Yes, look Alex."

I walked over and sat on the arm of his chair. In his hand the open locket revealed two tiny old pictures. Not burned or even scorched in the least. "Why she's beautiful, just like Willow. And look at you. Handsome devil. She's holding Willow isn't she?"

A tear fell from his eye as his lower lip trembled ever so slightly. I reached over gingerly and wiped it with my hand. "Would you tell me about her?"

Looking over first to Mama Willa and then back again to me, he lifted his head proudly, and began his incredible love story of his fair Rose.

"It was the early fall of 1969. A new family had moved into this farmhouse. The original owners had gotten transferred up north somewhere. I had been out in the woods most of the day collecting some herbs, on Mama's medicine list. Being the inquisitive young man that I was, I made it a point to cross through these woods to get a look at the new neighbors. Rumor was, they had a daughter that was as pretty as the harvest moon on a star filled night. Right they were too. You know that path you take going out to your favorite place in the woods?"

"Yeah," I said, glued to his every word.

"At the edge of the woods, well that's where I first laid eyes on my Rose. I can still remember what she was wearing that day. Some bell-bottomed jeans with embroider patterns sewn on them and a pink tank top. Her shiny brunette hair was pulled back into a ponytail that flopped back and forth, as she chased after her younger brother in the yard. She acted so young for her years. I always adored that about her. She had an energy that beat all I'd ever seen. I was twenty-nine at the time, and a confirmed bachelor by choice."

Mama Willa cut in, "Yep, he'd had every girl for fifty miles around this mountain chasing after him since he'd been sixteen years old. Guess Thomas didn't feel the need to settle down, until he met Rose. She put the fragrance in his life."

"That she did Mama." He smiled and gazed off to the far corner of the room, as though he saw his Rose standing there, before continuing his story. "It was about three months later before we were properly introduced. Ma had asked me to come and help her out at the café that day. She never asks for help unless there was something special going on, so I found it a bit unusual for her to ask that day. But I got down there before the lunch crowd hit.

That day the Grey family came in at Mama's request for a welcome to Aliceston's Mountain free meal. Mama was waiting on the customers out front, and I was assisting a deliveryman in the back. Now Alex, Mama gets this peculiar look on her face, one that I had learned to recognize when she was up to something. She comes up to me and says, "Take this out to that family by the front window. The ones in front of the flower box."

"Yes ma'am," and then I noticed that look on her face. "What's with the look Ma?"

"No look Thomas, just happiness expressing itself on my face. Go on about ya self."

"I shook my head and proceeded to take the food out to the Grey's table. No sooner than I'd gotten through those swinging doors my eyes met with Rose's. My heart skipped a few beats. All dressed up today, I thought to myself. The most beautiful woman to ever come to this mountain. Pushing my shoulders back and holding my head tall, I introduced myself, and placed the plates of pip-ing hot fried catfish down in front of them."

"Running Horse, now that's not your real name is it?" Her father asked me with a belittling tone in his voice.

"But before I could speak for myself, my Rose defended me."

"Well Father, I think it's the most lovely name I've ever heard of. Of course it's his real name. Don't you know that it's a name that he has earned? You must share your story with me sometime Mr. Running Horse. Her voice was as grace-ful as the lilies of the valley."

"She stole my heart right then and there. So you see Alex, I understand how you feel about my Willow. It was the same for me with her Mother. Her Mother, Rose, was so outgoing and strong-willed. She did what she wanted and when she wanted. To her Father's dismay, I'm happy to say. After she finished her meal, she marched right into the kitchen and invited me to a picnic the next day in the meadow, behind her house. He pointed out the window showing me the spot. As she left the kitchen to go back out front with her family, I spied Mama watching me intensively with a bear's grim on her face. So this is why you had me come to the café today? I thanked Mama with a hug and told her what she already knew. I have a date with Rose tomorrow."

"Will you be taking her some flowers?" she asked me.

"Yes Mama. The next day assured me of what my heart had been trying to tell me. I was in love with Rose Grey. We dated for the next seven months. She loved these hills. She loved me. She loved my family. That's when I decided I wanted to ask her to be my wife. Mama and Pa thought the world of Rose. It was perfect, except for one thing." He paused and gave me a troubled stare.

"What, what, Running Horse?"

"Her Father did not want an Indian dating his daughter, much less marrying his daughter. But I was determined to do the honorable thing and ask his permis-sion anyway. It was the right thing to do. Mama told me he would never approve.

"I drove into Asheville and picked out an engagement ring for my Rose. I had managed to save a substantial sum of money over the years, with my business in Asheville, so I hunted for a ring befitting my Princess. With ring in hand that night, I asked Rose to marry me. Under the stars, out in a canoe on the Ocon-aluftee River, drifting lazily while listening to *You've Made Me So Very Happy*, by Blood, Sweat and Tears, on our portable cassette tape player, I proposed. She said, "Yes," and made me the happiest man in the world."

"Ahhh, but what about her Father?" I inquired.

"I'm coming to that. The next day I went over after supper. Rose was sitting in the swing on the porch, anxiously awaiting my arrival. We were both nervous, but I was intent on seeking her Father's approval. I asked Rose to stay out on the porch, while I went inside to speak with her Father. But she'd have nothing to do with my staying outside request. My goodness no, she was a little spitfire, and she was coming inside with me to speak to her Father.

When I asked him for her hand in marriage, he laughed right in my face, while gulping his scotch on the rocks. He said he'd not have any daughter of his marry some heathen Indian, and destroy his family's good name.

"Utterly disparaging and a complete damnation," he had added for a final blow.

"For the first time in my life I felt a rage flame in my gut that took all the strength I had to maintain. An angry humiliating force that was crushing me from the inside out.

"Instantly Rose got in front of me, and told her Father she'd not have him speak to the man she loved and the man she would marry in that cruel manner. My heart filled with pride as she added that she'd leave his house and never come back, if he did not apologize and talk to me with respect. Her eyes burned, while she stood there defiantly facing her Father.

"Her Father's face fumed bright red with pompous indignation, as he pointed to the door and loudly told us both to go. I looked down at the sadness that had consumed my Rose and tried to console her. I told her to stay with her family. You see I didn't want her to have to choose between them and me. But then she told me the words that still echo in my heart to this day. She said that I was her family now.

"Looking stoically into her Father's eyes she said, "We know who is responsible for splitting this family up. You shall have it your way Father. I'll come by to pack some clothes tomorrow, while you are away in town. Come on let's go."

"With her hand in mine we left the house, and got into my Camaro and drove away. I felt terrible, but she soothed me with her loving heart. We stayed with my folks for the next month until our wedding day. Rose slept in with my sister, Joy. All our close kin helped me build a cabin, over there next to the property line that adjoined her folks. She wanted to be able to see her Mother and brother whenever her Father wasn't around. Her Father refused to let her Mother come to our wedding, but we tricked him into believing it was scheduled on the week following the actual date. Rose was so glad that her Mother was there.

"Once back from our honeymoon we moved into our little cabin. I had built it just the way Rose wanted. We planned to add on later. She got pregnant within two months after we were married. That's when I bought her the locket you found up there. She loved surprises and I loved giving them to her. She brought me so much happiness that I would have done anything for her.

"When little Willow was born we were both sure that her Father would want to see his grandchild. Obstinate man continued his stupid alienation. He did allow her Mother to visit once each week, and we continued sneaking over when he wasn't around. I added on another bedroom and enlarged the kitchen when Willow was a year old.

"Music filled our home each evening. Rose played the piano expertly. From Beethoven to The Beatles, she could master them all. She had planned to be a music professor before she met me. I had given her a new piano our first Christmas together."

His eyes were now misting over, and his bright smile had turned to a painful expression. "Are you okay? Do you need to stop now?" I asked him with concern.

"No, I'm okay. Thanks…It was a cold January morning, Willow had been sick through most of the night with a fever and vomiting. Normally each Monday, Rose rode along with me to Asheville, while I conducted business. She taught piano lessons in a room over the library on Mondays every week. It was good for her to get out and use her gifted talent. Mama Willa would keep baby Willow for us until the next day, since we didn't get home until late those nights. We'd usually go out to eat, do some shopping or go to a movie, before we headed home. It was our special time.

"But on this particular Monday, Rose said that she felt exhausted and her head was splitting. She had been up most of the night with baby Willow. Still, she was determined to go with me into town, in spite of herself. Rose didn't want to disappoint her piano students or me. She was always putting those she loved ahead of herself.

Mama came over to see about little Willow and brought some herbs to bring down her fever, and stop the vomiting. Bundling her up, she took our little papoose back home with her. I had lain down and stroked Rose's head until she drifted off to sleep, and then I slipped out the front door to let her rest that day. I thought then that it was the right thing to do. I stopped by Ma's and asked her to check on her later that day.

"Little did any of us know that her Father had gotten drunk and decided to come over, while he thought we were not at home, and burn our cabin down. While Rose slept peacefully inside, her Father poured kerosene all around the outside, and then threw torches onto the roof. He crept back through the woods that morning like a skunk, and when he got home he told his wife, "I left a surprise for the Indians next door when they get back tonight." It took his wife over thirty minutes to get the evil deed he had committed out of him, before she called Mama Willa with the news of his senseless act.

"Mama shouted into the phone, "Rose is asleep in there! Oh God help us."

"By the time Ma and Pa got there, it was too late for anyone to help. She was gone."

Seeing me weeping he stopped to comfort me. "There, there now, it's okay. I've come to peace with it. Anyway she got through to me through you, didn't she? She's happy our daughter has found the same magnificent love that we had, and in many ways still do Alex."

I didn't want to express any disbelief, but I had to ask them. "Do you really believe she sent this as a sign? I want to believe all this. I really do."

Mama Willa chimed in, "Then remember Alexandra, just listen with your heart."

CHAPTER 15

▼

As I climbed into bed around nine-thirty and stretched out my mind flashed like a slideshow, rapidly moving from one picture story to another. Beginning with the shattering news of Frannie's death. There would be no coffin. No body remained to be buried from the aftermath of the explosion. Please God; I pray she never felt any pain…Flashing to the way the horses gave a bow of reverence as I left them today. Did I really see that? Had it just been my active imagination? I questioned myself. Flashing to the sudden visit of Running Horse and Mama Willa, ready to share my grief and surround me with their love. How did they know I was hurting? How do they know these things? The next flash was a snapshot of my Willow Rose, and a smile returned to my face. I knew she would have been with me too, if I hadn't talked her out of it. Her spirit was with me. I could feel it. Flashing onward to the sad yet loving story of Rose Grey Sykes. Was the locket really her way of giving her approval of me? I wanted so hard to believe. The slideshow ended and left me with loving thoughts.

These gentle people, the Cherokees of Aliceston Mountain. Such kind, loving and intelligent people. Protective and proud of their ancient customs, but a unique willingness at the same time to teach all who earnestly sought to listen with their hearts and connect with God's life-force. I silently prayed and thanked God for all my many blessings, and asked Him to take good care of our Frannie. From the wisdom inspired by my new Cherokee family I was convinced that Frannie would keep her promise and be watching over me. My soul was expanding in this mountain forest to heights I'd never before conceptualized. God had taken on a new and more central meaning in my life…a peace came over me. I even thought I heard music coming from that peace.

From my bedroom's quiet darkness, Robin Hood abruptly ran to the window that looked out over the meadow. "What is it boy?" Getting up I joined him. "You hear it too. It really is music. Let's open the window."

His tail beat me about my legs with each excited circle he turned, while I raised the window. A harmonious parade of comforting tones drifted in with the fresh night air. Night crickets weaved their stereo chirps into the music. Almost an angelic presence enfolded me as I stood there listening. Seeing a small fire out behind the main barn the silhouette of Running Horse loomed up at me, as he played his echoing melodic tones on a flute. Its tune carried adrift a myriad of provoking emotions. So this is what he meant by sending Frannie a tribute to express my love to the heavens tonight. What a wonderful tributary for her and also a gift of joy for me. Peaceful and chimerical, the calming music transcended me for the next hour. While his mellow sounds continued, I ventured back to bed with the window remaining open, and the music still pacifying my soul into a restful slumber.

I slept in late the next morning. That I accredited to the healing flute music that had sailed through my window, from Running Horse last night. I packed a few clothes before going downstairs. I needed a black outfit or something similar for Frannie's ceremony tomorrow evening. Then some kicking around clothes for whatever else Be's and I might do. I hauled my suitcase and hangered clothes down the steps with me, and parked them by the front door. I let Robin Hood outside and went into the kitchen to fix us some breakfast. I really didn't feel up to cooking this morning, so I just fixed a bowl of cereal, and drank the last of the pink grapefruit juice.

Just as I was returning to open the door to let my boy back in, he surprised me. By golly, if he didn't open that door and come back in by himself. "Hey, how'd you do that? Well, you're just too smart for your own good, aren't you boy?" Shaking my head in amazement, I looked outside to see if someone had opened the door for him. Not seeing anyone, I praised him for his clever learning skills. "Com'on and let's fix your breakfast smarty pants."

After breakfast we walked briskly to the barn to see Running Horse, so we could thank him for last night's one-man concert that had touched our spirits. As always he was notably humble. He knew I was on my way to Chapel Hill for the next few days, and said that he would feed Robin Hood for me. We hugged paternally and as I turned to leave he asked. "Will you be seeing Willow while you're in the area?"

Turning back, "I'd love to if she could find the time. I'll call and leave her a message when I get down the road a piece."

"She'll make the time for you Alex. Mama Willa interrupted another one of her meetings again last night, after we left your house. She told Mama that she couldn't get you off her mind and wanted to see you in the worse way. She wants that darn trial over. Said she needs to be with you."

"Gosh, I've upset her. She doesn't need my troubles taking up her time or clouding up her mind. This is her last important trial, and she doesn't need to be preoccupied with other things."

"I wouldn't be telling her that if I were you Alex. She's like her Mother when it comes to that. Kinda like a mama bear, if you know what I mean." He bared his teeth in a big sinister growl.

"Ohhh, thanks for the warning," I said, while laughing respectfully at his exaggerated display.

It was nearly one o'clock when I loaded my things into the Hummer. As I walked back to the porch, Robin Hood seemed to detect I was leaving him again. His sullen look expressed his love for me. "Now stay here boy. Guard the house for us. Okay?" I hugged his neck and kissed his long cold nose. "Stay," I said, pointing to the porch. Rolling the window down when I got in the truck, I repeated, "Stay Robin Hood." As I drove a way, he sat looking so downhearted with his floppy ears out to the side, and his big hazel eyes watching me earnestly, but obediently obeying this new command. I loved that dog. I hated leaving him, but I knew BeBe's cat, Skipper, would not appreciate a seventy-pound dog crashing his domain. My boy was looking good and healthy now that he was getting a solid dependable diet mixed with lots of love and attention. He was thriving on it. But of course as Mama Willa had told me, you always get back what you give to God's creatures.

I was moving along at a swift pace on highway 19 and nearing interstate 40. Once I hit the interstate I'd have another three hour drive before I'd make it to BeBe's door. But it was a clear sunny day and I was enjoying the feel of my new Hummer on the road. I found a great station on my satellite radio, and sung along with the music. My squeaky vocal abilities would frighten the dead, but I belted the tunes away in my solitude. I'll have to wait until I get to heaven before I'll ever be able to make a joyful noise. Thank goodness, God loves me anyway.

Another hour down the road and my phone began to ring. Noting it was my Indian Princess, I answered with a chipper voice, delighted to be hearing from her. She said she had cleared her schedule for the next couple of hours to take a nap, since they had worked through most of the previous night. But instead she'd decided to spend that time on the phone with me. Gosh, if I could have just reached through that phone and kissed her, I would have. We spent the next two hours getting caught up on events and sharing our feelings. Sometimes her voice was so sultry it tingled my whole body. I could feel my smile stretching the width of my face. She erased all my pain. It seemed like the two hours flew by. Neither of us wanted to say good-bye. She had kept me company until I was only a couple of miles from Be's. We'd made plans to see each other Friday evening. I'd drive to Greensboro and spend the night at her place. My body quivered with excitement at the thought, knowing it would be an evening and night filled with loving surprises.

Pulling into the drive of Be's stately colonial home was familiar and comforting. Once inside I called to let her know that I had arrived. Little Debbie answered. "Oh, hi Alex. Good drive over?"

"Yeah, it was. Thank you. I just wanted to tell Be's I'm at her house now."

"I'll let her know for you. She's at a closing right now."

"She told me that. Guess I forgot. So much on my mind here lately."

"I'm really sorry about Fran. I know how close you guys were."

"I still can't believe it Debbie. But I'll come to terms with it sooner or later. Not much choice is there?" Sensing my anguish, she changed the subject.

"How's the farm coming along?"

"Great. You need to come out sometime. It's the best medicine you could ask for, at least for me it has been. The people there are unreal. Biggest hearts you could ever imagine."

"Sounds like you've found your true home in the world Alex."

"Yep, I think you're right Deb. Thanks for giving the message to BeBe. Good talking with you. Take care now. Bye-bye."

I uncorked a bottle of 1995 Bolla Valpolicella. Be's always had a case of it in her closet wine cellar. We had first discovered this pleasantly inexpensive quality wine when we visited Italy, about six years ago. A small town called Soave was its home. We both loved its fruity sweetness and bouquet of complexity. I poured some in a crystal wine glass, which came from a set I had given her a few years back. Whiffing its malty toffee aroma, I sat the glass on the counter to breathe.

I found a couple of rib eye steaks in the frig; so I marinaded them using the mixture of spices and oil she kept in a bottle in her refrigerator door. Two nice size potatoes sat next to the sink, so I washed them off, and preheated the oven for baking. I got everything ready to go for when Be's got home.

We nearly got drunk that night recalling stories of our Frannie days. We hit the gamut of feelings. There were tears mixed with lots of hearty laughter. But at eleven we called it a night and went to our rooms, where sleep came easily with the wine sedative we had drank in quantity.

The next day at the Baptist Church in Rose Hill, the pews were filled in the large auditorium. Several framed pictures lined the front of the pulpit. Chronologically arranged from birth to only months before her death, including one picture of the three of us that had been taken at her going away party before she set off for Iraq. There were our three faces beaming with huge smiles. We had no idea this day awaited us. The rock-like lump in my throat made me ache, as I tried to hold back the river of tears that wanted to pour out. But I sat there silently, while I went through Kleenex after Kleenex. The service had been beautiful, as far as those services can be. After an officer presented the flag to Frannie's Mother, the minister concluded the memorial service. I felt light-headed as I rose to go and visit with her family. I held on to the pew in front of me until the spell faded. BeBe let me hold her arm as we made our way over to Frannie's Mom. With hugs and more tears we promised to stay in touch....

At nine o'clock that evening we entered Legends, to give Frannie her final going away party. She would have wanted all of us to laugh, dance, and toast her with smiles, not tears on our faces. That's just how Frannie was. She always wanted to make other people happy. Her Mother had sent most of the pictures over, and the club displayed them in a field of rainbow colored flowers to her honor. The club even gave everyone a round on the house, and proclaimed it from Frannie. I visited with friends I hadn't seen in ages and found myself actually having fun. It was about ten o'clock when Abby entered the club. Be's spotted her first.

"Don't look now, but I think Abby just got here. And it looks like she's aiming for you; cause Al she's coming this way. Keep your cool buddy."

"No problem." Some arms went around my waist and then around my neck as I turned to acknowledge her. "Hi Abby." Before I could speak another word she planted a kiss forcefully on my lips. Eyes of those closest to me locked in on the scene. Like a minute frozen in time it seemed. Briefly I was the center of attention. Nonchalantly, I withdrew several steps back from her and continued with small talk. "Nice to see you. You're looking lovely as usual."

"I've missed you Alex. I heard that you quit your job and moved to the country. That truly shocked me."

"You know me, always full of surprises," I returned, trying to keep the talk light as I looked everywhere but at her.

"Sweetheart, about that awful last night at the house. I never intended for anything like that to happen. Remember, you always said that Joe wasn't the brightest crayon in the box. I'm so sorry." She touched the small scar above my lip. "I'd love to kiss it and make it all better."

Gently I removed her hand. "No, it's fine. I'm doing fine Abby. I adore my new place. All is right with the world. Everything happens for the best I believe." I didn't want to tell her too much. Anyway she was acting like we could just pick back up with things the way they used to be, and I didn't want to give her any false impressions to entice that belief.

"Buy a girl a drink for old times sake then?"

"Sure, what would you like?"

"You know what I like." She cozied up against me and eyed me seductively.

"White Russian?"

"Yes dear. I'm going to go and sit at that table right over there and wait on you. Hurry back." With that she walked slowly away, while glancing over her shoulder back to me.

How could she think I would welcome her back into my life? I had to get away from her. The only feelings remaining for her weren't exactly pleasant. Sure, I had forgiven her and Joe too, but I didn't want to play this little game of Ring Around the Rosie with her tonight. I made up my mind I'd tell her I was in a relationship, if she kept persisting with her coy advances. Finding BeBe on the way to the bar, "Save me girlfriend. Abby is acting like no big deal about the past. I think she's actually hitting on me. HELP!"

"She knows she gave up a good thing. Want me to tag along with you and chaperone?"

"Please." Together we walked over to Abby's table, and I placed her drink in front of her.

"Sit here next to me," she said patting the bench next to her.

That did it. I was going to have to tell her. "Abby, I think I should tell you that I'm in another relationship."

"Well hell's bells, that didn't take you long, now did it? Is she here," she asked looking around, shaking her hair back and forth in a sudden outburst.

"No, I'm here with Be's, for Frannie."

"Have you moved her in with you? Is that why you moved? You were probably cheating on me all a long, weren't you? I should have known. You were just waiting on an opportunity to kick me out. And to think I thought that I still loved you. Too bad that scar on your face didn't run all the way up your head."

"You're all wrong Abby." Seeing her seething, I retreated to avoid further confrontation. Walking with Be's towards the bar, Abby's cocktail glass crashed at the back of my feet, splashing and attracting the convergence of nearly every eye in the club. "Shit, let's get out of here. That woman is absolutely nuts," I said to Be's.

The bar manager, Kevin, asked me if I wanted him to make her leave the club. "No Kevin, she'll cool down in a few minutes. But thanks."

"I think she's been smoking some more of that wacky weed. It's wrecking her brain or at least what's left of it. I was proud of you for just walking away Al. But you're right about one thing, she's gone crazy," Be's said shaking her head slowly, registering disbelief at Abby's almost volcanic eruption.

"Could you believe she tried to accuse me of cheating on her? Wow, that fish bowl she calls a head is full of dead fish. Let's not talk about her anymore. This is Frannie's party."

We joined a group of our friends and were able to enjoy the next couple of hours, up until Abby's spectacle of a departure left its mark on me. Evidently Abby had consumed far too much that evening. The sway of her walk and the volume of her voice emitted proof of it. I tried to slough her off, but she was determined to get a piece of me before she exited. With her purse she whacked the back of my head, and then proceeded to address me with profanities spewing like vomit.

"Tell your new little slut, I'm glad to be rid of you. And one more thing, tell her she'd better enjoy you while she can, because I have another brother that just might take you out for good this time."

Kevin rounded the bar and escorted her from the club. She laughed manically all the way into the night air. And the chill of it dawdled.

"She just threatened you Al. We all heard her. Maybe you should tell the police." Everyone started talking all at once about Abby's vicious exhibition.

"Oh, that's just the booze and drugs talking," I said trying to laugh off the ordeal.

"Are you sure?" Be's looked worried.

"Well, let's hope so. She probably won't even remember saying that tomorrow."

Kevin came back in. He had put her into a taxi. "She's tighter than a jar of glue. I'd watch over my shoulder if I were you Alex. That girl ain't right."

CHAPTER 16

▼

As I tried to sleep that night Abby's angry face haunted me, even when I tried to fill my thoughts with my beautiful Willow Rose. Still, Abby's words and torrent cackling images hung around my mind like a noose of consumption. Tossing and turning, flipping my pillow over and over again, the vivid reflections irritated the crap out of me.

Finally around three in the morning I gave up in defeat. Dragging a blanket behind me, I went to the kitchen and made a cup of cocoa. Sipping on the sweet treat I made my way to Be's plasma screen television. Keeping the volume low I kicked back into the reclining section of her couch, and watched an old movie starring, Goldie Hawn titled *Private Benjamin*. It was exactly what I needed to take my mind off of the negative effects Abby's words had enshrouded me with earlier. I laughed my way through most of it. After the movie I fell asleep for the next three hours, until Be's found me on the couch. It was about eight in the morning. I saw her tiptoeing around the entertainment room trying not to wake me. Then she saw my eyes watching her.

"Hey Alex, whatcha doing on the couch?"

"Had trouble falling asleep last night, so I came out to watch some TV. That old movie, *Private Benjamin*, was on. I think I laughed myself to sleep."

"Why couldn't you sleep?"

"I guess it was the whole Abby fiasco. Her temper-tantrum tormented me, while I laid in bed, so I came out here to be rid of her."

"Like I told you last night Al, you should take her threat seriously. She's already proven she'll get someone to hurt you. I'd call our lawyer, Tim, and have him put a restraining order on her, if I were you."

"Well, I don't think we need to go quite that far Be's."

"Then at least call Tim, and tell him about what happened last night, just in case she rears her ugly head again in the future."

"He'll think I've gone daft."

"No he won't. He came to the hospital to check on you, while you were still unconscious, when she had you hurt before. You really need to let him know." She stood there with her hands on her hips, and her mouth pursed pursuing my compliance.

"Alright, you've convinced me. I'll call and thank him for the nice flowers he sent me, and follow that gratitude up with this bit of news. Like you said, just to have it down on record."

We'd grown up with Tim, and since he'd become an attorney we had always had him handle all our legal matters. So I gave him a call, while Be's had her ear glued on the other extension, ready to put her two cents worth in on our conversation. Tim said that I should seriously contemplate taking Be's suggestion about the restraining order. That made her give me a smug look of I told you so. "Well Tim, thanks for the advice. But for now, let's just let it ride. If she makes any more advances we'll move forward with the restraining order. You've got her threat documented. I really don't think she'll do any more foolishness. Least wise, let's hope not."

After we hung up, Be's gave me a condescending glare of frustration as she passed me on her way to the kitchen. "I think you're making a mistake, but hey, you know best. You lived with her. How many eggs do you want this morning buddy?"

"Two over easy please. Let's change the subject. We've rented her way too much space in our heads this morning."

We dressed after breakfast and rode over to Eno City Park, and took a long hike beside the Eno River banks, amongst the daylilies and azaleas, dwarfed by the tremendously fragrant southern magnolias. Partridgeberries crept across the granite bluffs guarding the sequence of friendly rapids that dotted our trail. A couple of inexperienced kayakers entertained us as they floundered in the currents. Together we kept close eyes on them, just in case they needed rescuing. The mid-morning sun felt good on our faces.

After finishing our hike we checked out the reconstructed 1778 working gristmill, taking pictures of one another on the bridge overlooking it. The Hugh Mangum Museum of Photography, which we had hoped to walk through, was closed during the week, along with the old Blacksmith Shop. So we had to settle for peeking through the windows. Be's and I both liked history and botany facts and trivia. That was the nerdy side of us, or so some thought. We however thought it showed our maturity and depth. It only added balance to our child-like curiosity. And it gave us the time to just enjoy being together.

Once arriving back to the house, BeBe helped me carry my clothes out to my truck. "Today was fun Al. I miss all the things we used to do together."

"Me too. Sorry you can't come to the pig pulling party this weekend for Willow. But I'm glad we got to spend a couple of days together. We can thank Frannie for that. When can you come for a visit?"

"This is my busy season with school out and all, but I'll make time soon. Anyway you and Willow need some alone time girlfriend. It's great seeing you happy again. You take care of yourself, and tell Willow hello. Oh yeah, and ask her if she's got a friend available like her I could meet," she said with a happy but serious expression.

"You got it good buddy." We waved and I was off.

Once getting on the interstate, I rang up my number one cellmate and left a message on her voice-mail. "Hi my Indian Princess. I know you're in court for the verdict today. I'm positive the jury will come back with not guilty, on all counts. There's not a doubt in my mind. The newspapers agree with me too. Then you can come home for good. Just wanted to leave you a message and let you know that I'm on my way over to your apartment now. I've got the directions you gave me, and I'll knock on your neighbor's door for the key. I should be there by five o'clock. The traffic's not too bad, especially for a Friday. Hope you won't mind if I freshen up a bit when I get there. Can't wait to get you in my arms again. I've missed you something terrible. See you soon my love. Bye-bye for now."

I daydreamed of our evening together, so much so while driving, that I nearly missed my exit. Almost cutting a guy off to get over to make my turn, I yelled, "Sorry," like the guy could hear me. I knew for sure he must have been telling me off, as he traveled down the highway. West Wendover Avenue. Not far now. There it was, Steeplechase of Adam's Farm. She'd sold her house a few months ago in preparation of moving back home to Aliceston. As I drove into the complex, I noticed the grounds were neatly landscaped with island gardens, surrounded by lush green grass and well-maintained facilities. The streets were lined with trees. So this was her home away from home? But not for much longer, thank goodness. Parking as she had instructed me, in her designated area, I made my way to her friend Sam's door. He quickly answered after one ring of the bell. "Hi, I'm Alex, Willow's back home friend."

"Hi Alex. I've heard a lot of nice things about you. You look exactly as she described. Would you like to come in and have a seat? Are you thirsty from your drive?"

"That's very kind of you Sam, but I'd best go on up to the apartment. Need to freshen up before Willow gets home. Thank you so much for the invitation though. Perhaps some other time?"

"Sure dear. Here's the key. Let me know if you need anything else."

"Yes sir. Thanks again." What a kind man, I thought as I raced up the steps carrying my clothes.

Opening the door of her apartment my anticipation grew, knowing that I was so close to being by Willow's side again. A giant arrangement of roses and daisies covered the living room coffee table, standing nearly two feet tall. The attached card had my name on it. Reading the message my soul jumped merriously around in my bones.

It read: To Ms. Alexandra of Nottingham Forest. These flowers are no match for the love in my heart for you, but I hope they express the beautiful colors and fragrant sweetness you have brought into my life. See you tonight. Forever yours, Princess Willow Rose…

With an enormous smile circling around my entire head I searched for the bedroom so I could take a shower, and change into an appropriate outfit for going out to eat that evening. She had said that she made reservations at the restaurant, 223 South Elm. My Princess wanted to introduce me to something called stuffed Bobwhite quail. Afterwards we'd go dancing at the Sky Bar. I was so completely enamored with her that I'd eat monkey stew and dance in Haw River, if she asked me too. But I'd heard that 223 South Elm was an outstanding restaurant, and that the Sky Bar was a wonderful women's bar.

I was going to get all decked out so that she'd be proud to be seen with me. Once I stepped inside the shower, there was a note taped just below the fountain showerhead. There were seven words: I wish I were here with YOU!! My body tightened pleasantly at the thought.

After getting all dolled up, I stood back to take a long look in the dresser mirror. My hair behaved it self, as though it knew this was a special occasion. The black riding jacket I wore, was over a cotton mandarin collared v-neck shirt, and was fitly accompanied by my gray pants with paisley swirls. Not bad for a rush job, I thought. I sprayed perfume, stepping in and out of it, to get just enough. Feeling satisfied with the results I strode to the kitchen. Dry mouth was setting in now, probably from the nervousness of my impending rendezvous. God bless her little pea-picking heart, as my dear Mother used to say. Another note was taped to the refrigerator. This one said: Have a glass of wine my sweet Alex. And if I'm not home by the time you finish, have yourself another. I love you, and tonight I will show you just how much…

Now I was drowning in estrogen. She could stir my estrus without a single touch. A landslide of emotions emerged, and my heart was resonating with love. "Gosh, when is she going to get here," I said aloud, as I walked out on the screened deck to watch for her car. The sun was going down as I sat back in the lemony cushioned patio chair, and listened to the traffic down the road. I drank the wonderful French burgundy wine. She must be a Burg, because she has excellent taste in wine. Juicy black cherries, with earthy components, leapt out with intensity, as I chewed the wine to get the richness of it. For the next twenty minutes I watched the night stars begin to appear and spread across the sky. Just as I was beginning to get up to go inside to pour another glass of wine, I thought I saw her car turning into the complex. Sure enough, there came my Princess. I knew she saw me too, because I could feel her smile radiate up to me.

My heart started dancing with delight. My hands began to shake with the impatience of holding her. I watched her balletic movement up the sidewalk. Not so much a walk, but a glide. Quickly I went back inside. Her key was in the door before I could open it. When the door opened it was as if both our hearts jumped for one another's. Steaming HOT, she was more gorgeous than I had even remembered if that were possible. She dropped her purse and briefcase, shoving the door closed behind her with her foot, and came into my arms. I could feel her trembling. So we both clung to each other, until our trembling turned to passionate kissing. Low mourns of desire expressed in unison. I felt like I was on fire. My head was spinning from the sensations ready to explode inside of me. I had to push her gently back. "Do we really have to go out tonight?" I asked her, nearly breathless from desire.

"I wanted to introduce you to some people and show you the town, but I've changed my mind, if that's alright with you," she responded with sensual undertones.

"I wouldn't be able to keep my hands off of you. I want you more than food, water, wine or anything, Willow Rose. Can't you feel my heart grabbing for you?"

"Let's go to the bedroom," and with her hand she led me lovingly behind her. "You got all dressed up to go out. Are you sure?"

"Sure as rain Princess. Anyway, I only got dressed up for you."

I took my jacket off and laid it across her tapestry chair. Then I asked her if I could help her off with her clothes. As I slipped her cashmere candlelight cream top over her head, she began unbuttoning my shirt. I helped her remove her skirt, feeling her slim waist press in against me, as my hands unhooked her satiny cream brocaded bra. The sight of her golden breast sent electricity throughout my body. Our eyes were secured together in purpose. Feeling my breast set free, I guided her to the soft down pillowed bed. As she lay down, I slid my slacks off, and stood before her in black lace boy-cut panties.

"Come here," she said, and our fire blazed to towering heights. The hunger for each other escalated, with the first touch of our bodies. I felt her feverishly trying to remove my panties, and assisted her with the same fervor. Now skin-to-skin, our lovemaking met no obstacles. Gently we caressed, kissed, hugged and stroked every inch of one another, until the foreplay could endure no more, and our gentleness turned to abandonment. Each of us set on pleasing the other first, led to the spontaneous duality of pleasure and orgasm. Bodies heaving in satisfaction, but still wanting more. Over and over we brought each other to an island of gratification. We fell asleep, wrapped together like a Christmas package…

A couple of hours later she awoke me with gentle kisses, that once again ignited my very soul with ecstatic desire. We moved together so perfectly. Our bodies glistened from pleasure.

"Darling," she said, "Can you feel how much I love you?" Then her sweet face looked questioningly at me for a reply.

"I only pray that you love me half as much, as I love you my Princess." Her face lit up, and its beauty stilled my breath, as I lost myself in her soulful eyes.

Lying there in each other's arms, the phone suddenly rang. "Don't move I'll be right back." Then reaching over me she answered. "Hello, oh hi Grams. Yes she's here. No, you're not interrupting anything." She gave me a big smile on that one, and proceeded with the conversation. "Don't worry we'll be there by ten in the morning. Has Dad got the pigs on to roast yet? Wow, that many people coming. Yes ma'am, we won the case. I'll tell you more about it tomorrow. Okay, we love you too. Don't worry, we'll be careful on the road. Bye-bye." With that she hung up. "That was Grams. She wanted to make sure we'd be on time tomorrow. I think everyone on the mountain will be there."

"It must be something to have the whole town of Aliceston, coming to welcome you home Princess."

"Right, that enormous budding metropolis," she laughed.

"No, really Willow, they all love you. I understand why too. I wish I had grown up on that mountain."

"Well dear one, if you had been there, I never would have left," she said. Her words warmed my heart in a blanket of love.

CHAPTER 17

▼

The next morning we arrived back in Aliceston a few minutes before nine. Willow drove on to her Grams to get dressed for the party. I had tried to get her to tell me what to expect at the party as we followed one another down the highway. We chatted away on our phones all the way home, but never once did she offer me a clue about the party. Her mysterious ways allured me, and also drove me a little crazy at the same time.

Robin Hood had all but attacked me when I got out of my truck. He had heard me coming and met me up at the top of the drive, running along beside the truck, with his ears flapping and his tail beating in the wind. He never wavered or took his eyes off of me. The boy was growing so big that his front paws touched my shoulders, when he jumped up on me, giving him prime position to lick me slobbery on my mouth. Now his soft coat shined in the sunlight, and his eyes flickered with jollity at my return. "Okay fella, I missed you too. Good boy. Com'on inside with me." I talked to him while I was getting dressed as though he was a human friend and could comprehend my every word. And I trusted him not to reveal any of my secrets.

Almost dressed, I looked out the window and saw that Running Horse had Misty Morning and Warrior hitched up to a charming aged surrey, tied to the old willow tree below. The surrey appeared freshly painted green and red, matching the barns my neighbors had painted for me. Only the colors had been flip-flopped. The same colors made up the Scottish plaid top covering the wagon, while red tassels dangled beneath. It was reminiscent from the Currier and Ives collection of many years past. I guess this meant we were riding to the party in grand style. I simply cherished this way of life. Hurriedly, I ran downstairs and out the door to check out our transportation for the day.

Willow Rose drove up, and Robin Hood and I opened her car door. She had a big pork roast bone for Robin Hood and a marvelous kiss for me. Right out there under the giant willow tree in front of God and all His creatures. "Whoa, don't know if I deserved that wonderful greeting, but I'll take all I can get of that."

"You deserve that and so much more my sweet, sweet Alex. I'm so happy." She hugged me as tight as a vise. Turning and looking towards the surrey, she exclaimed, "Wow, Dad and Grams did a great job on the old surrey. Do you like it?"

"Yeah, it's something else. I need to get us one of those."

"No you don't."

"Why hon?"

"Because this is my gift to you. It's yours."

"What?" Stuttering with my words. "Gif...gift, you shouldn't be doing that. I love it, but this is too much."

"Nonsense, nothing is too much for you love. See how it goes perfectly with your barns?"

"Our barns, don't you mean?" I corrected her.

"Opps, our barns. Point made. Only one condition goes with the carriage."

"Anything Princess, what's that?"

"Just that you have to promise I'm the only one you'll be kissing in it. Is it a deal?"

"These lips are only meant for you." With that said, I kissed her tenderly. "Gosh, Willow Rose, you're really something else. You never cease to amaze me. You're all the gift I need. God has given me more than I could ever imagine."

"I feel the same way. We'd better get going. When Grams says ten o'clock she means not one minute later, or we'll have the dickens to pay."

I helped her up and climbed in beside her. I'd never drove a carriage, so she took the reins and gave me my first lesson. Of course, Robin Hood accompanied us down the road. It took some doing, but we managed to get him to jump up in the carriage with us after numerous pleas.

Once we got up to the main road we were joined by about twenty more horse-drawn wagons and other folks on horseback. It was like a parade. Willow handed me the reins, and down the road we went to the sounds of clomping horse's hooves. Then an old blue, rusty ford pickup truck pulled out ahead of us, pulling along a colorful decorated float. Eight people were perched on top playing musical instruments. Guitars, a banjo, fiddles, harmonicas and even an old washboard, as the country music filled the summer's air with ham-bone rhythms.

Willow put her arm around me in her glee. This was a surprise to her as well. The stunned happy expression on my face made my Willow Rose doubly excited. She continued to hang on to me as we approached the café. No one gave us any looks of discern. We were totally accepted for who we were. There's no words to fully express how wonderful that felt.

An enormous, red and white-striped carnival style tent was set-up just behind the café. Glorious smells wafted about. Evidently the pigs were cooked to perfection, judging from the lingering aromas that slapped at my nose. As we got within feet of the parking lot, people came out in plenty, with greetings and applause. They treated us like we were celebrities making our way to the red carpet. I was tickled beyond words. With her arm locked with mine we got down and returned the warm welcomes. The musicians played, *When Johnny Comes Marching Home Again*, and the crowd shouted, "Hurray!"

The band of musicians marched inside of the tent and continued to play. Before the beginning of the next song Mama Willa took to the small stage, and held up her hands to quite the crowd. She knew how to take control of a room. A hush fell, and Mama Willa made a little talk to get the party underway.

"Today my granddaughter has come back home for good. She's discovered that true love grows in these rich soils, on Aliceston Mountain. She's returned home to continue with her heritage and the ways of our ancestors. Along with her is her twin flame, which most of you have already met, Alexandra Nottingham. Together, they will bring good things to our land as they further stir the soils of these hills, with their God given talents, and the love that burns in their hearts. So today let's celebrate, and show these gals what a real party is. Welcome home baby-girl. Welcome home Alexandra."

Everyone applauded and the music kicked back up lively, churning out into the dog day of summer.

Commingled with Grams' fanfare of delicacies was a potluck paradise. I'd never seen so much food spread out in one place. Picking and pulling lavish helpings off one of those roasted pigs was a treat in its self. Darn, if that wasn't the best BBQ I'd ever eaten. Now the deserts were fit for a king. You name it and it was there. From heavenly hash and shoofly pie, to mountain rum cake, the list was long and scrumptious. We ate until we hurt ourselves. Man oh man, was I stuffed like a Thanksgiving turkey. Grams said that God would forgive me, since I was a first time pig picker.

They cleared away an area in front of the stage and a hoedown began. The two-finger picking guitar players got the jam session going. Willow Rose and her Dad started it. Without saying a word, Grams grabbed me. I didn't know what the heck I was doing, but I knew I was having one of the best times of my life. Mama Willa surprised me with her spryness. For an eighty year old, she really had some moves. My new mountain friends could cut quite a rug. Uncle Opie and his brother, Charlie, had been in the apple Snapple wine and were ready to party. They kept Willow and I out on that dance floor for most of the afternoon. Uncle Opie had gotten his new false teeth, and he smiled all the time now. He looked ten years younger, at least.

Everyone's laughter overflowed the tent. Robin Hood sat enduringly by a picnic table next to the dance floor, and closely watched my every movement. I couldn't understand why he wasn't interested in the six or seven other dogs lollygagging about the party. When Willow and I finally sat down to catch our breath, he put his head on my knees. "What's wrong fella? Here let me get you some scraps to eat." I patted him and bent down to place a paper plate filled with food. "You're a good boy. Eat this." And without hesitation he complied.

Having worked up a huge thirst we decided to switch from Pepsi to Miller Lite. It was ice cold and satisfied our parched throats. Winding our way outside we met up with Running Horse and joined his horseshoe pitching team, which included Uncle Opie and Charlie. The five of us put the hurt on the other team. I did all right for an ex-city girl, which surprised even me.

Afterwards, we went over to the pig chasing and mud pin that had been set up especially for today. Children were slipping and sliding around in there to the laughter of their parents, flocking around the pin. With my back to the tent I hadn't noticed that practically everyone had moved outside from the tent. Then the PA system came on, and I turned to see what was happening. Seeing all the people, I turned to Willow, "What's going on?"

"Just wait, you'll see," and a foxy grin spread across her face.

Running Horse's voice echoed and boomed; "Now we all know it's customary for anyone new to our mountain to pick a partner and enter the pig pin. They both must catch a baby pig, individually, before we can officially declare the new person an Aliceston town member. So Alex, why don't you pick your partner, and let's get this show on the road."

Seeing I had been had I threw up my arms and said, "I wouldn't think of doing anything without my Willow Rose." The crowd roared with laughter as I held out my hand, and displayed a foxy-grin of my own this time.

"I knew you'd pick me. Let's catch ourselves a pig." With that we both took off our shoes and climbed into the slop jar of mucky mire.

"Have you got any pointers for me, since you got me into this?"

With a bewitching smile, she answered, "You might want to keep your mouth closed. Stuff flies around in here, if you get my drift."

"Would that be your drift I'm smelling, my sneaky Indian Princess?" Her broad smile confirmed the answer I already knew.

Running Horse's loud, "Sooie, sooie," sounded, and the crowd needled us into action. I followed Willow's lead and scampered after one of those baby pigs. Skidding and stumbling repeatedly, face down in the mud, to the joyous whales of laughter coming from my neighbors.

I saw Willow carrying a little pig in her arms and continued in pursuit of my own. I could hear her coaching me over the laughter of the crowd. Robin Hood's bark let me know he was pulling for me too. Wiping the mud from my eyes I cornered one in the pin, and got down on my knees blocking his escape with my fluttering arms. Determined, I lunged forward and caught the little yelling critter by his back legs, and then scouped him into my arms holding him up proudly for all to see.

You'd have thought that I had won the Indy 500 as the cheers, whistles, and applause resounded. Seeing my Princess for the first time standing there all covered in mud and straw, made me laugh so hard, I almost cried. We both just stared at one another and laughed uncontrollably. We almost strangled ourselves laughing so hard. Grams and Running Horse were patting us on our backs to help us get air, while they still continued with their own laughter.

"Whew-wee, laughter does a body good. If you young'ems don't look a sight. Think we might have to hose these two off, Thomas."

"Think you're right about that Mama." Holding his sides from laughter, he added, "Welcome to Aliceston Alex. Guess I need to give you girls a ride home in the back of my pick-up truck, so you can get cleaned up. You're smelling a bit ripe around the gills."

Never minding the dirty and smelly mess we were, the town's folks hugged and waved us good-bye, as we rode away in the back of the truck. We could see the laughter on Running Horse's face each time he glanced at us in his rear view mirror. We were indeed a spectacle. Arriving home Robin Hood jumped down, as we slid out the rear.

"See y'all later," and with that Running Horse left us in a cloud of dust.

"I suppose we really should hose down before we go inside, don't you think?" I inquired of my Willow Rose. Reaching for her hand we walked around back.

"I'm sure this is going to be cold. Do you want me to spray you down, or do you want to spray yourself?"

"It would probably be less shocking to my system if I sprayed my own self. Thanks for asking," she said while reaching for the hose.

I turned on the faucet, and the water's spray had mud dropping in clumps from her slim body. After several minutes she was pretty well cleaned up. That's when I saw that foxy grin return and light up her face. I knew then what was coming. Before I could getaway she was soaking me down, and laughing the whole time. Already wet I gave in, and let her have some fun. Then I grabbed that hose and chased her giving her back some of her own medicine. Slipping, she fell to the ground. Immediately, I released the nozzle and dropped the hose, and ran to her side thinking she was hurt. "Are you alright?"

Then reaching up with an 'I gotcha grin', she put her arms around my neck, and pulled my face to hers planting an affectionate kiss in surrender. "My little pig in a poke. Let's go inside and get in the shower," she said.

We laughed in the tub's shower from the day's celebration, while we washed each other with Grams' homemade lavender soap. Then the laughter ceased, and other emotions of a more serious nature erupted our pleasure zones.

We'd barely gotten out of the shower when Robin Hood alerted us to a knock at the front door. "I'll get it Princess." So I hastily threw on some jeans and a t-shirt and went to see whom it was.

"Didn't catch y'all at a bad time, did we?" There stood Mama Willa and Running Horse, with platters of food in their arms. "We just wanted to drop off some of this food from the party. You can freeze some of it. Willow knows how."

Willow entered. "I'll take care of it Grams. Thanks for the wonderful party today. You know I really do feel at home, and I'm looking forward to my life here."

"Yeah, me too," I piped in.

Hugs were spread around the room. I'd never had so many hugs before coming to Aliceston Mountain.

"Well then, we'll be running along. Willow, will you be staying here tonight?"

"Yes ma'am. Alex wants me to move in here with her seeing this is the place where Mama once lived. And we don't want to spend anymore time apart."

"Oh, sure honey-child. Been expecting it. We'll help you next week get your things moved over and straightened out, if you'd like. It's the way it's meant to be. Good-night baby girls." Their toothy smiles showered us with their approval.

We stood on the front steps and watched them drive over the hill. Then suddenly I picked my Princess up and carried her over the threshold inside. "This is your home now."

Willow heated up some of the leftovers for our dinner. We dined in almost complete silence, worn out from a full day of play and love. Afterwards, I washed dishes as she dried. While she finished putting away the dishes, I poured us a glass of wine and took the glasses into the living room. She joined me on the couch as the CD I had put on played romantic lyrics and soft music in the background. We shared our hopes and dreams for the future. I would write and she would paint. I'd seen some awesome artwork at her Grams' home, but never had I realized she was the artist. "Why haven't you ever told me?"

"I needed to complete my other job first. Now I can be an artist. Just like it was for you with your writing."

"Okay, now I understand, but you've done such wonderful works before, whereas I've only just begun."

"Sweet, sweet Alex, that was just me practicing. There are so many things on this mountain that I truly never saw with the eyes I look through now. It's through these eyes that I want to paint. They see the Technicolor detail, where before I only saw in monochrome. You'll see my love. Anyway we are both painters. You'll paint with your words."

"I cherish you Willow Rose. Your words are like comforting music to my heart. All melodies I've longed to hear."

The next morning we joined Mama Willa and Running Horse in the surrey and rode over to a small brown church. A cross pointing to heaven topped its steeple. It was down a dirt road I'd never traveled, not far from the house. It stood idealistically like the 'Church In The Wildwood,' my grandfather used to sing about while strumming his old mandolin. It's stain-glassed windows sparkled rainbowedly in the sun's brilliance that morning. The surrounding meadow crowned its glory. The sign out front, Bear Creek Valley Baptist Church, grabbed my attention. "Mama Willa, where'd they get the name for the church?"

"Lordy, no ones asked me that in a coon's age, child. Well, let's see now. My daddy and his brothers built this church in the early 1900's. While they were building it a big old mean black bear came right down that ridge yonder, and treed their youngest brother, Wiley. Hearing his screams and seeing his predicament they all took hold of hammers, shovels and the likes thereof, and took off to the rescue. Yelling in our native language as they ran towards that old bear, *a le wi s do di yona*. Well sir, they scared that old bear so badly he high tailed it back up the mountain, and never stopped until he reached the top. We never saw that bear no more after that. Then there's that creek right in back of the church there. Well, there you have it, Bear Creek Valley Baptist Church. Fitting don't you think?"

"Yeah, great story, but exactly what were they yelling?"

"STOP BEAR. They yelled it over and over as they chased after him."

"I remember the first time you told me that story Grams. I wouldn't play outside the church for a long time in fear of a bear coming after me," Willow added.

"That was my intention baby-girl. Kept me from having to traipse along after you," Mama Willa said, with her steely wise and caring eyes.

While her Dad tied up the wagon we ventured inside the church with Grams, and took the pew that was obviously reserved for this family. Padding the pew were pillows covered in the same green-checkered gingham material used at the café. A well-worn bible topped each pillow. There was a lot of greeting going on until Reverend Carlton walked up to the pulpit clearing his throat audibly, which signaled the beginning of the service. Sister Rachel took her place at the organ, and began the hymns with *Blessed Assurance, Jesus Is Mine*, followed by *The Sweet By And By*.

"I see the newest member of Aliceston has joined us this morning. Sister Alexandra, welcome," nodding to me with a flashing smile. "We certainly all enjoyed your initiation yesterday along with Sister Willow. Mighty fine pig catching I might add." That brought laughter from the pews. He continued on with other announcements, followed by a bible sword drill for the children occupying the first three rows, on the left hand side of the church. Sister Rachel preceded Reverend Carlton's sermon with another hymn. The familiarity I felt with these people only grew as we broke bread together. I knew there were angels within these walls. Sister Rachel had to one of them, because an iridescent glow encircled her as she sat humbly at the organ. Momentarily I closed my eyes, and thanked Jesus for leading me to this place and these people.

At the end of the service everyone visited outside after shaking the reverend's hand and thanking him for a good message. It was all so quaint in the most marvelous way...

We went back to Mama Willa's house for dinner. After a big bowl of Brunswick stew that Grams had made last evening from the leftover pig pull, Willow and I decided to walk back home through the woods to give our food a chance to digest.

Walking hand in hand through the forest home, she stopped and faced me. "Alex, I think our love will grow stronger and more beautiful over time as its roots reach deeply into the nourishing soils of this land. Look at these trees, so tall and strong. Grams says, that we are each our own tree. I see within you good fruits. Fruits that you will use to help many others. I read part of your manuscript you had sitting by the bed. I hope you don't mind. Your insightful words stirred me. You described a scene I want to paint for you."

Her words of loving praise completed a void that my heart had been seeking. She believed in me. All I could do at that moment was grab her and hang on to her, as if my life depended upon it. I drew her to me with every ounce of love within me. "I love you Willow Rose. God how I love you. You've spoken the words I've always wanted to hear. Thank you my love."

Standing in that majestic forest the two o'clock sun's rays pierced between the towering trees, and bathed us with vivid brilliance. Gazing upwards, Willow said, "See, God is blessing us Alex."

"I believe that too," and we kissed in the glow…

For the next two months our love flourished as we shared everything together. Long walks exploring nature, horseback rides, picnicking in the woods, naps by the stream, swimming and fishing on the lake, gathering herbs for our folks, and working side by side writing and painting. Domestic bliss lit up our home, and loving laughter filled its walls. Our two spirits thrived in devotion to one another.

Robin Hood adopted my Willow Rose as his second mother and shared his doggie love. And the feelings of endearment were mutual. She cooked special dishes meant just for him. Yep, she spoiled him and me too. We were in hog heaven.

Mellow yellow skies were gently leading in the changing of the season. Soon the annual onslaught of leaf peekers would invade our mountainous area. Our neighbors were setting up stands near the highway, in preparation for selling their handcrafted goods. Patchwork quilts, cornhusk dolls, sling shots, old outhouse reproductions, aprons, fine crafted furniture and toys, birdhouses, jellies and jams, and apple cider made up a few of the wares for sell. They took up about a block, on each side of Grams' café. Pumpkins surrounded the stands, like brilliant orange linoleum. Mums, the size of snow cones, decorated nearly every other table. Excitement was building in anticipation. Our little town kept mostly to itself, except for this harvest festival. The festival's popularity had grown over the years, and this year they expected about five thousand people spiraling their way around our mountain.

Many of our neighbors worked all year long making their wares for this one event. Monies made throughout this one-weekend festival kept them going until the next year. These dear people were blessed with things that no amount of money could ever buy. Surely, they are the salt of the earth. Everyone shared around here. A cornucopia of blessings and love was spread around this mountain.

Willow was helping Grams with the baking, and I ran errands with Running Horse and stocked the inventory. I had the delivery truck take a load over to our house, since we were running out of room at the café. This little Apple Dumpling Café would be jumping in a couple of days. Grams said that people would be standing in line to get in. So Running Horse and Uncle Opie built a desert booth outside for those only wanting something sweet, or maybe just something to wet their whistle. That would leave the tables inside for those ordering a full meal. I'd agreed to wait the tables with them, only after they promised not to give me a hard time if I messed up a few orders. This was going to be another whole new experience, but I was looking forward to it. Spending this time with my family felt nothing but good.

Mama Willa told us to go home about six that evening, and to take tomorrow off to get rested up for the demands our customers would be putting on us. We tried to get her to go home and let us stay and work, but she'd have none of that. And as Willow had taught me, you can't out stubborn Mama Willa. Everyone on this mountain knows that. When she makes up her mind about something, you'd have an easier time draining the ocean with a Dixie paper cup, than changing her mind. Best to learn that lesson right up front to save yourself some time, and a whole bunch of grief.

On the way out we ran into Sister Rachel. She was unloading baskets of doll clothes she had meticulously made in various sizes, along with mason jars filled with a variety of concoctions to sale at the festival, from her green Volvo's trunk and backseat. We helped her get her things to her stand, and she rewarded us with a quart-size jar of her prized homemade apple butter, which she was notorious for in these hills. It was so good that even Mama Willa gave up making it, and traded her free café meals in return for keeping the café stocked. Grams always said, "If you can't beat'em, join'em."

The days were getting shorter. As we rounded the evergreen curve down to the house, the moon was rising and putting the sky gently to sleep. Darkness began to cloak our haven. "Something's odd," I said. "Where's Robin Hood? It's so not like him not to meet us at the top of the hill. Something's not right." Parking the truck in haste I jumped out of to call him. "Robin, here fella. Where are you?"

Willow joined me, and we circled the house calling his name repeatedly. She saw the look of concern that consumed my face as I continued yelling for him.

"Try not to worry, we'll find him," she said, while trying to comfort me. "I'll call Dad on his cell phone. He can find anyone." She got on the phone to him right away. "Dad, we need your help. Robin Hood isn't coming when we call him. We're awfully worried. Okay Dad, thanks. He's on his way Alex. Come on and let's sit on the porch and wait."

"You sit love, please. I'm too uptight to sit still right now." Rubbing my chin briskly in my fret and walking in circles, I began to scream frantically. "Robin Hood, come on boy."

Her Dad must have flown from the cafe. We heard his truck and when he rounded the evergreens he was being followed by several more trucks and cars. I ran to meet him. "Running Horse, something has to be wrong! He's always here to meet me. You know that." A dozen or more of our neighbors gathered around, while Running Horse gave out the plan of the search. He had those without flashlights fetch a knotty pine torch from the barn, to light their way through the woods.

"I'm going with you Running Horse," and ran to grab my flashlight from my truck. "Princess, I'm going with your Dad. Stay here in case our little fella gets back. Call me if he does."

She stroked my cheek tenderly, as she had done the first day that I'd met her. "Don't worry Alex, Dad will find him."

"I know. I just hope he's okay when we find him." I ran to catch up with the hunting party scanning out in different directions. Running Horse waited on me at the edge of the woods flagging his torch to show me the way. I followed along behind him and observed his every move. He'd bend to pick up Robin's tracks, and then stand again to proceed. He'd touch a broken twig or low laying branch, and look up at me while lighting his find for me to see. Then nodding me on, we'd walk silently while he tracked in deep thought. Out of respect and not wanting to distract him, I kept my anxiety to myself. Tracking for almost an hour now, we were beginning to see a set of much larger tracks appear on the trail. Running Horse sensed my fear.

"Looks like he's being chased by another preying cat. See how the tracks are getting spread apart? He's running and the cat is in pursuit." He saw the tears coming down my face and continued in earnest pursuit.

"Crazy dog, what's he out here messing with an old cat for?" Wiping my eyes on my shirtsleeve, I continued close behind him.

"It's his nature Alex. Earlier this evening that cat was out by the barn, and Robin Hood's trying to protect your home. This time he's messing with something that's meaner than he is, but plott hounds are ferocious animals. If anything can overcome mean, it's his love for you."

We came to an area several yards ahead, and our lights revealed blood and fur. "They got into it here Alex. Judging from the cat's fur spread about, I'd say Robin Hood tore into him.

"Then he's alright, isn't he? He whipped up on that old cat, didn't he?"

"To be honest with you Alex, there are two types of blood here. But don't let that scare you. I'd predict Robin Hood put the fear of God in that cat."

"How big do you think the cat is?" I feared his answer, but I had to know.

"Paws these size indicate about a hundred pounds. I've heard of plott hounds tackling something twice their size or more, so Robin Hood should hold his own. Look, the tracks are moving in two different directions now. Stay close, we're going to go after your boy, but that wounded cat might turn back this way. We don't want him sneaking back around us."

I picked up the biggest stick I could find lying on the ground. I was determined to bash that cat's head in if he did come back. Knowing that I was safe with Running Horse, my brave cells took over and heightened my courage level. I held the stick firmly in my right hand, my knuckles whitening for battle.

"Shhh, listen," touching my shoulder gently and pointing. I was stilled and my ears perked to hear a whimpering coming from the direction he was pointing.

"That's him, it has to be. He's hurt." We stepped lively in the sound's direction. We were close. I called out to Robin Hood, while tears trickled down my cheeks. Then a bark of recognition. "Oh that's him. Where is he?" I followed Running Horse as he went speedily up ahead and crouched down on his knees. Removing some brush from the side of the hill with his hands, he feverishly tore at some nailed together planks across the entrance to an old coalmine.

Shining his torch inside, he turned to me, "He's in there. Looks like he's hurt pretty bad. Hold this, and I'll crawl in and get him."

Shining my flashlight and the torch so he could see his way, I saw my mangled boy panting and lying in blood. "It's going to be okay fella. We're going home and we'll get you fixed right up as good as new." I prayed I was right.

Crawling back out with my fella, Running Horse's face depicted the severity of my boy's wounds. My dog's eyes though matted with blood, took hold of my face with the love he gave me so unconditionally. Those remarkable canine eyes that had come to mean so much to me. I lit the way back to the house as blood continued to drip along the path, while he was carried in the hardy arms of Running Horse.

Grams met us at the clearing with the pickup truck. We placed him carefully in the back on some hay and drove him to the barn, while I cradled his head in my lap. Willow had kettles heating over a large fire burning at the entrance to the barn, where her Dad slept most nights. Standing beside her were Uncle Opie and Charlie. The others had recently gone home, when Mama Willa instructed Willow to call them back in from the search. Don't ask me how she did it, but she had had a vision that we had found Robin Hood. It was that vision that spurred her to get things set up, with Willow's assistance to take care of our patient. As he was lifted from my lap and carried into the barn, I was only inches behind.

My sweet Willow Rose stopped me at the door and brought her loving arms around me, along with these words. "I want you to come and sit by the fire with me. Grams and Dad need space now to take care of Robin Hood. You must trust them to do this. They have the ways of our ancestors to guide them in the healing. I wouldn't tell you this if it were not so." Her compassionate touch added to the confirmation of her words.

Without speaking, Uncle Opie came out of the barn, gave us a respectful nod, and with gloved hands took one of the boiling kettles back into the barn. I stared intently into the fire as I listened to the chanting coming from within the barn.

Willow clued me in about what was happening. "They are having a ceremony of purification for our boy, my dear Alex. It will cleanse his body."

"But what's that I smell?"

"That is a part of the ceremony. We call it smudging. You smell the sage burning. The smoke is releasing energy and carrying any impurities away. Everyone in there is receiving a spiritual cleansing. This will promote healing. You'll see my love. He's in the best of care."

Although I believed her words, my mind could not erase the gashes that had expelled so much blood. Some of which now soaked my shirt and pants and covered my hands. Almost like she'd read my thoughts, she pulled me from the glum of it.

"Let's get you cleaned up. Please come to the house with me. I promise he'll be fine. Please Alex."

Looking into her soft eyes I stood up, "Okay. Sorry I'm so bummed out."

"I'd expect nothing less from you. You have every reason to be. Just let me take care of you, while they take care of him." After getting me into the tub she'd nearly filled to the brim with warm water and some relaxing bath salts, she gathered my blood stained clothes, kissed me and went downstairs, leaving me to my thoughts.

I slid my head beneath the water and held my breath to rinse my hair. Opening my eyes and looking up through the water I saw someone in the room with me. Startled, I sprang up out of the water like a bottle rocket. There was no one there. I pulled the shower curtain close up to me as I continued to inspect the room. Had my grief brought on illusions?

A couple of minutes later, Willow Rose came into the room bringing me a glass of wine. "What's wrong Al? You look like you've seen a ghost."

I looked at her and asked, "Were you in here a minute or so ago?"

"Not since I took your clothes downstairs. Why?"

"Don't think I'm crazy but I was rinsing my hair under water, and while still submerged I thought I saw someone else in the room with me. But when I came up there was no one in here. It totally freaked me."

"Whom did they look like?"

I thought back for a moment. "Gees, I didn't get that good of a look since I was underneath the water. It didn't look like you, or I wouldn't have gotten freaked out. Kinda like a man, I think."

"We should tell Dad about it."

"No, please don't do that Willow Rose. I was probably just seeing a shadow or something. I don't want him thinking I've gone nuts."

"Dad or even Grams would never think that of you. Sometimes these are signs, but if you don't want me to tell, I won't. Try to relax. Here drink your wine. You want me to stay up here with you?"

"What and protect me from the bogey man?"

"I just want you to know that I take what you tell me seriously my love."

"I'm sorry. I know you do. It's just that I've never had anyone that has cared so much about me, the way you do. You're a gift from above my love."

When I came downstairs she had prepared me a sandwich with a glass of milk. Sitting at the table we shared childhood memories, as I tried to get a few bites of the sandwich in me. Unexpectantly the subject of my Mother was questioned. "I've never heard you talk about your Mother that much. What does she do?" Willow innocently asked me.

Biting my lips first in hesitancy, I then replied, "She died when I was twelve years old."

"Ohh, I'm sorry. I shouldn't have brought it up."

"No, that's perfectly fine. You need to know. It's a part of who I am. Are you sure you want to hear all this?"

"If it wouldn't be unsettling for you."

"I just never talk about it much. I've pretty much buried the thoughts."

"Buried feelings have a way of staying alive, and we can't heal, or move forward with our lives until we confront them. I can tell by your eyes that this isn't going to be a happy story." Her genuine look of concern consoled my apprehension.

"You're right, it isn't a happy story. Nonetheless, it would probably do me good to break free of the chains that those haunting remembrances have wrapped around my heart. I want to be able to give my complete heart to you, without those chains holding pieces of my heart captive. Time for those memories to come out and face the hurt they've created for most of my life."

Grabbing her hand I continued, "I've never told this story to anyone." I took a giant sigh. "Okay then, here goes. My Mom moved out and left my Dad a couple of years before she died. I'll go back before they got married to give you a better understanding of my Mom. Her parents had been farmers deep in the country, up around Rocky Mount. Her Mother had made her drop out of school in the eighth grade. There were nine other younger brothers and sisters. Since she was the oldest, she was given the responsibility of caring for all of them on the farm. They were very poor. Hand to mouth most times with so many children to feed. Anyway, she never got to have much of a childhood. Mom went through a lot of hardships growing up so impoverished. Heck, she even had her baby brother die in her arms. She had tried to save him after the other kids ran and told her he was in trouble down at the fishing pond. Poor Mom, she never forgave herself for not getting there in time.

Finally years later, when she was able to break away, she went to work at Burlington Industries in Burlington, at the age of eighteen. That's where Dad met her. So you see she grew up hard and married young. After two children and ten years of marriage, she got antsy and wanted to kick up her heels. I suppose her deprived childhood had a great deal to do with that. Anyway she got party fever. Dad was very conservative and partying down wasn't his style. He took his obligations far more seriously than Mom. It wasn't that she didn't love Bonnie and me. I think Mom just tried to thread the needle of her life with wet spaghetti. She didn't know any better. I'm not trying to make excuses for what she did, but I can't be mad at her either. I loved her way too much.

My memory of the day she left is so vivid up to a certain point, like it was yesterday, you know? I had my skinny little girl arms woven tightly around her legs, as I lay in the floor begging her not to go. But even my tear soaked face, and agonizing Mommie pleas wouldn't stop her. That's where I draw a blank. I guess I've mentally blocked out her actually walking out the door and driving away. However, when she walked out that door she took pieces of my heart with her, without realizing it. In my young mind I always believed she was coming back. Bonnie and I stayed with Dad. We'd spend a weekend each month with her. I cherished those visits.

Two years later, Dad came in our bedroom one morning to wake us up for school as usual, but as we got up from our beds, he asked us to sit back down. "You don't have to go to school today," he said. Immediately I ran to the window thinking it had snowed, and school had been cancelled. But there was no snow. Turning back and looking into his face, I saw a tear roll down his cheek. I know he didn't know how to tell us, but his words, "Your Mother died last night," tore a hole in my heart the size of a football field. They play over and over again in my head to this very day."

My sweet Willow Rose put her arms around me and held me, as I sobbed like I was twelve years old again. Holding me tight to her chest, she cried along with me. Swallowing my tears, I went on. "They said that Mom killed herself with a gun, but I've never believed that story. I've always believed that sorry low-down son of a bitch, she was dating murdered her."

Gasping slightly, Willow requested, "Why's that love?"

"Well, Mom was left-handed and she was shot in the right temple. Makes no sense. No one would take a gun like this, and stretch it around like this, I said animating the awkwardness of the movements. She lived in a duplex, and the neighbors next door heard a loud noise, like a firecracker. Then several seconds' later tires squealing out of the driveway. That had to be the gunshot they heard. You know, she was coming to pick me up for the weekend in two days. Of course that never happened. Consequently, I retreated inside myself so deep. No one knew that. I covered it like an Academy Award winning actress. All this resulted in me putting a protective barrier around my heart. I never wanted to let anyone mean that much to me again, thinking that would shield me from abandonment, rejection and heartbreak. What I didn't realize at the time was that barrier would also keep all that hurt chained to my heart, and cripple future relationships. I don't want anything to happen to us my beloved."

"My precious Alex, through your own words you have unraveled those chains, and they are vanishing into the night, never to return. The only good those chains ever did for you was to keep your heart for me. In a way, I suppose I should thank them, but I'm sorry you've endured so many years of pain. It's all gone now. Let me protect your heart with velvet heartstrings. I promise you, you'll never have to worry about me going anywhere without you." She rocked me back and forth in her sweet arms, and I felt my enormous burden lifted.

Suddenly, the front door sprang open, and we both jumped. Uncle Opie burst in. "Got a little fella out in the barn trying to git up and come see about his mama. Thought I'd better come and fetch ya."

"Oh, thank God. He's doing alright then, right?"

"Right as rain. Tweren't nearly as bad as it looked. Com'on, git a move on it."

We ran to the barn, hand in hand, with Uncle Opie hauling us. Standing there all bandaged up on the end of a leash with Mama Willa on the other end was my tail-wagging friend. Dropping to my knees I received his wet kisses with a new appreciation. "Is he going to be alright Grams?"

"That's a tough hound dog you got there. He'll be sore for a few days, but that old cat probably got the worse end of that battle. He's lost a lot of blood, but we got to him in good time."

I hugged Grams, Running Horse, Uncle Opie and Charlie with the utmost respect and thankfulness I could muster up.

CHAPTER 18

▼

Saturday Robin Hood was feeling well enough to tag along with us to the festival. He stayed concealed on a loop rug; Grams had made for him and placed behind the back door, inside the kitchen of the cafe. That way if the food inspector decided to pay the café a visit he could make a swift exodus outside. My dog was the main topic of conversation among the townsfolk. They were calling him a hero, and I beamed with pride as though he were my son. Of course, everyone was still concerned about that wounded cat that might be lurking about the mountain, and the men folk talked about setting some traps.

By ten o'clock that morning the whole mountain was flocking with people. We were up to our eyeballs with hungry people inside the café. Grams had been totally correct about the leaf peekers being some demanding folks. They growled as loud as their stomachs, and we obliged them with whatever their hungry hearts desired.

"Good glory bees, they're coming out of the woodwork. Land sakes, I believe we're gonna set a record this year. How you children doing?"

Willow spoke up, "We're fine Grams. Alex is acting like a pro at this. You should see her in action out there."

"Gee, thanks, Princess."

Yes siree, nature sure was putting on a fetching show this year. The trees were the stage and we were the audience. Smokeless flames of red, yellow and orange covered these mountains, sipping in the blue Carolina sky. Today the Apple Dumpling Café became the Garden Of Eat'em on this majestic mountain. Our town was like a cathedral of nature that everyone wanted to visit. And to think that I was a part of all this. Grams says nature is the mirror that reflects God. Her glowing understanding of life was inspirational to those lucky enough to be a part of her peaceful journey.

The day moved along at a hectic pace. We had been practicing for several days using the colloquial hillbilly language, the leaf peekers expected from us, and we were performing well. My Willow Rose looked darling in her overalls, with her hair in pigtails tied with gingham ribbons. Grams homemade biscuits slathered in chocolate gravy were in high demand. She heaped generous portions on their plates, and customers left the café smiling and holding their bellies that swell with satisfaction. We were working hard, but having fun at the same time.

Uncle Opie meandered through ever so often picking his banjo, and mouthing his harmonica to some down home bluegrass tunes. He was good at it too. We had become great friends. He never missed an opportunity to pick on me, and today would be no different. He had taped a sign on my back, unbeknown to me, that said, *Will Dance for a Quarter.* I wondered why people were throwing quarters at me. I just figured it was some mountain custom, until a little boy told me about the sign on my back. Reaching back awkwardly I managed to snag it. Immediately, I darted my eyes across the room to the grinning face of Uncle Opie. He shrugged his narrow shoulders comically and continued with his music.

"All in good clean fun my sweet," Willow said, as she passed me carrying a tray load of hot plates filled with Grams' signature chicken and dumplings.

"How long have I been walking around with that on my back?"

"At least a couple of hours."

"Why didn't you tell me?"

"And spoil Uncle Opie's fun? Besides, I don't think you would have told me. Now would you?"

She had me there. The bells jingled on the front door as customers came and went. About an hour later, I couldn't believe my eyes when in walked Abby with her sister, Gwen, and brother, Nate. Another girl I didn't know accompanied them. Abby's eyes met mine with cold animosity, almost like she knew I was inside the café. They stood there waiting for a table to clear, and I could feel her frosty stare following me. As I passed Willow, I whispered, "Come to the back with me, fast."

"What in the world? Your face is stark white. Are you okay? Grams, something's wrong with Alex."

Grams dropped her spatula and was at my side with Willow. "Dear Lord child, the blood has done drained right outta your face."

"Abby is out there with some others. I don't know how she knew I was here. I just know she's going to create a bad scene."

"That'd be the pugnacious old girlfriend."

"You're being too kind Grams. She's a total bitch. Forgive my language."

"I understand dear. I've used that word a couple of times myself. Here, you and Willow take a break. I'll get Thomas and Uncle Opie to fill in for you until they leave. Trust me, they won't be creating any stink with us."

"I'll go out there and tell her she's not welcome here," Willow said.

"No baby girl. That's what she wants us to do. It would only give her an opportunity to stir her anger a little more. Let us take care of this gal. Go on out back and walk around the festival."

"I have got to see this Abby," Willow said.

"Let me walk out with you," Grams said, walking with her arm around Willow to check things out in the front.

"Watch out she's got a toiletic mouth," I said as they left the kitchen.

"Maybe her toilet needs flushing," Willow responded over her shoulder with a twinkle in her eyes.

Gnawing fears welled up in me. How did she find me? This couldn't just be a happenstance. She wouldn't say anything out of the way to my family, would she? If she did, I'd have to confront her. Please Lord; make Abby keep her mealy mouth shut. I hadn't told Willow about the bar incident at Frannie's memorial party. I wanted to guard her from that part of my past. Now I was wishing I had told her.

Walking back in, Willow took my hand. "She'd be a pretty girl if she wasn't leaking so much hate from her pores. She wears her hate like a cape. You know what the bible says, anger is in the bosom of fools. What a shame. Let's get outta here."

As we were leaving I petted my fella and told him, "Stay Robin Hood. You don't need to be overdoing it today. Lay back down boy. We won't be long."

The evening air was cool and felt good. The crowds were thinning as the sun was about ready to call it a day. "Willow Rose, I haven't told you everything about Abby. Now I realize I should have, and I'm sorry that I didn't. I wanted to protect you. I never in a million years thought she'd show up here in Aliceston."

"I already know what you're going to say my love. BeBe accidentally let it slip the last time she was here, while you were upstairs taking a bath. She thought you had already told me. It's all right. I probably would have done the same thing. Funny how sometimes our good intentions mock us."

"Isn't that the truth?"

"However Alex, I'm concerned about Abby. A rational person wouldn't be so blatantly persistent. To show up here is extremely bold. I'm afraid we haven't seen the last of her."

"I'm so sorry Princess. I wouldn't have allowed this to ever happen."

"It's not your fault. Let's get a glass of Charlie's hard cider. He brews the best."

After washing down the cider, as we rounded the festival, we headed back to see if the coast was clear. Bad timing. Dead ahead coming straight at us was Abby and her entourage.

"Oh shit. Here she comes."

Running Horse was close behind them. "Alex, we need your help inside," he said trying to give us an excuse to avoid confrontation.

"We're on our way." We made our way hastily past their stinging haughty expressions, and Abby's paltry comments followed on our heels.

"So you've gone country. Guess that's the little bumpkin you wallow around in the mud with. Just to let you know you can run, but you can't hide. Mountain trash."

I stopped dead in my tracks.

"Let it be Al. Her words mean nothing to me," Willow appealed to my heated grimace.

"I can't Willow Rose." Turning and walking towards Abby, while Running Horse followed me, I protested Abby's nasty mud slinging, "You can say whatever you want to about me, but don't you dare speak that way about my Willow Rose. She's everything you're not or could ever be. Go home and leave us alone. You don't belong here."

"You can say that again. There's no hillbilly blood in me. You've gone to the pigs Alex."

Lord knows, I wanted to open fire on her, but instead I chose the high road and added calmly, "Then it's the best place I've ever been. I have nothing further to say to you." As I turned to walk away she sputtered more venom.

"See you got yourself an Injun body guard. What's his name? Geronimo?" Her co-conspirators laughed in favor of her cheap audacity.

I was preparing to turn around again to defend Running Horse's honor, when he reached for my arm considerately. "Let her have the last say Alex. She'd be best keeping her words tender and sweet, in case she should ever have to eat them one day."

"That's right Alex, run away," her words bounced behind us, and her icy laughter taunted me.

Entering the café, Mama Willa put her warm fleshy arms about me. "There, there, sweet child. Pay no never mind to that vicious girl. I do believe she has grits for brains, and maybe a couple of scrambled eggs thrown in to fill in the gaps."

"There you go being too nice again, Grams. She has something that rhymes with grits for brains. I'm so sorry you guys had to get caught up in this mess."

"That's what family is for Alexandra. Isn't that right Thomas?"

"Yes ma'am. You did yourself proud out there Alex. I know it took far more courage not to let go on her, than it would have to verbally attack her. You displayed great strength of character." He patted my back lovingly.

"Thanks all of you for sticking by me. What did I ever see in her, sure beats the you know what out of me."

"Sometimes you have to have a bad love before you can appreciate a good love," Grams said.

"You make a good point Grams." Hugging Willow closely to me to display my understanding, "I know I have the perfect love now, and I'm going to cherish her for all my days."

That night when Willow and I got home we threw a movie in the DVD and cuddled up on the couch. After the movie I made us some cherry milkshakes and took them out on the porch.

My Princess sounded from inside the house, "I'll be right out. I need to get something."

"Need any help," I asked, as I sat in the swing slurping my shake.

"No, I can handle it." Seconds later she came out the door carrying a large picture frame, turned opposite my direction. "I was going to save this for Christmas, but after the kind of week you've had I want to give it to you now. Hopefully it'll cheer you up."

"Oh sweetheart, you cheer me up just by being with me."

"I painted this especially for you. It's what I envisioned when I read part of your book that day. Remember when I told you I wanted to paint it for you?"

"Sure Princess, I remember."

Turning the painting around slowly, her gaze was fixed on my expression, eager to see my reaction. I was astounded. Her brush expressed the gentleness of her soul, and the visions she possessed. The canvas pulled me into it instantly, and absorbed me speechless in its dimensional qualities. I could hear the music of the rustling leaves on the magnificently defined trees, and feel the connectedness this brilliant painting achieved. The detail was captivating. "It's the most beautiful painting I've ever laid eyes on. It's the forest of life isn't it?"

"Yes precious, it's what your words fabricated in my mind. Did I get it right? Is it what you envisioned?" Her black eyes welled with tears.

"Oh, Princess, it's perfect. It's that and so much more. It touches my heart. Gracious, you're more talented than I perceived possible. If I could write one-tenth as well as you paint, I'd be blessed."

"This is your writing Alex, only mixed with a little paint stirred by my devotion. It's what we can do together."

"You make everything we do together beautiful. It goes right over the mantle. In fact, I'm going to put it up right this minute. Just give me time to run out to the barn and get the ladder. Be right back. Oh, but first let's put this down. There we go." Then I reached for her and kissed her with the overflowing love, pumping from the fountain of my heart. "Willow Rose, you stir up a dust storm of emotions in me woman. I'll share them with you tonight."

"That's a promise I'm going to hold you to. Now run on to the barn and hurry back," she said.

"Okay love. Keep Robin Hood in the house so he doesn't hurt himself chasing along after me. I'll just be a minute." I could hear my boy barking from the house in frustration as I headed off. Playfully I skipped all the way to the barn. I swung open the barn door and went to the sidewall to retrieve the stepladder. As I stretched to release it from its perch, I whistled with happiness. Suddenly the overhead light went out startling me. Gees, what a time for the light to burn out, I thought. The barn door was still open, and the lights from the outside filtered in enough for me to see how to make my way towards the door, while carrying the ladder in both hands.

"Stop right there Alex!" Sharp words seemingly came out of nowhere.

Their punching effect shocked me, and I immediately dropped the ladder. "Who's there?" I asked with a demanding voice.

"Turn around and put your hands behind your back," the intruder snarled back at me. "That is unless you want to do this the hard way." I didn't recognize the husky sounding voice.

"Just tell me who you are and what you want."

"If you don't want that little slut of yours up in the house to get hurt, you'd better do as you're told."

That voice sounded familiar. "Abby, is that you?" Two silhouettes moved towards me in slow motion, moments before someone grabbed me with brute force from behind. Arms around my neck choking me as I fought violently trying to break free. Then something was placed over my head. The odor it exuded burned my throat. I couldn't breath. I was suffocating and thought they were killing me. Is this how it ends Lord?

CHAPTER 19

▼

"Robin Hood, what do you think is taking your mama so long out there in the barn?" Willow said, making her way to the front porch. "That's strange, there's no light on in the barn. Alex dear, where are you?" Robin Hood was desperately trying to get out of the screen door that Willow leaned against. "No boy, you've got to stay inside. Alex, Alex," she yelled out into the darkness. "I don't like the feeling I'm getting boy. Get back and let me in. Is that why you were barking so much?" Hurriedly, she dialed her Dad's number. "Papa, please come now! It's Alex; she went down to the barn about five minutes ago and hasn't returned! There's no lights on out there, and she doesn't answer when I call her!"

Hearing the fear in her voice and realizing that she hadn't called him Papa since she was eight years old, he knew she was frantic and scared. "Stay inside and lock the door. We'll be there in two minutes. Stay on the phone with Sister Rachel until we get there." Sister Rachel tried her best to calm Willow and together they said a short prayer.

Before they could say, "Amen," the yard was covered with the town folks of Aliceston Mountain, and droves more were pouring around the bend. Their headlights illuminated the barn as they came to park near the house. Willow bounded through the door and raced to Mama Willa's side.

"Oh Grams, I'm so afraid. I know something terrible is going on. I can just feel it." Her voice trembled.

Grams held her granddaughter and fought back the tears that wanted to wash from her own eyes. "Com'on back inside with me, and let the men folks check things out." Women and children piled in behind them into the house. Robin Hood managed to limp through the crowd out the door and shot straight for the barn, as fast as his still painful body would carry him. While inside the house a prayer circle was formed sending their prayers to God for Alex's safety.

Running Horse pushed on the light switch in the barn with his cell phone, and the light immediately came right on. Looking around he could smell something in the air that didn't fit in with the normal barn smells. Robin Hood's nose was planted into the barn's floor moving around like a metal detector. His bugle bark alerted the posse to his find. "What have you got there boy?" Running Horse picked up a pungent smelling rag with his hunting knife. The scent on the rag had Robin Hood coughing, rubbing his nose on the barn floor and rolling around unruly on the scattered hay. The gathering of men stood around in a semi-circle and watched as Running Horse and Uncle Opie investigated the find. "Appears a struggle took place here," he said glancing around the barn. "I'd say there were about four or five people involved and Alex was one of them."

"Whatcha make of this here rag? Smells like ammony to me," Uncle Opie said with a dismal face.

"I'd say you're likely right about that. They probably surprised her and put that rag doused with ammonia to her face to subdue her. Don't anyone touch that barn light switch. It may have some fingerprints on it." Standing back up he studied the area. "Looks like she lost consciousness here, and they started dragging her. Here someone picks her up. We'd better call the county sheriff's office. We don't want to mess up any evidence."

"But Running Horse, you know we can do ah better job at finding her than theys can. Sides, that's wasting portant time," Uncle Opie chewed out sternly.

All the other men raised their voices in agreement with Uncle Opie.

"I know, I know, and I agree with you too. We have to go by the law, but that doesn't mean we can't continue with our own search once we've told them. For now let's try not to frighten Willow or Mama anymore than is necessary."

"Yer reckon they'll be calling in the feds?" Uncle Opie asked.

"Likely so, since we have a kidnapping. Charlie go on up to the house and call the sheriff's office. Opie and I are going to put Robin Hood on the trail and see what he can pick up. The rest of you wait on the sheriff to arrive. I've got my phone with me so we can stay in contact. If Mama or Willow asks, tell them we're going to find her. Just keep praying. We're most likely going to need a miracle, but don't tell them that."

A voice from the barn door broke through the tense conversation. "I'm going with you Dad. I've heard everything that has been said. Don't try stopping me." Willow's determination was written across her face.

Putting his arm around her he said, "Okay everybody has a job to do. Let's get moving."

Robin Hood bellowed and led the three into the dark towering forest, never once letting his still injured body deter his search for Alex. Uncle Opie kept his magnum flashlight on Robin's every move, and they marched through the woods at a rapid pace. They all came to a stop at the old logging road about a half-mile up ahead. While Robin Hood ran his nose through the dirt staying on the scent, Running Horse surveyed the tracks imprinted in the dust with his lantern.

"They had a vehicle stashed here. There's four sets of footprints all going to the back of the car. It's either a very heavy car or a van of some type. See how the footprints leave the back. Three sets go to the front passenger side and one set to the driver's side. These here at the driver's door look like a man's footprints. Wearing much larger shoes than the others. Some kind of an athletic shoe. Look at the markings. I don't think Alex got in up there. I think she was put in the back. Let's put a circle of rocks around this area to protect it for the sheriff." Turning to comfort his daughter. "Are you sure you're all right baby-girl?"

"I'll never be all right again until we find Alex and the no good thugs that did this. Dad, it's those people from the café today, isn't it? I just know it has to be. We should have protected Alex better from them."

"You're right baby-girl, we should have. We just thought the poor two-timing ex-girlfriend was having a hissie fit. We should have taken her far more seriously. She's consumed with vengeance. I should have seen that today."

"Dad, Alex asked me not to tell you, but after all this I have too. The other night while you were helping Grams patch up Robin Hood, a curious thing occurred. Alex said that she was rinsing her hair under water in the bathtub and thought she saw someone in the room with her, as she looked up through the water. I asked her whom she thought it looked like, and she said a man. Do you think it could have been that brother of Abby's?"

"So," rubbing his hand over his jaw, "They've been scheming this. I think the story is coming together a little more clearly now. I'll see if these prints match up with any around the windows about the house, come first light. We should get back to the house and start planning."

"Dad, she'll be okay when we find her, won't she?" Her face pleading for his assurance.

Uncle Opie looked down to the ground and kicked at the dirt in apprehension, while listening for Running Horse's reply. Even Robin Hood's ears perked for an answer.

"The good Lord is on our side. You've got sixty or more people up to the house praying for her. You know He listens. Remember, if two or more pray in agreement for something, the Lord will hear and answer their prayers. We'll bring her home baby-girl." The foursome hiked solemnly back to the house. Entering the edge of the forest they could see several police cars with their blue lights lighting up the night in all directions.

A spotlight was swiftly focused on them. A loud speaker blared, "Stop right there, and put your hands up in the air where we can see them."

"Do as they say. They don't know who we are," Running Horse commanded. So all three raised their arms over their heads in compliance.

"Sheriff that be my son Thomas and grand-daughter, along with Uncle Opie coming back from their search. Put those guns down and let my kin comes on to the house for gracious sakes!"

"Okay men drop your guns, you heard the lady. Sorry ma'am but we can't be taking any chances. This is a serious matter."

"And I agree with you sheriff, but I can't have you taking aim at my innocent family. They're suffering enough already."

The sheriff nodded and said, "I understand Ms. Sykes."

"Call me Mama Willa. Everyone in these parts does. We'll round you and your deputies up some strong coffee to get you through the night."

"Thanks Ma'am."

Willow went to the comfort of her Grams, while Running Horse and Uncle Opie spoke at length with the sheriff and his men, sharing their findings and suspicions. The sheriff had already sent the rag into Doc Perry's office for identification of the compounds it had been doused with, and to see if it contained any usable fingerprints. He expected a report back by daylight. Mama Willa had told the sheriff about Abby and the events that took place earlier in the day. At the sheriff's request she'd found Alexandra's address book lying on a shelf in the kitchen, next to the old yellow wall phone. Before she turned it over to him she had jotted down several numbers and addresses that she figured might be useful to her family. She knew the family would be conducting its own search, no matter what any lawmen said to the contrary.

"Baby-girl I tried calling BeBe earlier but got no answer, not even on her cell phone. I think we should tell her what's happened."

"Yes Grams, we should. BeBe won't be back home until tomorrow. I think her plane gets back from Boston around noon. She's been out on a cruise with some tickets Alex gave her." Grams eyed her curiously and Willow explained.

"Alex had bought some tickets for her and Abby to celebrate their fifth anniversary, but you know what happened there. She didn't want to take me because she said that would be like I came in second place. I know that sounds crazy, but it's one more thing that endears her so to me. She cares so much about my feelings. I don't know what I'll do if we can't find her. Oh Grams." Willow sobbed uncontrollably now in her dear Grams' arms.

"Let it out sweet girl. Get it all out so we can get along with finding Alexandra."

At first light Running Horse and Uncle Opie circled the house looking for footprints. Out behind some bushes in back of the house, not seen from the driveway or the barns, they found the same athletic shoe prints from the old logging road last night. Uncle Opie tried the window and sure enough it opened right up with ease. "I'd say he came in this way." They both looked at each other and sighed while stretching their necks from side to side. The tension of all this had their muscles in knocks.

They didn't waste time sharing this bit of important information with Sheriff Terrell. As they stood there talking, a black sedan approached and stopped short of running them down. Popping out of the car were two young eager beavers with their hair slicked back, and their sun-glassed faces gazing austerely about the full scope of the farm. Large bold white letters on the backs of their black jackets immediately revealed their identities, FBI.

Flashing their badges one of them announced, "I'm Agent Pruitt and this is Agent Jones," extending his hand to Sheriff Terrell, while glancing over in Running Horse's direction and giving a dubious nod. "Have any reporters been here yet?"

"No, we've tried to keep this quite until you guys got here."

"Good job sheriff."

Then as if on cue two news media vans rounded the bend, stirring up dust as the sun dried the morning dew. Agent Pruitt must have been the senior agent, as he never let Agent Jones talk very much. "Speak of the devils, and here they come. Sheriff why don't you handle them for us while I speak to the family. Tell them the family has no comment at this time."

Inside of the house Mama Willa spotted the going ons outside, from the kitchen window over the sink. She gingerly placed her hands on Willow's shoulders slumped over the kitchen table. "Wake up child. I think the FBI and the news reporters are outside."

"What, have they found her?" she sat up hoping for good news while rubbing the restless sleep from her eyes.

"No baby-girl, but your Paw did find tracks around that window out back of the small bedroom."

"So Alex did see a man in the bathroom with her while she was bathing. What a creepy son of a bitch. He was in the house with us. Grams, I'd like to whale the ever loving life out of him."

"Now remember you're a Christian child."

"I know Grams, but they're picking on the wrong family now. If Robin Hood had been in the house he'd tore him a new butt hole. Puts a whole new meaning to going on the warpath. Now I understand its provocation."

Grams patted Willow's knees while she watched the red vanish from her angered granddaughter's face. "I had me a vision right over there in the kitchen this morning. I saw Alexandra lying in a bed in an old run down vacant building. I could see her chest moving up and down. Some skinny young girl, like the one tagging along with Abby yesterday was smoking a cigarette while standing in the doorway looking outside. Rusty old cars piled the hillside, and I could see what looked like a water tower with writing, but I couldn't make it out what it read. I saw the letters y and n. The other letters were faded so I couldn't make'em out. That was the final thing before my vision disappeared. So you see baby-girl she's alive. We've got a vision to point us the way."

"There's a lot of holes in it Grams."

"Wells then we be piecing them holes together. Now go and get your Paw and let's get started."

Willow dashed out bare-footed into the chilly autumn grass and raced for her Dad. Reporters took note and began herding in her direction as she caught up to her Dad.

"Are you Willow? Have you heard from the kidnappers? Have you found any blood? Do you think she's still alive?" Their questions were agonizing and Running Horse shielded his daughter with his jacket and led her away back to the house, leaving the sheriff and FBI to deal with the hungry for a story jackals.

All of the women and children except for Sister Rachel had gone to mind the festival and be on stand-by. She was busy making breakfast for the family that now sat at the kitchen table along with Uncle Opie.

"Dad, I'm going to get a flip chart in here so that we can diagram the evidence we've gathered so far. Then we can go from there. Grams, tell them about your vision while I go over to your house to pick up the flip chart."

"You'll not be going anywhere alone young lady. Uncle Opie and Robin Hood will go with you," her Dad insisted.

"Oh Dad, I'll be all right."

"I'm sure that's what Alex thought too."

Grams chimed in sternly, "Listen to your Paw, baby-girl."

Willow knew they were right and now wasn't a time to show her independence.

It had taken longer than anticipated to get back, because of the festival goers mixed in with the reporters, roadblocks and curious onlookers pulled to the sides of the two-lane road going through Aliceston. Uncle Opie kept the reporters at bay while Willow ran inside. He followed her carrying the easel and flip chart.

"Grams, we need to call Alex's sister, Bonnie, before she hears about this from the media. That would be devastating news to hear that way."

"Get her number for me. It's going to be devastating any way she hears it, but maybe coming from you, it'll numb the shock a bit."

"Oh Grams, you tell her, please!"

"No, sweet girl, this is something you must do since Alexandra is your companion. It's the right thing to do."

"All right, but what should I say? I've only spoken on the phone with her once."

"Speak from your heart my child." Grams dialed the number and handed the phone back to Willow. One ring, two rings, three rings and then "Hello."

"Hello Bonnie. This is Willow."

"Hey girl. Did my sis put you up to calling me?"

"Well in a way, I guess. I have something serious to tell you."

Now Alex had always told Willow that her sister Bonnie was thin skinned and prone to hysterics, so she knew she must choose her words wisely, but before she could speak Bonnie blurted in. "What's wrong with Alex? Did she have an accident? Oh my, is it bad?"

"Please, Bonnie, just listen for a minute until I can get the story conveyed. This is hard for me too."

Bonnie listened to Willow for the next several minutes as the details were described. She asked questions and Willow did her best to answer them without breaking down in tears.

"I have a feeling this will be on the noon news today, and I wanted to tell you first. Would you please tell your Father and let him know we're going to find her. I promise you that."

"What can I do to help?" Bonnie asked.

"Thanks Bonnie, but we have about fifty people floating around here now trying to help. You're welcome to come and stay at the house to be close by for news though, if you'd like. You can sit with Sister Rachel, and answer the telephone."

"I'll call my Dad right after we hang up Willow, and then I'll drive over this afternoon."

"That sounds fine, do you need directions?"

"Nope, Al sent me a map."

"It won't be hard telling where to turn off the road in Aliceston with all the police cars blocking the way. I'll give them your name so you won't have a problem getting in. Try not to worry Bonnie. Alex wouldn't want that."

"Thanks Willow, but I'm sure Al told you I'm a gigantic worry wart. But for you and Al I'll try to keep it under control. See you later on today. You stay strong too Willow. She really needs you. I know she loves you with all her heart."

"Thanks for those words Bonnie. Bye for now."

Sheriff Terrell came through the screen door waving sheets of paper as he walked over to the counter to pour himself a cup of coffee. "Got that substance analysis back from Doc Perry's office. Turns out you were right about the ammonia. NH3 compounds, likely a refrigerant of sorts. Not looking good Mr. Sykes. Doc says too much could cause grave danger. Exposure to 700 ppm according to toxicology reports, and we may have a homicide on our hands, depending on the length of exposure."

Willow ran from the room with Mama Willa in chase. "Now why'd you have to go and say a thing like that for?" Grams said, punishing the sheriff with hardened eyes as she left the kitchen.

"Sheriff that was a real cruel remark to make to this family. They're the stronghold on this mountain and they deserve more respect than that," Sister Rachel said, snatching the half full coffee cup from the sheriff's hand and placing it in the sink with a splash of discontent. She kept her back to him after that, desponded by his lack of empathy to her friends.

Running Horse stood up and dismissed the sheriff by walking him to the door and saying, "Sheriff Terrell, I realize you have a job to do, but I must insist that you be more careful with your choice of words around my womenfolk. This has shattered the very heart of my family, and I'll not allow you to add to that pain. Man to man, Sheriff?"

"Of course Running Horse, man to man. Please apologize to all of them for me and I'll deal mainly with you from now on."

"I'd appreciate that," and he closed the door and headed upstairs to find Willow.

Grams had Willow nearly dried up and back on track when he entered the bedroom. He stroked his daughter's hair to further diminish the bite of the sheriff's words. "Baby girl, Uncle Opie has got your chart set up downstairs. Let's piece this together and go and find Alex."

Sniffling, "Okay Dad, I'm ready."

Willow tore off and taped the large flip chart papers all around the kitchen walls and together they sequenced the events. Combining the evidence they had gathered so far and leaving blank sheets for the unknowns. The first chart indicated Alex seeing someone in the bathroom with her. Moving on to the festival. They listed every detail they could remember. Uncle Opie remembered a tattoo of a lizard on the hand of the skinny muddy-haired girl. "That's not your run of the mill identifying mark. It'll be easy to spot too," Willow added.

They kept at it for over two hours, rehashing over and over to shake their memories. The ammonia rag the sheriff said was a refrigerant of sorts. Who had access to such a chemical? The tires prints on the old logging road that appeared to look like a van, judging from the depth of the tire markings into the dirt, and the way the people's foot prints entered the vehicle. The athletic shoe print found on the logging road and also at the back window of the house. Mama Willa's vision played a lot into the location to begin searching. Abandoned building, rusty cars, hillside, water tower, skinny girl, and the letters y and n. "Sounds like car dump site. Maybe the building used to be a service station. Think so Dad?"

He answered his daughter. "Good deduction counselor. Now Sister Rachel, you're always doing those crossword puzzles. I bet you can figure out where that y and n fit into this puzzle."

"I'll get right on it. Do any of you have a North Carolina map handy?"

"There's one in the top drawer of the secretary in the living room. I'll get it for you Sister Rachel," Willow said.

A knock thumped on the front door. Running Horse opened the door and let the two FBI agents in. Agent Pruitt stressed to Running Horse, "I'd like to set up a command post in the living room. I'm expecting a ransom call, and we want to be ready. We'll try to stay out of your family's way as much as possible. We'll need to move the furniture around some to make room for our equipment."

"You'll need to address that with my daughter, Counselor Willow Sykes. This is where she lives with Alex."

"Oh, of course, so you're an attorney. Willow Sykes, I recognize that name. The attorney that won that big McMillan case over in Greensboro. Right? I'm impressed."

"Well, Agent Pruitt let's see you impress me and find my Alex."

"We'll do our best ma'am. Okay to setup here?"

"Just be careful. When you get through setting up, come on in the kitchen and we'll show you what we've come up with." As she left the room she could hear Agent Pruitt singing her praises to Agent Jones.

"She's a top-notch, high profile attorney. This Lady can teach us a few things, so pay attention Jones and let's not blotch this case," Agent Pruitt said with respect.

Jones spoke up, "But aren't these two lovers?"

"Yeah, so you have a problem with that? Where'd you grow up Jones? Some underground cave?" Pruitt asked in disbelief at his partner's bigoted attitude. Jones fell silent once again.

The telephone was ringing off the hook but no ransom calls, only well-wishers mixed with more reporters. Sister Rachel fielded the calls between trying to unscramble the y and n mystery. Grams baked cinnamon buns to keep busy. Reverend Carlton came over to pray with the family to supply moral and spiritual support. The lady's circle brought more food over than the family, lawmen, FBI and reporters could eat, even though they made a heaping attempt at it.

Agent Pruitt found Willow sitting out on the porch in the swing with misty eyes looking off into the distant sky. "Excuse me ma'am, but I thought I should let you know that Alex will be the lead in story on the twelve o'clock news in a few minutes. Most likely tomorrow morning's headline in the newspaper as well. I wanted to prepare you."

"Thanks Agent Pruitt. You can call me Willow."

"It would be my pleasure Willow."

Before heading back inside she took her cell phone and tried BeBe one more time, determined to get to her before she heard the news another way. She hadn't left any messages. This wasn't a message leaving subject. This time BeBe answered. "Hi Willow, what's up?"

"How was the trip Be's?" Willow questioned trying to gently lead into the alarming news.

"Oh it was wonderful, but you sound funny girl. What's going on?"

Willow lost it. "Forgive me a second."

This disturbed Be's, but she patiently waited for her return.

"There's no easy way to tell you this. It's coming on the news in ten minutes. Alex has been kidnapped, and we believe it was that sorry Abby and her brother."

"What the hell?" BeBe yelled.

Willow gave her the abridged story of what they knew.

"I'm coming straight there. I'm not even going home first. Give me two hours. I'll break every speed law there is. I'll be there by three o'clock. Damn her. I'll break Abby's neck for you Willow, when I get my hands on her."

"BeBe drive careful, please."

"Yeah sure. Have you called Tim, her lawyer yet?"

"No, I didn't think of that, but you're right he should know before the news hits. Would you call him for me?

"No problem. See you soon."

"Bye Be's."

Silently everyone in the room gathered in front of the television in anticipation of the newscast. As the news began Alex's face spread across the screen. Shocking gasps circled about the room with stinging reality. The newscaster sat somber and into the camera announced. "News has just been released that a well known local financial investor has been kidnapped from her home in Aliceston, North Carolina. Police reports indicate that she was kidnapped last night. Ms. Alexandra Frances Nottingham is thirty-fours years of age, and had recently moved from Chapel Hill to the peaceful small town of Aliceston, to fulfill her dream of writing. Last night the serenity that drew her to that mountain community was invaded upon in the darkness. No word has been received since her abduction. If you have seen or know any information regarding this crime, please call the FBI at the number on the bottom of your screen. We shall continue to keep you updated as we receive further details." At the end of the report no one spoke a word. Agent Pruitt turned the television off, and Reverend Carlton kneeled beside Willow and led those present in another prayer.

The harsh realness of the situation surged through every ounce of blood flowing through Willow's body; and the tears were gone, replaced by a steadfast resolution to bring her Alex home. She hadn't waited all her life to find her true love only to have her seized away by some demented devouring hussy. "Lord, I'm sorry for the anger that's come over me right now, but I'm going to use it as my strength to find Alex. Guide me Lord," she prayed to herself. She worked with Sister Rachel at the kitchen table until someone said that BeBe was pulling in. Then she ran to Be's car and threw her arms around her. "Gosh, you must have flown. Any Problems?"

"No, I called Judge Ward. I sold him a house a few months back, and Alex has helped him make a ton of money in the past. I told him what's happened, and he had a State Trooper catch up with me on the interstate and lead me all the way here. In fact there were three troopers in all. Two cleared the way and the other escorted me. You should have seen the looks I was getting. Tim's on his way, but don't expect him for at least another hour. He doesn't have an escort," Be's said smiling proudly at her resourcefulness.

"Come on in. You know everybody except for the police and FBI agents. But I know it won't be long before you know them too."

"Oh Willow, I think I might have some valuable information for you. You said."

Willow interrupted, "Wait a minute Be's, let's pull Dad into this. Dad BeBe's got some info for us. I'm sorry I cut you short," she patted Be's knee apologizing.

Be's and Running Horse hugged hurriedly. "What have you got for us BeBe," he asked her.

"Willow said that you thought the vehicle on the log road might be a van. Just so happens that Abby has an old 2000 Ford van that she uses in her catering business."

"Can you describe it to us?" Willow quizzed.

"Sure, it's white with painted signs on the back panel of each side reading, *Exclusive Catering*, in red letters. The phone number is listed on there too. Oh yeah, and there's a tag on the front that says, *Um, Um Good*, like a Campbell soup label."

"Bingo, we have our van. That should be easy to pick out." Willow said. "Agent Pruitt we need you to get a search warrant for Abby's home and van. What's her full name Be's?"

"It's Abigail Kathryn Adams."

Agent Pruitt stated, "How fitting having AKA for initials."

"Good One Pruitt, AKA, (also known as) police jargon," Willow explained to Grams. Willow spent the next minute briefing Agent Pruitt on the new information.

"I'll get right on that Willow," and Pruitt made a mad dash for his car with his shadow Jones trailing him.

Triumphant cheers sprang from the porch where Sister Rachel had retreated for some fresh air. They all met her at the door. "I've got it, surely to goodness I just know this is it. That y and n are two of the letters in Waynesville. See right in the middle. They have an old water tower there too. I've seen it a hundred times."

Willow, Grams and Running Horse grabbed Sister Rachel and together they jumped up and down in celebration.

BeBe had brought in her laptop and immediately brought up Waynesville onto the screen. She began a search for car dumps, which were listed under the heading of reclaimed auto markets. After locating the water tower on the map they found two addresses that just might be the area where they'd find Alex. Excitement was overtaking the gloomy fog that had prevailed the room. These new clues ignited their hopes.

The phone rang numerous times in the background, but their celebration covered the ringing, until Grams put her hands up in the air with a jerky movement. All talking ceased and Willow answered the phone. "Hello."

"I think I have something you want Willow. This is Willow, isn't it?"

"Yes, what do you have?"

"Don't be coy with me girl. Thing is, do you want her dead or alive?" The voice was muffled. "Better gather up two million dollars if you want her alive." Click and the phone went dead.

Hanging up Willow's face revealed the dismal horror of speaking with the kidnapper. "They want two million dollars."

"Two million dollars, holy shit! Oh I'm sorry," Be's said putting her hand over her mouth in regret for her outburst.

"Well, the agents are outside, but I don't think the kidnapper stayed on the line long enough to get a trace any way. Did they say they would call back?" Running Horse asked his daughter.

"No Dad, they just hung up."

"Okay, then, you'll have to stay here and wait for their next call. Tell them whatever you think they want to hear. Don't tell anyone, but Opie and I are going to sneak through the woods with Robin Hood and join up with some others. Sweetheart we're going to go and get Alex. If the lawmen ask, you don't need to lie, just tell them we had to go and fetch a few things. That wouldn't be a lie, would it Reverend?"

"If so Brother Thomas, I'm sure it's one that the Lord would forgive."

Alex's lawyer, Tim, and her sister, Bonnie, pulled up in separate cars outside and were greeted by the Sheriff. Hearing their car doors slam Grams, BeBe, Sister Rachel and Reverend Carlton went out to meet them in hopes of distracting the agents, while Opie and Running Horse left unseen through the back door with Robin Hood trailing them. Willow stayed by the phone daydreaming about having Alex back home safe in her arms again. It was the most peace she had felt since Alex kissed her and left for the barn the night before.

When the agents returned Willow told Agent Pruitt about the phone call, which set him on fire with Jones. "I told you to stay inside. Now look we've missed what we came out here to do. You screwed up big time Jones. I'm not going to be held responsible for this. It's your ass in the sling, not mind, you hear me?"

"Yes sir," was about all Jones could utter, as he folded his arms to his chest and chewed his lower lip.

Willow shook her head in disbelief at the inexperience in front of her and whispered under her breath, "Thank goodness for my family and friends. These are a couple of dingalings."

Tim and Bonnie sat frozen on the couch as Willow and BeBe outlined the entire story. Just as they were finishing, the telephone rang. Agent Pruitt snapped into action and motioned for Willow to answer on the third ring.

"Hello." Everyone in the room eyed her in utter stillness. "Yes we'll pay, but it will take a couple of days to cash in the stocks and get the cash."

The caller threatened into her ear, "You have until five o'clock tomorrow or she dies at five o'one. You'd better take me seriously. I'll call you back with where to take the money."

"Let me talk with Alex. I need to know that she's all right." But the caller slammed the receiver down. "He hung up when I asked to speak with Alex, damn him. Wants the money by five o'clock tomorrow or he say she dies at five o'one. Sounds like a man, but it could be Abby using one of those voice disguisers."

"Not long enough for a trace," Pruitt groaned running his hand through his hair in exasperation.

Tim answered his cell phone. "Yeah…okay…good, then you've got a couple of guys on the way over to her house? Great. Make sure the police go over the van with a fine toothcomb. We'll need tire prints. We're sure they abducted her with it. Should be some evidence left behind. Check her cell phone records. See if she's placed any calls to this house or anywhere around this area. Check out her alibis for last night. Call me as soon as you come up with anything. I'm trusting you to handle this for me Johnny." He snapped his phone closed and gave Willow a thumbs up.

"Where's your Dad and that other fellow," Pruitt questioned looking out the front door.

Grams answered persuasively, "I sent them on an errand for me. They'll be back shortly."

Seemed to satisfy him. The rest of us kept straight faces and went about changing the subject.

CHAPTER 20

▼

Uncle Opie drove his brother Charlie's old pickup truck down nineteen towards Waynesville, while Running Horse and Robin Hood sat speechless next to him. Four other trucks ventured close behind them. Shortly after getting onto the highway leading into Waynesville, Opie pulled off the road at the BP station. Nine men and Robin Hood rallied around Running Horse.

"Okay men, listen up, here's the plan. The first place we're going to check out is a couple of miles from here. If it's any of that bunch that showed up at the festival they'll recognize me, and most likely Opie too. So Rick, you and Jack are going to drive over and pull in like you're looking for old car parts. See if anything looks suspicious to you. Don't try to do anything, just check things out. Then get in your truck and head back here. Call me on your way, and we'll go from there. Remember, don't give our hand away." Rick and Jack drove down the road as the others watched pensively in expectancy.

"I'm going inside the store to ask the attendant if he's seen the catering van in this area." Robin Hood followed Running Horse inside the station. "Excuse me. Have you seen a white Ford van with red letters spelling out Exclusive Catering, in this area in the last couple of days?"

"Uh huh, early this morning. Stopped in here for some gas and then headed outta town," the attendant said after spitting a wad of chew tobacco in the garbage can at his feet.

"Do you recall the driver?"

"Yeah, what's he done?"

"We believe he's kidnapped our friend Alex, so if you can help us we'd appreciate it."

"You don't mean that lady that the television has been reporting on?"

"Yes, that's her. So what did the guy look like?"

"Y'all from Aliceston?"

"Yes, please go on." Running Horse was getting impatient.

"Let's see now. A burly guy with a buzz cut. I thought it strange because he was driving a catering van, but he had on a greasy Thompson's Refrigerant and Plumbing uniform. I remember that because my last name's Thompson. The guy had blood caked scratches on his face and arms. I told him he looked like he'd been in a catfight. He said that he'd got tangled up with some barbed wire underneath a house he'd been working on. He seemed uptight and in a hurry, but I didn't make much of it."

"Thanks," and Running Horse left fast paced towards his posse.

From an open door the attendant shouted after him, "You really think that could be the guy?"

The men watched hard as Running Horse approached. "We've got them. Those sorry sons of bitches. He was here this morning. Probably headed back to work to keep suspicions off of him. Now I know where he got the ammonia. The man inside said that he was wearing a Thompson's Refrigerant and Plumbing uniform. They're probably still using an ammonia refrigerant for coolant, I'd bet. And he was driving Abby's catering van. The guy said he had bloody scratches on his face and arms. That means Alex put up a good fight. I just hope that he didn't hurt her back in return." His phone rang. "All right then. When you get here we'll go back and get them.

Checked out men. Exactly the way Mama Willa saw it in her vision. Rick said that while they were walking around looking at bumpers on some of the old cars, a skinny muddy-haired girl came out smoking a cigarette and yelled at them. When they approached and told her they wanted to buy that old bumper out there, she told her it wasn't for sell, and to get the hell off her property. That's when they noticed the tattoo of a lizard on her hand. This is the group from the festival, just like we've figured all a long. Opie call Agent Pruitt and tell him we've found her, and we're going in."

Rick and Jack pulled in while Opie made the call. Running Horse prepared everyone for their role in the rescue. When Opie got off the phone he was digging in his ear with his finger. "Sakes alive that man can bellow. He says we're to wait until he gets here with the sheriff. I told him that dog won't hunt. Then he blasted me, so I hung up on the buffoon."

"Good job Opie. Rick says we can park around the curve from the site, and maneuver through the woods to the back of the building. He thinks there's only the girl there guarding Alex. She's never seen Robin Hood, so we'll send him in first. If he sees Alex, that girl had better watch out. If he'll rip into a wildcat, he'll tear her apart if she tries anything. I'll be close behind to stop him if necessary. Opie will follow me, while the rest of you surround the house in case she tries to getaway, or if there's more than one of them inside. Let's go get her!"

Cheers and fist went up into the crisp fall air. In moments the caravan was off speeding to the scene. Within minutes they were parked and making their way on foot through the woods. From the tree line they could see the back of the worn and tattered building, obviously abandoned many years before.

Running Horse knelt beside Robin Hood. "Your mama's in there with a real bad woman. Go over there and try to get in, and go to her until I come behind you. OK boy?" Without a moment of delay, Robin Hood did exactly as he'd been told, and even took it a step further. He went up to that door and with his mouth turned the doorknob, like he'd learned to do at the house. He pushed on the door, growling like a rabid wolf as he entered, exposing his sharp white fangs and blackish red gums. Terrified and taken off guard by his entrance, the lizard-tattooed hand of the gaunt kidnapping accomplice raised a revolver.

"Drop it missy, or old Betsy here's gonna blow your sorry head off," Uncle Opie said, aiming his double-barreled shotgun forcefully at her head. His twisted, angry face dared her to move. She dropped her gun, and Running Horse kicked it towards the door. Instantly, Rick picked it up and aimed it back at her.

Robin Hood had his head lying on Alex's bluish-whitened and still body, stretched out on a cot in the corner of the squalid, damp and detestable smelling room. All nine men watched as Running Horse picked her up in his arms and carried her outside. Sirens broke the tarnished grim moment, as he carried her to a soft bed of wild grass beside an old cedar tree, tears streaming down his anguished face.

An ambulance and a fire truck were part of the possession squealing to a halt. Several paramedics rushed to Alex's side. Robin Hood got on his haunches and bared his teeth furiously to defend.

"It's all right fella. They just want to help her. Make way boy." Robin Hood let the medics close, but he refused to leave his master's side. Then as if by some wonderful miracle Alex's eyes opened, and she saw her dog. Life came back into her face as she tried to reach for him, only to be overtaken by violent frothy coughing and wheezing.

"Lie back Miss. Let us help you," one of the paramedics said while checking her airway and pulse." Alex's breathing became rapid, and her face revealed fright as she fought to hold on. Her eyes rolled back, and once again she lost consciousness. "She's going into respiratory distress. We need that humidified oxygen! Let's get skin and eye irrigation started to treat these chemical burns." Acting as a team, one cut Alex's t-shirt from her chest, another began flushing her skin, while the other immobilized her and administered oxygen. Then they started intravenous fluids.

She looked so tiny lying there. All in all they worked on Alex for about twenty minutes before putting her on a backboard. Orange dust filled the air as a helicopter landed in the blocked road. They loaded her in a matter seconds and the helicopter took flight again. It took both Running Horse and Uncle Opie to hold Robin Hood back. His barks turned to agonizing howls breaking the hearts of the onlookers.

"They're going to help her fella," Opie said trying to calm him, while wiping his own teary eyes on the back of his hands. Then all their gazes focused on the copter moving away overhead in the distance.

Turning Running Horse asked the paramedic, "Will she be all right?"

"Too soon to tell sir. They'll need to perform several tests. I'd say she has aspiration pneumonia, but that's only my guess. She's been given some pretty strong sedatives too, judging from the size of her pupils. Her kidnappers probably used them to keep her unconscious and restrained. They'll take real good care of her at the hospital."

"Thanks for all that you and your partners did for her," Running Horse said shaking the medic's hand. Behind the medic he saw Agent Pruitt and Sheriff Terrell putting the cuffed lean creature woman they had captured in the back of a squad car. He made his way over to join them. "Did she tell you anything?"

"No, she's got her mouth zippered shut. We'll break her down at the station. How's Alex?" Agent Pruitt asked.

"Paramedic said that's it's too soon to tell, but she's a fighter. She'll pull through this. Where's your side-kick Jones?"

"He's at the BP station talking with the man you told us about. Oh yeah, Abby and Nate are in police custody. I just got the call. They arrested Abby's sister too. Looks like we've got the whole gang of them. You and your friends did a good job solving this case and catching the bad guys. I hate to admit it, but you didn't need us. I can see where Willow gets her astute talents. Speaking of Willow, have you called her?"

"No, but I'm going to call her right now. Thanks Agent Pruitt."

The phone rang back at the house, and Willow grabbed it first ring. "Hi baby girl. We've got Alex."

"He's got Alex," she shouted to the crowd.

"Praise the Lord," Grams and Sister Rachel said in harmonious union, while the rest of the room shouted in relief and exuberance.

"How is she Dad?"

"She's on a helicopter heading to the hospital in Asheville. I'm on my way there in two seconds. Let BeBe drive you and Mama over."

"Dad, you're not telling me something. I hear it in your voice. What is it?"

He had been hoping she wouldn't ask, but knowing that she would, and knew he'd have to tell her the truth. "She's in respiratory distress. She needs you. Then she'll be all right. You'll see. Here's some good news. Tell everyone that Abby; her brother, sister and that lizard girl have all been arrested. With the evidence we have against them they should be put away for a long, long time."

"Forever is what they deserve Dad."

Willow, Grams and Bonnie got into BeBe's car to make their way to the hospital. BeBe turned on the radio to break the soundless chatter of all their minds. "Right Here Waiting For You," by Richard Marx was playing, and its meaning prompted tears that quickly filled Willow's eyes. Be's immediately switched the radio station only to land on "I Will Always Love You," by Whitney Houston. She about broke her arm flipping the station again. This time, John Denver's melody of "Sunshine On My Shoulder," played as BeBe hit the off button on the radio. "I'm sorry Willow. I know those songs make you sad right now."

"That's okay. Alex is my heart's song. All the cheesy love songs in the world can't change that. They just remind me of her, and they no longer sound cheesy anymore."

Mama Willa unbuckled her seat belt from the back seat and reached forward for her granddaughter's hand, holding it to her gigantic and loving heart. "Don't worry child. Alexandra is strong and her will to get back to you is just as strong. Your love unites you."

About forty minutes later Be's let them out at the hospital emergency room entrance, while she went to park the car. Automated entry doors opened revealing Running Horse. He hugged his daughter with deep affection and concern. "They haven't been out to tell me anything yet. The nurses are hem hawing around my questions. Come on and sit down over here."

Willow's hands trembled, "Dad I want to find the chapel and say a prayer. Would you go with me?"

"Sure baby-girl. There's a sign at the end of the hall over there with an arrow. We'll follow that."

"Grams, you'll take care of Bonnie and Be's for me won't you?"

"Course child."

Finding the small chapel around the corner through some double doors they entered the sanctuary. Willow left her Dad's side and went straightway to the diminutive altar, and reverently got down on her knees. Seconds later her Dad was kneeling beside her, and silently they prayed together. Finishing and standing, Running Horse tried to sooth his daughter's tears. Abruptly candles flickered on the altar and just as suddenly went out. Father and daughter looked at one another with astonishment.

"Dad those candles weren't lit when we came in here, were they?"

"No Princess," he replied casting her a bewildered stare.

"And you didn't light them, right?"

"Right."

"Then Dad it's the sign I prayed for just now. I asked God to give me a sign that Alex was going to be okay. Thank you God. She's going to be okay. Oh Dad, I knew it! I just needed God to take away that cloud of doubt hounding me." She hugged her Dad with joy. "We've got to go and tell Grams." Willow ran back down the hallway to tell her Grams of the remarkable experience in the chapel.

Her Dad followed at a more leisurely pace, happy for God's special blissful message that filled their hearts with peace and love. He knew for certain now that his daughter's twin flame would pull through this dismal and terrorizing ordeal. For she was their Alex, another daughter to bring more of God's light into their lives. He could see his baby girl hugging her Grams with sheer happiness, as she shared the divine gift given them in the chapel. Bonnie and BeBe surveyed one another with skepticism, but the pull of the positive energy embraced them, and they joined in on the hugging ceremony. Now all the conversation was centered on when we take Alex home. Even the rain that began coming down in buckets outside, with crackling thunder penetrating the emergency room's walls didn't damper the repose that surrounded them.

Bonnie and BeBe made a run to the cafeteria to get coffee and soda pop for everyone. They'd barely gotten around the corner out of sight, when a doctor came out and called for the family of Ms. Nottingham. Willow sprang to attention, raising her hand in acknowledgment and meeting the doctor halfway, while her Dad helped Grams assemble with them.

"I'm Dr. Ruskin. We've run several tests on Ms. Nottingham. Her arterial blood gases, x-rays, blood count, oxygen saturation, and heart all sound good. We have called in a Pulmonologist to be on the safe side. We have her on a heart monitor, and we still have her on fluids to balance her electrolytes. It amazes me due to the high concentrations of vapors she breathed leading to asphyxiation from that bag being placed over her head, that she's sustained such minor respiratory injury. Not to mention all the sedatives they fed her."

"Bag, what bag?" Willow intervened.

"Oh, I assumed you'd been told that her captives placed a bag over her head containing an ammonia alkaline. Anyway, the burns she's received aren't corrosive, although she will experience some pain from the blisters. I didn't find any eye damage, which is another amazing outcome. But the pHs of her conjunctival fluids is normal. We might be able to call Alex a miracle. This is certainly one for the textbooks," the doctor reported through his clutched hands, huffing afterwards at the unbelievable outcome.

"When can I see her?" Willow pulled on the doctor's arm.

"You must be the Willow Rose she keeps asking for. She said to just look for the most beautiful woman out here. She was right. Come on back with me."

"Can they come too?"

"No, just one at a time right now. She's been through a trauma and really needs her rest. The drugs her abductors gave her are wearing off, but she's still a little hazy. She might talk a little out of her head, so be prepared. We're going to keep her overnight to monitor her. If the Pulmonologist gives us the all clear, we'll see about releasing her home with you tomorrow."

"Go on child. Your Paw and me will be fine. Tell her we love her," Mama Willa said pushing Willow along with the doctor. Thomas took his Mother's hand and together they watched as Willow walked down the long hallway with the doctor.

Willow was determined to be strong for Alex and wiped her puffed and weepy eyes. Reaching down into the pit of her heart she mustered up a radiant smile before entering the room with Dr. Ruskin. Alex didn't see Willow enter behind the doctor. Her sight was still blurry from the chemicals. "When will you let me see my Willow Rose?" Alex groggily and with a hoarse voice demanded pitifully.

"Funny you should ask me that," the doctor replied stepping to the side to bring Willow to light.

"My Princess, I was afraid I'd never see you again," Alex cried with tube pierced arms trying to reach for Willow.

"Take it easy now," the doctor said to no avail. Willow buried her face into Alex's neck and held her head gently in her hands. Then lifted her face within inches of her true loves and kissed her nose softly. Willow kept her smile, although her insides ached, looking at the swollen and red-blistered face that had endured so much in the past twenty-four hours. One eye was bandaged and ointment covered her face, but that one unbandaged, discerning eye exhibited the deep love in her heart louder than any words Willow had ever heard spoken.

Doctor Ruskin allowed Willow to stay by Alex's bedside all night. Pulling over a chair she rested, and held Alex's hand continuously through the night. Each time the nurses would enter throughout the night, Willow would kiss Alex and they would whisper, "I love you," before sleep came over them again.

The Pulmonologist arrived early the next morning at around six. He spent a couple of hours with Alex, while Willow went to have breakfast with her Dad and Grams. Bonnie and BeBe had left the night before after being given word that Alex was doing well.

"I hope everything checks out okay from this doctor too, so that Alex can come home with us today. She wants to come home so badly. They've been great, but being in a hospital stinks."

Grams spoke up, "So's the food." Thomas nodded in agreement and they all laughed. "It's good we laugh. God is good."

"Amen to that Grams! He's given me back my Alex."

CHAPTER 21

▼

Under the skillful daily care of Grams, Running Horse, Robin Hood, and my Willow Rose, my recovery thrived. I was a barrel of questions, as I lay in bed, eager to know how they had found me. My memory of the nightmare was sparse, due to being sedated the whole time. I wanted to know all the what, when, and wheres of how they pieced the sick and twisted puzzle together. I realized how very lucky and blessed I had been to have them on my side. Their tale of investigation fascinated me, and almost made me forget I was the one they had been looking for.

Within two days of being home I was out of bed, against their vocalized wishes. I think they would have kept me in that bed for a solid month, if I had let them. They about had a conniption fit when I asked Running Horse to hitch-up the wagon.

Grams admired my stubbornness and took up for me, so after a week I was touring BeBe and Bonnie around dusty roads and shaded paths in the surrey, with Robin Hood clinging to my every move. The last of the autumn's leaves drifted lazily in the cool breezes. Crunching sounds of the pignut hickory nuts underneath the wagon's wheels gave drum-like overtones to the accompanying mourning dove's songs overhead. I told lively stories I had learned from my new family as we clopped along the leave-strewn paths.

My new lease on life surprised my sister, whom had only known me to be a big go-getter. Kind of a rock'em sock'em kind of person. Always trying to make the earth move, type A personality, never taking no for an answer. This new laid-back version was far more to my sister's liking. Gone was my habitual talk of stocks, bonds, and conglomerates, that had preoccupied nearly every conversation I'd had with my sister in the past ten or so years. Things that truth be known, flew right over Bonnie's head, and frankly bored her to death.

Now my talk of the trees, animals, folklore and God's wonder brightened my words like poetic verse, and added a special charm to my smile, that even I took note of. Heck, Bonnie even said this place had changed me. Sis had a hard time believing that I had yielded the recent events so easily to the past, and moved on with my life. I pondered all these things as we headed into the sun on our way back to the house.

Then I felt a thumping on my shoulder and turned. Bonnie felt compelled to remark, "Sis, have I ever told you how proud I am of you?" Her words caught me unprepared, since we'd never been the lovey-dovey sister types. We were as opposite as the North and South Poles.

"Don't think I've ever heard those words come from your lips."

"I've been sitting back here watching you for the past hour, and something has come over you. This place agrees with you. Honestly, I'm a little jealous."

"Thanks Bonnie Lou. This place must be affecting you too, for you to go all mushy on me."

"Oh shut up Al. I was just trying to be nice," Bonnie said in her temperamental way.

"Now that's the Sis I know and love. Hand me one of those ciders Be's, please. Got another story for you." So we continued enjoying Mountain Dew skies as I narrated through the forest.

I had promised my ladylove that I'd be home before sundown. This was the first time I'd been without Willow's company since the hospital, and it had been like pulling teeth to get her to agree to let me go without her. But Mama Willa had intervened on my behalf. Besides Mama Willa needed Willow to go into Bryson City with her for some fangled reason. And a reason was never offered and I never questioned. Pulling the surrey through the clearing into the meadow I could see Willow and Grams parking under the Willow tree.

My heart lifted, and I cracked the whip high into the air and bellowed, "Heeiii," galloping the horses to the house while BeBe laughed, and Bonnie shouted colorful exclamations of protest. Drawing the reins tight to my chest and pulling on the brake, I leapt from the wagon and grabbed my Willow Rose. "Hi Princess. I missed you."

Grams teased us, "Two love-sick puppies, the both of yous. All my baby girl could say this afternoon was we need to get back home. Alex might need me."

"I do need her Grams."

BeBe helped Bonnie from the wagon as Bonnie complained. "You nearly knocked my teeth out butthead. Who taught you to drive like that?"

"Well Sis, I owe it all to my dear sweet Willow Rose."

Our house had been crowded with family and friends visiting during my recuperation, for the past couple of weeks. We had just waved good-bye to BeBe and watched her round the evergreens. Finally, for the first time since my abduction, the two of us were alone. The sun was gracing the spine of the mountains as it readied for the night. The late November full moon was taking its place in the evening sky, as it threw a kiss to the setting sun. Hand in hand we walked out to the pasture, and I made my first night visit to the barn since my kidnapping experience.

"I want to face the beast of that night and put it all behind me. Thanks for facing it with me." Walking into the barn, I looked to the ladder hanging on the side wall and then to the light overhead. "I remember I only thought the light had burnt out that night. I never suspected what happened next." Willow remained quite, and listened compassionately as I purged the memories. "I saw two people darkened in the night. Then I remember I couldn't breathe. That's the last thing I remember. Except for what I thought was a dream."

"What was your dream my sweet?"

"Well, it wasn't exactly a dream. I'll just tell you and let you decide for yourself. A voice communicated with me. It said, *You will rise above these difficulties and be rewarded with many pleasures. Rest, and I will take care of you. For I have heard the prayers from the mountain.* The words didn't enter my ears; they entered my heart. No words were spoken aloud. But my soul understood, and a peace overcame me. It's what I hung onto. I know now that it was Jesus, comforting me and healing me. You all said that the doctors couldn't explain my survival, from so much toxicity from the ammonia and sedatives. I don't have any residual losses. There's no other explanation."

Willow took my hands lovingly into hers. "He saved you for me. He knew that if anything had happened to you, I would have lost my will to go on. You're right He heard our prayers. For all of Aliceston Mountain lifted their voices in prayer, and cried to Him to save you. He gave Grams the vision to give to Dad to find you. He had Sister Rachel solve the y and n puzzle. He had Robin Hood open the door on that old building, and burst in slobbering and growling like a dog gone mad. Jesus saved you. He has special plans for you and us."

I embraced Willow Rose in my arms, and the silkiness of her hair felt like velvet to my face. Lacking his own attention, Robin Hood leaned against us with his full weight and knocked the both of us onto the hay floor. I caught my Willow Rose, and we nestled in the hay. The loft window was open above, and the full moon angled inside. Suddenly the barn light went out, causing me to jump involuntarily.

"It's me girls. Don't get spooked. Thought you might enjoy the peace of the moonlight," Running Horse said walking away from the barn.

Together we laughed and stared out the loft. We cuddled closer as the night chill had the temperatures dropping. The stars were the size of tennis balls casting enormous brilliance inside of the barn. "Looks like one of those mirrored balls on the walls, doesn't it Princess? May I have this dance?" I stood up and helped Willow to her feet.

"We don't have any music you silly romantic," Willow teased.

"But oh, yes, we do. We have the music of our hearts." Holding her in my arms, we danced, lost momentarily in the melodies our hearts played in stereo. The temperatures continued to plummet and even our potent love couldn't prevent the shivers that overtook us.

"Brrrrr!" we both let out simultaneously. The three of us raced to the house.

"Go on inside and get warm, I'll get some more firewood and bring it in," I told Willow, patting her on the backside flirtatiously.

"Better watch what you're doing there, unless you mean business," Willow returned.

"I'll show you business," I said keeping our banter going.

"How about I fix us a cup of Irish coffee?" Willow said, going into the kitchen to get the coffee started.

I heard her singing the country song by, Keith Urban, 'Days Go By,' and through the kitchen window I saw her two-stepping with the coffee can in her hands. "You'd better start living right now," she sang and hummed like a happy housewife. When she heard me come indoors she came to my side. "Can I help you?"

"That's all right, I've got it Princess. I love how your painting looks over the fireplace mantle. It amazes me that you painted it. But I'm not really surprised anymore with anything you do. Bet this old fireplace is going to gobble this wood up like hungry bear tonight. Look at the frost already glazing the windows. Hope your Dad doesn't try to sleep out in the barn tonight."

"He won't or Grams will tan his hide. He just wants to settle down the horses, and put their blankets on them. I'm positive he'll head to the house after that."

Willow turned on some steamy jazz music, and curled up on the sofa sipping her coffee. She sat back and watched as I got the fire going to a roaring flame. I could tell she was in deep thought. "What's on your mind Princess?"

"Oh, I was just thinking how very methodical you are in your way of doing things. You arranged those logs so uniformly. But, at least now you're relaxed about it. Your jaw isn't clenched tight and pulsating the way it used to. I see a child-like quality about you Precious. You know, I feel more collected now too. I think this mountain has reached out and covered us." Willow sighed in contentment. "We're so fortunate to have found one another."

I picked up my coffee cup to toast my Willow Rose. "I had never heard of a twin flame before I came to this mountain. Gracious, I'd never heard of half the things I've learned from you and your family."

"Our family," Willow corrected.

"Oh yes, our family, sorry. Seriously though dear, I love everything about you. I love our family, our boy here, our friends, our home and this mountain. I've always been searching for something. Never even knowing what it was I was searching for, that is until now. I've found it all in you and Nottingham Forest, right here on Aliceston Mountain. Thank you my everlasting love." And with a soft clink of our cups, I added. "Mighty good cup of coffee. Got a sweet bite to it."

With a look of glorified endearment, my sweet lady asked, "Alex, would you kiss me?"

"Oh Princess, just one kiss won't do." Instant lure swelled from our lips and drew our heated bodies closer and closer, until the heat turned to moistures of excitement. Hearts pounding so loudly, and moans of need stimulating each nerve, creating wanton desire. Clothes strewn about and full bodies touching. Climaxing time and time again, moving to the hot jazz like a trombone serenade. Exhausted, I held Willow's head to my chest as if she were a fragile china doll, and rubbed her beautiful black flowing hair delicately. "I thank God for you Willow Rose." And with that we both drifted into the comfort of the night.

Willow woke up at first light and silently unwrapped herself from me. My downward eyes saw her standing over me, as I pretended to still be asleep. She stood above me for several minutes and I heard her whisper, "I love the softness and cream-color of your skin. To think that your heart belongs to me is more than I ever fantasized." She leaned over and kissed the top of my head, and covered me with the afghan from the rocking chair, while I continued to play possum. I felt a little guilty as I watched her pick up the clothes tossed about the night before. However, I was enjoying this undetected spy game, and smiled in remembrance of the love we shared. Then she breezed naked up the stairs to bathe, as I watched her beautiful departure.

After her bath she returned downstairs to find me peaceful in deep sleep, or so she thought. She didn't try to wake me. Instead she went straight into the kitchen to get breakfast started. Robin Hood joined Willow in the kitchen the second his nose picked up the smell of the sausage frying.

"Guess you're ready for your breakfast this morning too, aren't you fella? Tell you what, let's wait until I get the sausage gravy made, and we'll pour some over your Kibbles'n Bits. How's that sound?" The fanning of his tail on the quarry tiles tapped out his approval.

Willow's humming coming from the kitchen sounded like angel songs to me as I yawned and stretched. And to have that topped off with the mouth-watering smells of breakfast waffling around, let me know that this was my heaven on earth. So, I wrapped the afghan around my torso and stepped into the kitchen. "Gees, it smells so good in here. How much longer before we eat?"

"Good, you're awake. Love your outfit. Time enough for you to go and get a bath, if you'll hurry," Willow said happily amused.

"Give me ten minutes?" I asked rubbing my sleepy eyes.

"I'll have it ready and waiting. Now shoo," she said jokingly as she chased me from the kitchen with the spatula.

I took off laughing in haste. "Damn woman, you sound just like your Grams!"

After breakfast I drove the surrey we had loaded with arts supplies, my laptop computer, a full picnic basket, cooler, blanket, and a radio to the spot where Willow wanted to paint that day. Robin Hood ran along side, while Willow rode Misty Morning leading our way through the woods and up the mountain. Dressed like a couple of lumberjacks to keep warm, we giggled and spoke incessantly until we reached a waterfall showered in the early morning's sun.

"Wow! Why haven't we been here before? This is absolutely awesome."

"I had plans on bringing you here the day after, you know, that awful time, but with everything that happened, well this is the first chance we've had. I knew you'd love it. But the waterfall isn't the main reason we're here."

I threw Willow a bewildered look. "What could be more glorious than this?"

"On the day before I was born my great Aunt Ruth died, from what the doctor said had been heart failure. Grams said it was really heartbreak. She and her sister had been very close, and Grams took Ruth's passing hard. Years before Aunt Ruth had made Grams give her a solemn promise that if anything ever happened to her, she'd bury her beneath the oak tree next to the waterfall, where the sun glistened most of the day. So on the afternoon of my birth Grams, Paw-Pa and Dad led their family and friends up here to bury Aunt Ruth. It was a windy March day, and Mama and I stayed back at the house for obvious reasons. See that oak tree there?" That was planted on the day that Aunt Ruth was born. That's one of the reasons she wanted to be buried beneath it."

"The big towering one beside that beautiful willow tree?" I asked, always fascinated by Willow's stories.

"That's it. It would be around ninety years old now. Dad planted that willow next to it the day they came up here, and Grams had him plant that fir tree at the same time. Looks like a majestic Christmas tree for the White House lawn, doesn't it?"

"Now that you mention it Princess, it does indeed."

"Do you remember when we first met, and Grams said that you were like a fir tree?" Willow said pointing to the tree.

My mouth flew open dumbfounded in retrospect, "You don't mean it. Couldn't possibly be."

"There's your proof dear-heart. The oak, the willow, and the fir standing together next to this gorgeous waterfall. Aunt Ruth, my Alex and me. That's what I want to paint. The symbolism it proclaims."

For several seconds we both stood speechless and just admired the beauty of the trees, that later that day would shade the waterfall.

"That's truly a magnificent sight. Don't think I've ever seen a trio of trees more grand, clumped together that way. The oak and the willow still have foliage this late in the year, and this high up. Unbelievable," I marveled.

"Our traditions say that the oak tree is courageous, strong, and unrelenting. Under the oak's branches the willow and fir have thrived and grown in beauty and strength. Our two flames are connected to Aunt Ruth's. I'm sure she's watching us with pride in her heart. She has been my guardian angel for all my life. This mountain and this forest is our destiny my love. It has everything we need for our happiness"

"I feel that way too, like I'm a part of this land."

We both worked together, side by side, as the noon sun warmed the air. Robin Hood interrupted with his bark of hunger as he jumped playfully around the picnic basket. "Our boy says it's time for lunch," Willow said, while soaking her paintbrushes and wiping her hands.

I stood up, stretched, and walked the stiffness from my knees. "Boy, the morning sure went fast. You know Princess, I've been wondering something."

"Ask away."

"Why did Grams think it was heart break that your Aunt Ruth died from?"

Willow explained. "Aunt Ruth's twin flame was a masculine Indian woman. They'd been childhood friends since they were toddlers, and so they grew up together on this mountain. By the time they were twenty they discovered there was more than friendship between them. One Saturday nearly twenty-five years later, Ollie, Aunt Ruth's twin flame, drove into Asheville. She went there to buy a special store-bought dress for my Aunt's forty-fifth birthday surprise party, that Grams was helping Ollie arrange. After buying the dress, Ollie headed for her car to return home. As she opened her car door she noticed that she was being followed.

Some good old boys didn't think much of Ollie's type, and they followed her out of town in two pick-up trucks. The roads back then were barely two lanes, and going around curves was dangerous enough without being pursued. They chased her and she sped up, but her old Desoto was in bad shape and it overheated. Smoke started piling out from under the hood. When she pulled off the road, both trucks slammed into her at full speed, and over the mountainside she crashed. Her car exploded when it landed over a hundred feet below, and her body was never found. The locals said that she was burned alive."

"How horrible. Your poor Aunt Ruth. Did they catch the no-goods that did it?"

"They did, but back then Indians were really treated badly. Those were unfortunate times. Basically the hoodlums got slapped on the wrist and let go."

"So that's why Grams said she died from a broken heart."

"Yes, but there is a happy ending to this story, if you believe in the ways of the Cherokee."

"I'm all ears Princess."

"Look at the oak tree a little closer, and you will see what was always meant to be. Go closer and look carefully."

"I don't see anything. Just a giant oak tree."

"Here Precious, let me show you. Put your hand here. Feel that? Now look up."

"Gees, I can't believe my eyes. It's two oak trees joined together as one. How'd that happen?"

"Grams says it was God's will. For only He can make a tree. It wasn't spotted until the first anniversary of Aunt Ruth's death. Grams trekked up here with Paw-Pa to pay her respects to her sister, and check on the trees they'd planted. Even though it had only been a year, another oak had attached its self and ran three fourths of the way up the tree. Its trunk was already half the size of the original oak. By the second year they were meshed as one in size, and have continued to grow as one every since. Aunt Ruth and Ollie were rejoined through death to journey together for eternity. The miracle of love."

"Willow Rose, I think that's the most extraordinary love story. I'd like to write that story as my next book. Do you think Grams would mind?"

"She'd be happier than a jay bird if you'd do that."

"Would you let me use your painting of this scene when you finish, as the cover of the book?"

"I would have been disappointed if you hadn't asked. It would make me proud."

"What if we called it, The Tree Of Hearts?" I suggested.

"The Tree Of Hearts, how inherently native. You're so shrewd."

Standing with hands clasped together, we continued to take in the magnitude of nature's divine wonder; appreciating the connectedness it brought us.

"Thanks for bringing me here and telling me this story. There we stand my Willow Rose, together, next to two other remarkable women. I guess it's true, isn't it? I finally get it."

"What's that Precious?"

"That we really are all like a tree in 'The Forest Of Life.'"

THE END

They are like trees planted by the rivers of water,
Which yield their fruit in its season;
And their leaves shall not wither;
In all that they do, they shall prosper...

—Psalms 1:3

978-0-595-34894-7
0-595-34894-7

Printed in the United States
69469LVS00004B/125